THE AUCTIONEER

Joan Samson

SIMON AND SCHUSTER · NEW YORK

The author acknowledges with thanks the grant from the Radcliffe Institute, which helped make the writing of this book possible.

PUBLISHED BY SIMON AND SCHUSTER
ROCKEFELLER CENTER, 630 FIFTH AVENUE
NEW YORK, NEW YORK 10020

DESIGNED BY EVE METZ
MANUFACTURED IN THE UNITED STATES OF AMERICA
1 2 3 4 5 6 7 8 9 10
LIBRARY OF CONGRESS CATALOGING IN PUBLICATION DATA

SAMSON, JOAN
THE AUCTIONEER.
I. TITLE.
PZ4.S1922AU [PS3569.A4667] 813'.5'4 75-23337
ISBN 0-671-22139-6

TO MY FATHER AND MOTHER

· 1 ·

THE FIRE ROSE in a perfect cone as if suspended by the wisp of smoke that ascended in a straight line to the high spring sky. Mim and John dragged whole dry saplings from the brush pile by the stone wall and heaved them into the flames, stepping back quickly as the dead leaves caught with a hiss.

Four-year-old Hildie heard the truck coming even before the old sheep dog did. She scampered to the edge of the road and waited impatiently. It was Gore's truck, moving fast, rutting deeply in the mud and throwing up a spray on either side. John and Mim converged behind Hildie, each taking stock of what might be wrong to bring the police chief out to the last farm on the road.

Bob Gore swung himself out and hooked his thumbs in the pockets of his jeans. He shifted from foot to foot for a moment as if his great belly were seeking a point of equilibrium. Gore had a taste for two things—trouble and gossip. By either route, he could talk away an afternoon without half trying. John glanced over his shoulder at the fire.

"Good day for burnin'," Gore said.

"Plenty of snow in the woods still, case it's that brings you round," John said, knowing full well it wasn't. "Figure to get my burnin' done before I have to mess with permits."

"Hell no," Gore said. "When was I ever one to go lookin' for trouble?" He grinned at the Moores.

They stood before him soberly. The father, his frame rounded like a stone by thirty years of routine, looked up at the policeman with a steady, slightly skeptical gaze, while the mother, whom the years of marriage and outdoor work had left straighter than ever, stared with blue eyes as clear and curious as those of the child leaning against her legs.

Gore cupped his hands around a match. "Thing is," he said, inhaling on a cigarette, "we're havin' an auction. A policeman's benefit."

John dug his hands deep into the front pockets of his overalls and hunched his shoulders. "But you're our only cop, Bobby," he said. "You already got yourself a swanky cruiser, and you don't fancy your uniform. What do you need an auction for?"

"Deputies," Gore said.

"Deputies!" repeated John.

Gore shrugged. "People ain't satisfied the way they used to be. What with the break-in up to the ledge, and then Rouse's woods on fire, and the holdup at Linden's . . ." Gore looked across at the splintered reflection of the fire in the pond. "Course it's the murder on the Fawkes place last spring that done it."

Hildie, impatient, began to dance to and fro, pulling on Mim's arm until Mim began to sway to the child's rhythm.

"Only murder Harlowe's had in a hundred years," John said. "And that by an outsider for sure. So's that other stuff, most like."

"Still, times are changin'," Gore said. "Murder right smack in the center of town? Such a fine old home too. There was people after me all along to stop Amelia rentin' rooms. Then, when she went and got herself strangled . . ."

"No way to stop her," soothed Mim. "Not when old Adeline Fayette's been takin' in tourists these twenty years."

"Guess if young Nick Fawkes couldn't steady Amelia down, weren't much point to other folks gettin' their ears boxed," John said.

"Maybe she needed the money," Mim said, running a hand thoughtfully through her short curls. "Left like that with the two kids . . ."

8

"Who's to say?" Gore said. He shifted his weight. "The troopers don't lift a finger. 'Lots of unsolved crimes,' they tell you. But everyone watches too much television. They get to expectin' me to scurry round scarin' up clues. Every poor slob with a job to do's supposed to be some hotshot detective. Well, I got news—"

"If everybody in town was a deputy, there'd still be trouble," John said. He eyed his tidy white farmhouse. "And we got our fair share of peace in Harlowe too."

"Not like we used to," Gore said. "It's gettin' worse. And not just here. You know that Perly Dunsmore that finally bought the Fawkes place? Well, he's an auctioneer. Been to half the cities in the world. And he says it's gettin' worse all over. Every place growin' and fillin' up with strangers. Look at Powlton. Doubled in five years."

"What?" John said. "From four hundred to eight hundred? That's just on account of that trailer park."

"Come on, Johnny," Gore said. "Can't hurt to have a deputy or two." He grinned. "At least it'd be somebody to share the blame. And if we raise the money at auction, it'll be no skin off your teeth. We won't even touch the town budget."

John examined Gore. "Ain't like you to be dreamin' up changes, Bobby," he said. "Now that new fellow—"

"A policeman's benefit's a smart idea. That's the main thing," Gore said, pausing to pitch his cigarette toward the fire. "And I recall you gave the firemen an old plow last year."

John chuckled. "Worth about three and a half cents," he said. "Some Sunday farmer paid twelve bucks for it. Must be plannin' to go west in a covered wagon."

"That's the kind of thing," Gore said, spitting a speck of tobacco to one side.

"How about the old wheels?" Mim asked.

John nodded. "Must be five or six of them."

"Someone can make chandeliers out of them," Mim informed Gore, her face merry. "Or paint them blue and plant them at the bottom of their driveway for the snowplow to knock over."

Gore leaned back on his heels, his jowly face reverting to its usual slackness. "Swell," he said.

The wheels were in the woodshed. John and Gore took two

apiece and carried them to the truck. Mim ran past them laughing, chasing the last wheel which was rolling down the front lawn like a hoop. Gore opened up the tailgate of his truck and lifted the wheels in, one after another. "Thanks," he said, giving the top wheel an affectionate pat. "I'll lay odds these'll bring ten bucks once this new auctioneer gets goin'."

Mim and Hildie stared past Gore at a carton full of chipped dishes, a badly cracked pine worktable, and an oversized easy chair leaking stuffing from one arm.

"Why's he takin' away our wheels?" Hildie asked as he drove away.

"Auctioneer's goin' to sell them," John said.

"Why?" Hildie asked.

John knit his brows and shrugged.

"For money, love," Mim said. "But it's nothin' to do with the likes of us. Nothin' at all."

It was mud season. In the woods there was still a fair snow cover, though it was receding in dark circles from the trees as the trunks warmed in the lengthening days. But Moore's pasture, which turned a steep face to the southeast, was already bare except for sparkling heaps here and there where drifts had been, and the meadow at the bottom where snow lingered near the stream. The soggy ground, matted with the roots of last year's hay, gave like a sponge underfoot. The sun drew the moisture from woods and field and stream and pond, and set it loose in the air. But the sky remained deep and dry and blue. It was the time of year when mittens and caps and indoor heat seem stale. A thousand outdoor chores crop up and country people feel groundswells of new strength.

On Thursday afternoon, when Gore came again, John and Mim were halfway up the pasture where it leveled out a bit, deciding where to put the patch of Hubbard squash they planned on for a cash crop that year, where to set the corn, where to plant the shell beans and potatoes. Hildie squatted at the edge of last year's potato patch, pushing her hands into the icy mud and watching the impressions fill with water. Only Ma, too stiff with arthritis for the out-of-doors, could bear to remain in the dry front room by the wood stove watching television. She hardly quickened to the weather any more, except to comment on what she saw through the front window. Besides, she would no more miss her programs than let pass the rare scraps of gossip that came her way.

When Gore got out of his truck, the Moores waved and started down the hill, Hildie and Lassie trotting ahead.

"What's he after now?" John muttered.

"Got to tell you how his blessed auction went." Mim laughed. "He should of been the town crier instead of the town cop."

Ma had heard the truck too and was rapping on the window, beckoning furiously, her image faded to gray by the weathered plastic tacked over the glass for insulation.

Inside, the house was faintly pungent with woodsmoke. Over the years the stoves had deposited a crust of dull black on the ceilings and sifted soot into the crevices between the scrubbed floorboards. It was a house that had been lived in for generations by the same family, and treasures from various eras cluttered every surface. Even on top of the television set, a kerosene lamp with a fluted base and a tall etched chimney jostled wax flowers under a dusty dome, three Hummel figurines, and a plastic replica of the Statue of Liberty. There was a light rhythm of clocks ticking against each other—the cuckoo clock, the eight-day clock with columbine painted on the glass, and the grandfather clock in the hall. The various chimes and the chirp of the cuckoo were no longer synchronized, and the house was filled with random sounds the Moores barely heard, a counterpoint to the birdsong that filtered in from outside.

In the front room, Ma sat bolt upright in the precise center of a bright slipcovered couch. She seemed to have shrunk since her clothes were put on. The collar of her flannel bathrobe stood out like a monk's cowl around her drawn neck, and her fuzzy pink bedroom slippers seemed four sizes larger than the feet that held them so carefully side by side on the bleached floor. She seemed more like a child than a grandmother.

Gore stood, enormous and grinning, in the center of the room,

11

dwarfing his surroundings. Ma held out her hands to him with the force of a command until he took his own hands out of his pockets and leaned over to grasp hers. "How are you, Mrs. Moore?" he asked.

"Not so good," sighed Ma. "I ain't got the go I used to." Her weary voice contrasted with her small hazel eyes—sharp as a bobcat's—watching Bob Gore from under her tangle of gray hair.

Hildie sprang onto the couch and curled up against Ma. Without taking her eyes off Gore, Ma reached out a knobby hand and, with a few pats, straightened Hildie around until she quieted down and folded her hands in her lap.

Mim perched on the edge of a straight chair near the door and John took the piano bench.

"And you, Bobby," Ma was saying. "What's new? Anything you can hope to tell us in less than a day or two?"

"Perly Dunsmore's what's new, Mrs. Moore," Gore said, settling his broad self comfortably in the rocking chair. "He's the newest thing Harlowe's seen in years." He beamed, as if the auctioneer were a glistening new possession, a special find, a bargain worthy of the envy of any neighbor who knew value when he saw it.

"Who?" Ma said, raising her brows. "You mean that crazy fool moved into the Fawkes place all by hisself?"

Gore lit a cigarette, located a flowerpot by his left elbow to flick the ashes into, and seemed to expand just slightly. He took a breath.

"Don't wear us plumb out now, Bobby," Ma said, but her voice was no longer weary.

"Good turnout?" John asked.

"Wonderful," Gore said, taking a deep breath. "It was one absolutely wonderful auction." He chuckled. "You wouldn't believe how that Perly Dunsmore gets the most for everything. What an auctioneer! I never saw nothin' to beat it. He gets up there on that bandstand and I don't know him, hardly. He's like one of them fish can puff itself up to four times its ordinary size. Sharp as a whip, he is. And what a talker! Makes me seem like the silent type."

"They talk different," John said, "these city dudes. They drink crankcase oil for breakfast."

"Oh, but Perly's a New Hampshire boy," Gore said. "From Elvira, up to the Canadian border. Ain't much we can tell him about the country."

"Thought he was some big-deal consultant," John said. "That's what Arthur Stinson says. And he ought to know after all the time he spent paintin' and scrapin' that place."

"Well, Perly ain't ordinary," Gore said. "Fact, there's a man could do any damn thing he set his mind to. But he growed up on a New Hampshire farm like all the rest of us. It's just that he lit out when he weren't much more than a chicken. Made his way everywhere you can think of. Mexico, Alaska, Vegas, Venezuela. All over. And all over America too. Once in a while he'd run an auction, I guess, but most of the time he was some kind of consultant that tells people how to manage their land. He just kept wanderin'. Must of thought he'd find somethin' better."

Ma snorted.

"Seems like he didn't, ma'am," Gore said. "Because here he is, ready to settle right back where he started from. Fact, that's how he knew about the Fawkes place. He stayed there once about a year back, when Amelia was rentin' out rooms. And he was smart enough to see Harlowe's as good a place as any."

"They say the Fawkes place was quite a bargain," John said.

"Still, he's a bit on the odd side, you ask me," Mim said. "Movin' into that big house all alone with just that dog. Specially after all this time no one'd even cut the grass."

"Guess murders in the night don't mean nothin' to him," Ma said.

Gore shrugged. "He knows it don't mean nothin' one way or the other about what Harlowe's really like."

"So why Harlowe?" John asked. "Instead of Powlton, say, or over Peterborough way where it's so much fancier?"

"Oh, Perly's got ideas," Gore said. "You should hear him talk."

"You ought to bring him out," Ma said.

"You'd like him," Gore said. "He's got that way about him women like. And he'd see the value of a well-kept farm like this."

13

"That's 'cause he don't have to do the keepin'," John said. "Is it him you're plannin' on for deputy?"

"I asked, but he ain't interested," Gore said.

"He's just after tellin' you what to do. He ain't interested in the actual labor," John said.

Gore frowned. "Red Mudgett's back," he said. "He's lookin' for somethin', and you remember he was always so smart?"

"Bobby," cried Ma. "You ain't gone and hired Red Mudgett? Why you ain't got no more sense than the rest of the Gores."

"Perly thought he'd be good," Gore said, fishing in his pocket for a cigarette.

Hildie had wiggled to the floor in front of Gore and sat with her arm around Lassie. She watched entranced as he lit a second cigarette from the end of the first.

"Why he's the rottenest egg this town's turned out since I was big enough to hear tell," Ma said. "And if anyone knows, it's me. I had him in my Sunday School class a good three years."

"I figure Mudgett's a reformed character," Gore said.

"You figure, or this Dunsmore fellow figures?" John said.

"Well, he's got a wife now," Gore said. He pulled out a handkerchief and wiped his brow. "Some wife too." He gave Mim an appraising look. She smiled, a trace of color coming through the light freckles on the bridge of her nose. "I don't know, Johnny," he said. "If you and him can do so well, maybe there's even hope for me."

"Funny," John said. "I pegged Red as one would never marry. Nor was I thinkin', the way he always talked, he'd ever want to see the likes of Harlowe again."

"Speakin' of which," Ma said, "don't you think it a mite peculiar that this new auctioneer'd come here instead of back to his own town where everybody knows him?"

Gore let the question hang fire a moment. "It's a pretty depressed area right now, northern New Hampshire," he said.

"Guess you don't call this depressed," John said, gesturing toward the barn.

"There's changes comin' here," Gore said. "Don't forget the summer people. And all the new ones stayin' the winter now too."

Gore leaned back in his chair. "Like I told you, Perly knows about land. And there's big things brewin' in Harlowe to do with land. It's comin', I tell you. You know them towns down near Massachusetts? They've got as bad as the city. Vandalism all the time and traffic and filth. . . . Perly figures he can help Harlowe get to growin' right before it strikes us full on."

"What if Harlowe don't care to grow at all?" John said.

"You better go dynamite the interstate then," Gore said, looking apologetically at Ma. "With Boston, and I guess everyplace, spreadin' like gypsy moths in June . . ." He leaned forward in his chair. "Besides," he said, "would *you* like to live in the city?"

"Not me," John said.

"Course not." Gore settled back. "Perly figures the only reason city folk make such a mess everywhere they go is that they need just what we got. They come here lookin' for some good country values. A group of real people to feel part of. Some kind of connection. But we keep them at arm's length now, never let them into things—"

"He just moved in," John said. "He plannin' to set up as a welcome committee already? Or is he goin' to set you up at the edge of town to give out daisies—from your new cruiser maybe?"

"Damn it, John," Gore said. "You was always such a one to mock. With all the new people comin' in, how can it hurt to have someone around knows what he's doin'?"

"What's he got in mind for himself's what I'd like to know," John said.

"You ain't got the picture of this Perly straight at all," Gore said. "The thing is, he's sort of a do-gooder. After me all the time to swear off beer and cigarettes. Like one of them old-fashioned preachers, ought to be wearin' a black hat and a collar. He's got this idea if we bring back auctions for a start, and square dances, and quiltin' bees, and potluck suppers . . . Remember them spellin' bees we used to have before they closed the old school?"

"Me and you," John said, "we always used to go down near the first ones. You hankerin' to go back to that?"

"Then he's got this thing about farmin', and well water, and firewood, and clear air. To his mind, all that's part and parcel with Christian values."

Mim chewed on the knuckle of her thumb uneasily.

Gore lit another cigarette and drew on it so that his whole front lifted six inches. He looked down at Hildie, then turned to gaze uncomfortably at the plastic daisies hanging between the front windows. "Fact, he was after me to ask who all would send their little ones if he started a Sunday School."

"I taught Sunday School thirty-five years, for my part," Ma said.

"Well I know it," Gore said, nodding.

"Course Hildie'd go to Sunday School," Ma said. "She'd love that. And she needs it bad."

Hildie felt her grandmother's complacent glance, caught her lip in her teeth, and scuttled to her mother.

There was a loud snap in the stove and the hollow sound of the fire momentarily blazing, not a comforting sound since the room was already too warm for everyone but Ma.

"That what you're doin' here?" John asked, starting to laugh. "Collectin' kids for a Sunday School class?"

"Well, not exactly," Gore said. "Thing is, we thought we'd give it another go next Saturday."

"Another auction?" John asked, his laughter cut short.

Gore shrugged.

"I thought the one you had was fine," John said.

"If one's good, two's better," Gore said, resettling his bulk in the chair. "We're thinkin' we might hold even more."

"For the police again?" John asked.

Gore rummaged in his back pocket for his handkerchief again. "If you wait till crime gets out of hand before you get around to more police . . ."

Ma nodded enthusiastically. "Why it's just like Janice Pulver was sayin' about how Farmer's Mutual had to raise its prices because of payin' so much on account of them hippies campin' out all over the place. Never mind Amelia strangled like that."

"Well, things are gettin' more complicated," Gore said, turning to Ma with gratitude. "That's about all I know."

"Why, we can give them that old buffet," Ma said. "What'd we ever do with that anyway?"

On the days when nobody went to town, John walked the quarter of a mile to the mailbox as he had since he was barely bigger than Hildie. Usually it was empty. But on the Friday after Gore's second visit, when he lifted Hildie to look, she pulled out a letter. She ran home ahead of him in the sunshine, so agile now that John could no longer keep up with her without breaking into a run himself, and he was some years past that. His boots crunched rhythmically in the sandy mud as he followed, his broad face content as his child widened the gap between them, waving the letter high over her head like a flag.

Hildie threw the letter triumphantly into Ma's lap and waited for John to sit in the rocker so she could climb into his lap. Mim leaned against the piano in her apron. Ma read aloud:

Dear John, Miriam, Mrs. Moore, and Hildie:
    The wheels you contributed to the policeman's auction brought a surprisingly good price. I would like to remit some of the money to you as a recompense for your generosity.
    Bob thinks the auction was a great success. I certainly hope it will contribute to Harlowe's future safety.
    As you no doubt know, I am the new owner of the former Fawkes place on the Parade and very much hope that we will meet as neighbors soon and see a lot of one another.

Sincerely,
Perly Dunsmore

Enclosed was a check for three dollars. "More than the firemen ever do," John said, turning the check over and righting it again.

"He's sure got Bob Gore all wrapped up and tied with a yellow ribbon," Mim said.

"That's nothin' to sneeze at," Ma said. "For all his talk, Bobby got the share of sense for the whole nineteen of them Gore kids. And if he'd a lit out of Harlowe like the rest, we'd have old Toby on the dole sure."

"How 'bout the cows, Ma?" John said, winking at Mim. "We'd

17

of had the cows on the dole too. Might's well shoot Toby out-right as take his cows away."

"Crazy how that barn don't fall on them," Mim said.

"Everybody from Harlowe knows it's goin' to stand as long as Toby," snapped Ma.

"Bob's not the worst cop you could have," John said. "He's sure to be up in a flash if you call."

"He'd be scared of missin' somethin'," Ma said.

"Kind of mean, ain't it?" John said. "All these seven years he's been dreamin' of havin' a real honest-to-gosh crime to solve. And now he's got a whopper—a stranglin'—not to mention the break-in and the holdup. And poor old Bobby ain't scared up so much as a suspect."

"Fanny says he was so cross he wouldn't even talk about it," Mim said. "Not even when he'd had a few. Not that I blame him. Downright humiliatin', right there in the biggest house in town like that."

Ma turned to John. "Do you recall that spell back when old Nicholas Fawkes used the big barn for auctions?" she asked. "That makes a sort of a tradition, don't it? Maybe this Perly Dunsmore ain't such a fool after all. You ought to go on down to the store a bit more often. See what you can find out."

John shook his head and grinned. "You're workin' up a power-ful curiosity about this fellow, Ma," he said.

"Can't say I ever thought about it just like that before, did you, John?" Mim asked. "That what they're really after is to get to be like us?"

"Who?" John asked.

"All the people movin' from the city to the country," she said.

John and Mim were climbing up the pasture to replace any fallen stones in the back wall so the cows wouldn't stray into the woods. It was always a good hike to the top, but that morning there was a fog curtaining their progress, and it seemed a journey. The child walked between them, subdued, keeping their hands tight in her own. An invisible phoebe called over and over as if counting their quiet footsteps up and up on the steep brown island fading into whiteness, and occasionally crows cried in the distance.

Halfway up, they turned, as they always did, to look out over the pond, but it was lost completely in the fog. "Look at the house," Hildie whispered.

"Looks nice," Mim said.

What they saw was a white cape set into the side of the hill with a fence of tall hand-carved pickets across the back. The mist bleached away the weathering on the paint, the rusty tin over the woodshed, the missing bricks in the chimney, the plastic over the windows, even the tangle of last year's morning-glory vines still clinging to the fence.

"Looks all polished up," John said.

"Like summer folks had got their hands on it." Mim laughed and turned to climb again.

Eventually, the small walled cemetery under the cherry tree emerged through the fog. "Look out," Mim warned as they approached, catching Hildie before she stepped into the brown remains of last year's poison ivy. "We ought to spray that," she said, "before it gets a hold this summer."

"Before Ma goes," John murmured. "Now there would be a pretty mess."

"Might not suit your pa either and all the ones before him to be lyin' like that in such a bed of poison."

But the child had turned to look down again. "It's gone!" she cried. "The house is gone!"

"No more than you're gone from it." John laughed. He caught her up to carry on his shoulders. "Look at the willows, pet. See that smudgy yellow? They'll be greenin' up and we'll have spring before we're halfway ready." They headed toward the high back wall of the pasture, scanning it carefully for broken places. But most of the granite chunks remained in their accustomed places, fastened by a sinewy net of Concord grape vines.

"All things considered, I don't half mind," Mim said.

"What?" asked John.

"Bein' the way we are," she said.

19

·2·

As MUD GAVE WAY to black flies and black flies to mosquitoes, Bob Gore came again, and yet again.

The Moores heard about the auctions at Linden's store. Every week more people came, more people smitten with the romance of a country life, part of the same blind force that, since before Hildie was born, had been tearing up the hillsides with bulldozers and setting in the trailers and tiny modular houses designed to look traditional. Some of the new people drove halfway to Boston every day to work along the outer belt highway. Some manned the bright glass and steel factories going in along Route 37 as it made its way south. And more and more summer people poured in off the interstate every weekend, invading Linden's store in flimsy striped and polka-dot clothes, complaining about the price of produce, and gobbling up the plastic balls and pinwheels and inflatable elephants that Hildie loved so.

When Gore came, John led him down under the barn to the cavernous area that housed a century's collection of broken rockers, tables with legs missing, cracked mirrors, rusted cider presses, and outdated tools. "How long you figure you can get people to buy this rummage, Bobby?" John asked one week.

"I wonder myself sometimes," Gore admitted. He stopped to light a cigarette and watched the smoke curling up into the cobwebs overhead. "Perly's like a magician, but still . . ."

"Hard for me to figure people with nothin' better to do in spring than go to auctions."

"Well, they ain't farmers," Gore said. "Sets you on your heels to see all the city folk pourin' into the Parade on a Saturday. The towns around here are growin' all right. And even the people just drove up for a weekend can't seem to think what to do with a Saturday. Mow the lawn, cart the garbage to the dump, complain about the bugs. What the hell? I guess Perly's right. The auctions make them feel a part of things."

"I can't say the checks ain't welcome," John said.

"What Perly says is it's just buyin' and sellin' in the best American tradition, and we give them a better show than a discount store, which is where they'd be in the city on a Saturday. Guess some people just like to part with money."

"You plannin' to goldplate your cruiser, or what?" John asked, unearthing an old soapstone sink and indicating that Gore should lift one end.

"Manpower," Gore said. "I've got me five deputies now."

"*Five!*" John said.

"Well, like Perly says, 'Prevention's the best cure,'" Gore said, running his hand over the gray stone appraisingly. "I told you we got Mudgett, and now we got Jimmy Ward, Sonny Pike, Jim Carroll, and your neighbor there, Mickey Cogswell."

"Tough lot," John said, frowning.

"Perly says," Gore said, looking up at John, "it's men like that make people want to bring up their sons in Harlowe."

John lifted his end of the heavy sink and helped Gore carry it out to the truck.

"When you goin' to come and see our man in action?" Gore asked. "He's a regular wizard. Puts a spell on a crowd so they can't help what they do."

"But, Bobby," John said, "you come to us every Thursday bustin' at the seams with every slick thing that man's said all week. What do we need to see him for?"

The Moores found few free moments in spring. Spring was the time when they laid the foundations for another year of living.

John plowed up and reseeded the quarter of the pasture that was most grown up in hawkweed and daisies. Mim pruned and sprayed the apple trees. John harrowed and manured the garden and the new patch for the squash. And Mim and Hildie planted, pressing the seeds into the wet earth by hand. They took down the plastic covers from the windows, and hung up a swing for Hildie and an old tire. They planted flowers in front of the house and in the bigger garden across the road that they still called Ma's garden, though now it was Mim instead of Ma who cut the flowers to sell to the church. And, of course, they milked the cows in the mornings and drove them up into the pasture, then brought them back and milked them again in the evening.

The child went with them everywhere, sitting on her own stool near them as they milked, keeping out of reach of Sunshine's tail and asking endless questions or singing idly to herself. John and Mim listened quietly and answered when they could, resting their heads against the warm flanks of the cows and leaning into the rhythm of milking the seven cows.

They were married over a decade before Hildie was born, and the quick fair child was so unlike her parents that Ma teased her, telling her she must be the changeling child of a dandelion. John and Mim had planned a big family. It was a part of growing to put out branches, as many as possible. When they were married, the price of milk was holding and nothing seemed difficult. Even when the milk stopped paying, they would have accepted children as part of the course of things, had they come along. But, by the time Hildie was born, their plans had faded to an almost forgotten ache, not from longing for a child so much as from a sense that they had been passed over by the rhythms of the earth, like the apple tree that bloomed so prettily but could not be coaxed to bear.

John and Mim had always gone to the fields and the woods and the barn together and fallen into step like brothers to do what had to be done. And practically from the time Hildie was born, they continued their habit, taking the baby with them or leaving her sleeping with her grandmother, by then too crippled to care for a child, but able enough to ring the gong to summon them when she woke up. When Hildie was tiny, Mim carried her on her back or tethered her to a stake like a goat, and when she grew older, she seemed to stay nearby just naturally. And, in a way they hadn't expected and never mentioned, it made them feel complete, even happy, to have the child about.

In the evening the family talked, as they did every year when spring gripped them with energy and stirrings of ambition, about tearing out the big central chimney and putting in a real bathroom with a tub and an electric hot water heater. If Mim could get a few days of cleaning for the new summer people, or sell a few more flowers—if John could get more time from the town running the grader or the snowplow, or a few more jobs helping Cogswell, then they could pay for it. That year they also talked about the auctioneer—about his plans for the town. There was an excitement to his coming that seemed of a piece with the quickening of spring. It reconciled them to Bob Gore's visits to hear him talk about the things that were happening just beyond the edges of their farm.

"That's what I always said," claimed Ma. "That all them people are comin' here on account of this is where America began. They get to see that all that fast livin' ain't worth the trouble it starts."

"That's why you watch all them jack-a-dandies on your programs like they was givin' out the word of God," John teased.

"And what would you have me do, with my legs no more use than two popple sticks?" Ma cried.

"If the auction checks came out to just a mite more," Mim said, "could be we'd get our bathroom after all."

But finally they decided, as they always did when the days grew warmer and lazier, that any change should wait until they had the money in hand.

One Saturday morning, their curiosity got the better of their list of chores. John and Mim and Hildie took a bar of Ivory soap down to the pond and cleaned up. Afterward, scrubbed from scalp to toes, they dressed to go to town—John in clean khakis, Mim in a flowered skirt and yellow blouse, and Hildie in a hand-me-down dotted swiss dress from one of the Cogswell girls. Mim gave Ma a sponge bath and helped her to pull her lisle stockings over her lumpy legs and lace up the black dress shoes.

Secretly, Mim liked going to town, but she wondered if her clothes were right, if she would say something foolish to somebody. She remembered the way people had looked at her when she first came to Harlowe, and she brushed furiously at her hair, as if that would somehow soften the laugh lines around her eyes and make her seventeen again. Now that it was too late, it would have been all right to be admired. Although she had grown up in Powlton, only one town away, she had always felt out of step in Harlowe. John did not hunt or play poker, and she, in turn, did not take part in bake sales or sewing circles. When the others her age had been raising babies, baking, and fancying up their homes, she had known only planting and milking and cutting wood. "No children," she knew they had commented over their sewing. "Too pretty, that's why." Then, when the others, with children in high school, were putting in formica counters and central heat, she was finally raising a baby, continuing to cook and heat with wood, and finding things quite all right and cheaper the way they were. And, although she and John sold flowers to the church, because Ma always had sold flowers to the church, they didn't feel the need to attend.

If anyone had asked, Mim would have said she was friends with Agnes Cogswell. In summer the Cogswells were their nearest neighbors. Two or three times a year—at least once during blueberry season and once at Christmas—Mim went over and spent a day there. And occasionally Agnes called her up with some question or tidbit of gossip. Agnes wasn't fashionable either, though not because she didn't try. Agnes' problem was that she overdid everything to the point where she scared people away. But Mim, in a quiet way, appreciated her affection and enjoyed visiting in the harum-scarum household with its six noisy children.

Four abreast on the seat of the old green truck, the Moores were all silent as they rattled over the dirt road toward town— Ma with discomfort, John and Mim with their thoughts, and Hildie with eagerness. The auctions were being held on the

Parade like the firemen's auctions. Although they were early, the road that circled the green was parked solid on all four sides, and a good group of people milled around examining the things for sale clustered around the bandstand.

"Balloons!" cried Hildie, jumping ahead of the others as they walked slowly toward the auction.

There was only a smattering of Harlowe people among the summer people and strangers—little girls in pink shorts and jerseys and new sneakers covered with stars, boys in crisp new jeans sporting bright cap pistols, lean couples in baggy clothes, fat ladies with jangling bracelets, and a few serious antique dealers in dark jackets.

"Please, Papa, please," Hildie cried. "I need a balloon."

It was Mudgett selling the balloons. John followed Hildie and gave up the thirty cents. He made no mention of the fact that Mudgett had been gone for nearly twenty years.

"Be very careful now," Mudgett warned. "If you let go, the balloon will float right up into the sky and disappear just like a bad child."

Flat on his hip lay a neat black leather holster like the one Gore wore when he answered trouble calls. "You need a pistol to sell balloons, Red?" asked John.

"Never can tell," said Mudgett and straightened up without a smile, his dark eyes dull as charcoal, his once red hair long since tarnished to brown like neglected copper.

John shook his head as they walked toward the chairs to settle Ma. "Red always had that way," he said. "When he was in school, he just had to look at you to set you squirmin' without half knowin' why."

Mim helped Ma into a chair and hooked her canes over the rungs beneath her.

"Like quicksilver with the Bible verses, that boy," Ma said. "One look and he could rattle them off better'n the preacher. In the preacher's way too—so close it made your flesh crawl. Oh, he was wicked fresh."

"You still got it in for him 'cause you caught him takin' off on you that time," John said, grinning.

25

Ma shook her head. "Some boy he was. Too big for his britches even then. He was settin' up to get out of Harlowe before he was half growed."

"Guess he found out the rest of the world's no different," John said. "Don't know of anyone glad to see him back."

"Fanny says that girl he married's from Manchester, and she's showin' already," Mim said.

"Him a father," John said, his foot up on the chair in front of Ma, his elbow on his knee. "God help the child. He used to have this dog. Remember, Ma? One of them black-and-white spotted hounds. He wanted that dog to be a killer. Tried and tried to make him mean. But nothin' would do. The dog just put his tail between his legs and shivered. At school we'd all stand around, our eyes buggin' out to watch Red punish the beast. Once in winter, he lowered the dog into the well. And once he dragged him up to the roof of the schoolhouse and let him slide down and fall. He finally killed him feedin' him broken glass. He pulled the dog the whole way to school in a wagon so we could all see him vomit blood."

"Well, I know other men was fresh when they was boys," Ma said. "A baby may soften him up some. I know someone turned soft as a grape." Her eyes darted here and there in queer contrast with her slow body. "Now you young people get over there and take a look at what's for sale," she said. "I see a bed frame looks quite fancy."

So John and Mim and Hildie moved toward the bandstand and wandered among the things set out for sale.

"A heap of barns gettin' cleaned this year," John said.

"Why do you suppose anyone'd put this out to the barn?" Mim asked, running her hand down the cornerpost of the fine spool bed Ma had spotted. It was beautifully oiled and finished. "This is a darn sight better than what I call rummage."

Hildie found a cast-off red wagon and arranged her sturdy self in it. She ran her hand lovingly around its rusted rim. "Not even one little thing?" she pleaded, for her parents had warned her they would not buy her anything.

"Might not go for much," Mim said.

"We'll see," John said, heading back toward Ma.

Hildie followed, pulling the wagon behind her. Then she set

herself to kneeling in it, sitting in it, trying out the handle and all the wheels, her green balloon bobbing overhead.

A ripple of attention passed through the crowd. On the porch of the old Fawkes place stood the auctioneer. He was as tall as Gore, but trim and upright. Despite his red plaid shirt open at the neck, there was something sharply formal about his stance which set him apart from the country Saturday slackness of the people waiting for him. His features were fine and tense and his skin was burned almost as brown as his hair. He stood looking out over the crowd, his hands in his pockets. Directly over his head, elaborate carved fretwork hung from the eaves, laced in and out with thick brown stalks of wisteria. Above the porch was the central window, and higher still, at the peak of the roof, a weather vane with a lynx turning restlessly in a light breeze beneath a pointed lightning rod. At the auctioneer's heel sat a young golden retriever, the tip of her tail moving in tentative friendliness as she waited to walk with him into the crowd.

Finally, a half smile of welcome on his lips, the auctioneer moved down his front steps, across the road, and into the crowd between his house and the bandstand.

The people were beginning to fill in the seats and to settle themselves for the auction. They opened a way before Dunsmore, and he paused to nod and shake hands with everyone from Harlowe.

When he reached the Moores, he stopped and looked at them. "The Moores, perhaps?" he said. "From up on Constance Hill?"

John looked at Mim.

"Lord sake," Ma cried. "How'd you know that?"

The auctioneer threw back his head and laughed. "I've been hoping you'd come. You folks do keep to yourselves. I've met almost everyone else by now. And I've heard about Hildie's corn-silk hair." He reached out and placed a broad palm on Hildie's head.

Hildie stood with her mouth open and allowed herself to be caressed.

The auctioneer stepped back and put his hands on his hips.

"Do you like that red wagon, little lady?" he asked.

Hildie clapped her thumb into her mouth and lifted trusting blue eyes to the auctioneer in assent.

"Now there's a lady knows her own mind," he said to Mim with a broad smile, his dark eye catching momentarily on her face. "Now, Hildie. If you'll just give up that precious wagon. Oh, only for a minute or two, don't worry. I'll kick off the whole shebang with your little wagon. That way your daddy can buy it for you right off."

But instead of letting go, Hildie plumped her bottom firmly into the bed of the wagon and hung on.

"Now, Hildie, I'm a man of sterling honor, can't you tell?" he asked.

Hildie caught her bottom lip in a shy smile.

He lifted her out of the wagon, kissing her on the forehead as he set her down next to Mim.

He held out his hand to John. John, caught off guard, paused for an awkward second, then shook hands. "So glad to meet you folks at last," said the auctioneer.

"We've heard it's quite a show," John mumbled.

Then the auctioneer picked up the rusty wagon and carried it off with him. The dog turned to follow. Hildie watched for a second, then turned and headed off herself after the auctioneer, the dog, and the precious wagon.

"Hildie," John called sharply, but the child didn't turn.

"Let her be," Ma said. "What harm can come to her in Harlowe?"

Perly Dunsmore climbed up the stairs onto the bandstand and rapped his gavel on the wooden railing. Hildie followed him up. He paused and lifted her high onto a bureau behind him where she stuck her thumb back into her mouth and kept a sharp eye on her wagon. The dog lay down at his feet.

Mim turned to John with a grin, but he tipped back in his chair with annoyance.

"This little girl here is Hildie Moore," said Dunsmore, his words lengthening into a drawl, and his air of distance dissolving so completely that the lines of his face seemed literally to rearrange themselves. The deep timbre of his voice took on a burly quality, and he was transformed before their eyes into someone who was clearly born to be an auctioneer.

"Now Hildie Moore is a very special pal of mine," he went on, "and she's picked out this fine little magical chariot here to kick off the bidding at this auction—on this most sensational cotton-picking high falutin lollapalooza of a Saturday auction Harlowe's seen yet. Now, what am I offered for this all-American humdinger of a wagon, the dream of every big-eyed thumb-sucking whipper-snapper this side of Powlton?"

Hildie blushed. She took her thumb out of her mouth and sat on her hand for safekeeping. On Perly Dunsmore's left, Gore held up the wagon for everyone to see.

"Fifty cents," John called.

"Fifty, fifty. Do I hear a big round shiny silver dollar?" Perly's voice gained momentum like metal wheels rolling over the joints in a railroad track.

A young woman in shorts and a halter stood at the edge of the crowd with a little boy in a white sailor suit. "Seventy-five," she said.

"Seventy-five, seventy-five. Come on, folks. Let's not be scrimy. Remember this is for the little ones. Where's that big round shiny silver dollar?"

John raised a hand.

"Dollar, dollar. Do I hear a dollar and a quarter?" chanted the auctioneer.

The woman nodded, and her little boy jumped on the end of her hand.

"Yes sirree, this is more like it. A little elbow grease on this gilt-edged rust, a little spit and polish on the squeaky wheels, a little muscle power on this bent axle right here, and this little old chariot here'll be fit for a gladiator. And now I'd like to hear a couple of big round shiny silver dollars and then I'll hand the lucky winner keys and registration, bill of sale and license plates. Who knows, folks, where the rusty wheels will take you."

"Dollar and a half," called John.

"Dollar and a half. Dollar and a half. Do I hear two? Going,

going, going, gone. For a dollar and a half to the prettiest little lassie I've had my hands on in many a day." Perly caught up Hildie from her perch behind him and swung her high over his head for everyone to see, then handed her over the railing to Mudgett who swooped her down and settled her in the small rusted wagon.

A teenaged boy with hair almost to his shoulders pulled the wagon down the grassy aisle to where the Moores were sitting, and John paid him. "You Jimmy Ward's boy?" John asked.

The boy nodded.

"All you kids got those freckles just like your pa," said Ma. "I'd know a Ward a mile away."

"Dad's a deputy, I hear," John said. "Always get a turnout like this?"

"Nope," said the boy. "But now they're puttin' notices in all the papers. Even the Boston papers." He grinned and shook his head in the direction of the bandstand. "He always carries on like that. Guess that's the main thing brings them out."

"An old-time Yankee auction," Perly was saying—his body swaying in a strange stillness, his words flying out over the crowd with a life all their own—"is the crossroads of America. An old-time Yankee auction is where the best of the old meets the best of the new. It's where recycling meets up with the old saying, 'Use it up, wear it out, make it do, or do without.' It's where the best of the old-timers meet the best of the newcomers. You've got people on your right and people on your left. You've all got things to offer, and I sincerely hope that this here seventh old-time Harlowe auction will help you get together.

"Now I have here a piece of genuine Americana. An old-fashioned beautifully worked hand-cranked milk separator." Mudgett lifted the heavy separator and balanced it precariously on the railing of the bandstand while Perly showed it off. "Look at that pewter fancywork, at the quality of the porcelain in the bowl. Nowadays, they don't bother to make machines beautiful to look at. But there was a time when they cared about the boy who had to stand there and crank, so they decorated the separator with leaves and flowers to rest his eyes and calm his soul."

"Never mind the malarkey, Perly," called Sam Parry from just behind the Moores. At seventy, Sam was white-haired but still hale. His age showed only in that, since his children had left home, he found it harder with every passing year to hold his tongue. "Does the blamed thing *work?*"

"Like a charm," Perly said. "In those days they made machines to last." He turned the crank. "Perfect working order. Look at this."

"Sounds a bit squeaky," Sam said. "How do I know the innards are workin'?"

"Because I say so," Perly said. "And my word's as good as the fact, though if you're nervous I'll write you out an ironclad guarantee. This machine's been running for a heap of years, and it's probably got a longer journey yet to go than most of us."

Sam bid a dollar, muttering to his wife and anyone else who might be listening, "That Sears electric thing I got from Paul Geness is no damn good."

"Serves you right," said his wife. "You know he gets that stuff from the dump."

"A dollar!" Perly laughed. He shrugged his shoulders. "Course we have to start somewhere, but this is a genuine antique worth at least a hundred. Now I want you all to consider what a conversation piece this would make in your playroom or your dining area. Teach your children the centrifugal principles. Teach them how they did things in the olden days. And you can rest assured that no one else you know will have one like it. There probably aren't a dozen machines like this one extant in all the vast stretches of America."

"Ten dollars," bid a small woman wearing a tight minidress and a glossy high-piled hairdo of dark curls.

Perly spotted her in the crowd and spoke directly to her. "This is a piece that will stop people in their tracks. Picture it mounted next to your basement bar. Entertain your company by cranking punch out of it. Yes, ma'am, you can't go wrong on this. I have ten now, I have ten. Do I hear fifteen?"

"Eleven," Sam called. "If you're so sure the blessed thing works, why you sellin' it for a conversation piece?" He went on mumbling.

"Holy smokes. A conversation piece. What kind of fool needs a conversation piece. If talk don't come natural, why bother?"

"Never your problem," commented his wife.

"Eleven. Eleven," Perly was intoning. "Now remember an antique like this will just keep right on growing in value as time goes on. What's more, it's still working, so if times get hard, you can always buy a cow and separate your own milk."

"Tarnation," Sam said. "I already *got* cows."

"I have eleven. Do I hear fifteen?"

Perly kept an eye on the woman with the curls, but from the chairs on the other side of the aisle, a man in a blue seersucker jacket raised his pipe to signal fifteen.

"Fifteen, fifteen. Do I hear twenty?"

"Sixteen," Sam called loud and clear, "and robbery at that."

"Sixteen, do I hear twenty?"

The woman with the curls nodded to the twenty.

"Twenty, twenty. Do I hear twenty-five?"

The man gave him the twenty-five, and the woman went up to twenty-six. The man countered with twenty-seven, and there was a pause.

"Twenty-seven, twenty-seven," Perly cried, "and a bargain at twice the price. Who'll give me thirty?"

The woman with the curls nodded.

Perly turned to the man again. "Thirty, thirty, give me thirty-five and you'll have something you can pass on to your children's children."

But the man shook his head.

"Sold," shouted Perly. "For thirty dollars, to the little woman who knows a bargain when she sees one."

"Who don't know when she's been had," growled Sam to no one in particular.

"And now, folks, hold your horses," called the auctioneer. "There's one more brave old American custom that an auction helps to keep alive. Americans have always jumped at their chances where they found them and that's what keeps their blood flowing stronger and quicker than any other blood. I've been in forty countries and I know it's true. Americans have never been afraid to risk their money where their hearts are, and that's why we're the richest country in the world. Now I've got something here that just might pay big dividends. I've got three surprise boxes here and each and every one of you is going to get a chance to bid. Here's your double or nothing bid. You never know. I heard of a man once bought a strongbox for forty dollars and when he pried it open it had seventy-five thousand dollars in it. Seventy-five thousand dollars that the judge ruled his by law. It could happen to anyone—to me, to you. So what am I offered for this Campbell soup carton filled with surprises? A thimble, a screwdriver, a bundle of quilting squares, a pair of long johns— who knows? Maybe a gold nugget. Fifty cents, fifty cents. Let me hear a dollar. . . ."

The Thursday after the auction, the Moores were up in the garden setting out tomatoes and onions and planting beans.

"I figure there's about two good boxes of old tools down there still and then that'll be about it with us and the auctions," John said.

"I don't know," Mim said, leaning back on her heels and pushing her wispy brown curls out of her face. "We could start on the attic. Make a clean sweep while we're at it."

"Got to save somethin' for another year," John said.

"Another year," Mim said. "Someone or other's been savin' that rummage for another year since longer than Ma can remember. We can get somethin' for it if we let it go now."

John was using a crowbar to sink the stakes for the tomatoes and beans. Now he pried out a rock the size of his head and heaved it off to one side.

"Save it," Mim went on, "and Hildie's children's children will be sniffin' through there every rainy day just like you did as a boy. Beaver traps and broken mirrors. That's no place for kids, and Hildie's already jumpin' to be up there every chance she gets."

Gradually they recognized the sound of a motor approaching. They stood up to see who it was before they committed themselves to walk down the field. In summer, curious people drove

33

the back roads just to see what was at the end of them. They would turn around in the Moores' dooryard. Ma would peer out her window. Hildie would stare from the shadow of the barn. And the sightseers would gaze soberly back as though what they saw were as insensible as the black-and-white images of a television documentary.

But this time the motor was Gore's. And this time he had Perly Dunsmore with him.

Hildie started down the hill at a run, and Mim and John walked quickly after her.

Gore's truck stopped in the dooryard, the passenger door opened, and the auctioneer's golden retriever bounded out. Lassie backed off, barking wildly. The retriever moved cautiously toward Lassie. Lassie stopped, and the two dogs circled each other, their tails held high.

Behind the picket fence that ran between the house and the barn, Hildie stopped, struck shy, as the tall auctioneer unfolded himself from the truck and stooped with a smile to greet her.

"Do you like your red wagon, Hildie?" he coaxed.

Hildie nodded and came out from behind the fence, but still stood at a distance sucking her thumb.

"Come and see what I have for you," said the auctioneer, digging into his pocket.

Hildie took her thumb out of her mouth and waited for her parents. She took Mim's hand, and moved with them toward Gore and Dunsmore.

Gore was leaning on the door of the truck. "How'd you like the way Perly scared that tourist half to death with the idea of scrubbin' off a little rust?" he greeted John.

Perly opened his palm to Hildie. In it was a piece of pink bubble gum wrapped in green plastic.

Hildie glanced up at Mim, then smiled and reached for the gum. Perly stroked her cheek and winked at her, then stood up.

"Sure is a pretty place," Perly said to John and Mim. "Everything everyone says about it's true." He looked out past the house to the pasture with the garden halfway up on the level place. "Just had to come out and see for myself."

Hildie was sidling up to the dogs. They were still sniffing each other warily. The hair on Lassie's broad back was bristled and her short legs were tensed.

"That's Dixie," Perly said to the child. The big fawn dog came to his side when he mentioned her name, though she kept her amber eyes longingly on Lassie. "Shake hands with Hildie, Dixie," he said. The dog sat down and held out her paw for Hildie. Hildie held her ground for an instant, then turned and buried her face against her mother. The auctioneer winked at Mim as she caught the child and sheltered her.

"Show them how she says her prayers, Perly," Gore said. "This here's the smartest damn dog . . ."

"Pray, Dixie," Perly ordered. The dog balanced herself on her hind legs like a terrier, pressed her paws together, pointed her nose at the wisp of smoke curling from the chimney of the house, and howled.

Hildie laughed and jumped up and down with delight, bouncing into Gore's knee in her excitement.

"Mind yourself now, Hildie," Mim scolded. But her own face was bright with pleasure. "Would you come in and say hello to Ma?" she asked, raising her eyes shyly to meet the auctioneer's.

While Mim and Hildie led the auctioneer inside like a visiting dignitary, John and Gore went to fetch the boxes of tools from under the barn.

"Sign on any more deputies?" John asked.

"Jack Speare and Ezra Stone," Gore said.

"You must be plannin' to start a circus," John said, taking up a wooden crate and tossing in the rusty odds and ends still scattered around among the rat droppings and stale bits of straw.

"Somethin' like," Gore said.

John shook his head. "Your business, I guess," he said. "Long's the auctions pay and my taxes don't go up." He dropped one crate by the door and picked up a bushel basket for what was left. "I just hope you know what you're doin'."

"You oughta thank me," Gore said. "This place looks a whale of a lot better'n six weeks ago."

John straightened up and looked around. "Guess we'll sweep out and put in some chicks down here," he said.

He took the basket and Gore took the box. They carried them out and set them in the bed of the truck next to a peeling blue bureau. "Well, that'll be it for this year," John said.

Gore slammed the tailgate shut. "You mean you ain't got nothin' up there in that attic?" Gore asked, squinting up at the little window under the roof over the kitchen.

John followed his gaze to the dusty window, then looked back at Gore, who was studying the hairs on the back of his hand. "Might and I might not," he said. "But I guess that's all for this year when it comes to me and the auctions."

Gore lit a cigarette.

Hildie, Mim, and the auctioneer came out the back door with a burst of laughter.

"Doesn't it beat all the way they keep on buying this junk?" Perly said to John, striding down the path with Hildie at his side and Mim following.

Mim pushed the hair off her forehead and grinned at John. "Must be the auctioneer," she said.

"That it is," Gore said, relieved. "A real humdinger. You saw yourself."

"It's good healthy fun," Perly said. He picked up Hildie and peered at her with his dark lively eyes. She giggled and squirmed to be free. "Got a goodbye kiss for your sugar daddy?" he asked. And Hildie obliged with a quick peck on his dark sideburn, then leaped out of his arms.

"Any chance that Hildie can come to my Sunday School class starting this Sunday at ten o'clock?" Perly asked John.

"Oh, how fine," Mim said. "Would you like that?" she asked Hildie.

Hildie danced noncommittally, holding tight to Mim's hand.

Perly sat on his heels and asked, "Would you like that, little friend?"

"Will Dixie come?" Hildie asked.

36

"You bet," he said. "And we'll tell stories too—Moses in the bulrushes, wise old Solomon, King Herod and the baby Jesus. It's almost like living lots of lives at once, telling stories is."

That week John and Mim swept out the lower level of the barn and built a chicken coop to replace the one out back that had fallen in an ice storm three winters before. On Wednesday, John took Hildie down to the Farmers' Exchange and picked up two dozen baby chicks.

"In any kind of common sense way, chickens ain't worth their keep," Ma said after the cows were milked, supper over, and Hildie in bed. "But there's somethin' about havin' a cock crowin' out there while it's still pitch black in the mornin'. Him so full of the devil while you're still tryin' to wipe the sticks of sleep out of your eyes . . ."

"Now we're not about to fuss with no roosters, Ma," John said. They were drinking tea at the table by the window, looking out over the pond, still as glass in the last light.

"I don't suppose," she said. "It's somethin' like what Perly says. We lost the old-time values, to go out and pay good money for chicks already incubated when you keep one good rooster and they'll come along in their own natural way."

"I'd like to know by which old-time values Harlowe needs such a heap of deputies," John said.

"There you go, John," Mim said. "Lookin' for worries again."

"Not me," John said. "We're quit of the auctions for our part. It's nothin' to me what they do in town."

·3·

BUT WHEN, on the following Thursday as the Moores were finishing lunch, Gore's truck came roaring into the yard again, John's face darkened. "What the hell?" he said.

Again Perly was with Gore.

Hildie cried out with delight and ran out the door and down the path with Lassie to nuzzle Dixie. Mim was about to follow when John moved in front of her and blocked the door. He cocked his head to one side and waited for the men to come to the door.

But they moved to the back of the truck. Gore opened the tailgate and climbed heavily into the truck. Perly took the end of a tired red plush couch and guided it to the ground as Gore pushed.

"You wait here," John said to Mim and moved slowly down the path.

Mim followed him.

"What's this?" John asked.

Perly turned to him with a smile. "Well, when this came into the barn, I just happened to notice that it was about the right height for your mother. When your joints are stiff, you don't want a couch that's too low. Thought you might like to trade this for your couch and rest your mother's bones a little."

"Course that's up to Ma," John said, eying the rather worn upholstery charily. "Could be it's more comfortable. Hard to say."

Mim said nothing. She was thinking of the new flowered slip-cover she had spent three days making for Ma's old couch only the winter before.

Confronted with the new couch, Ma looked a little alarmed. Perly helped her to her feet. "If it's not right," he soothed, "we'll take it back and keep on watching till the right one comes along."

While Perly watched, Ma sat herself on the new couch with the help of her canes, then she got herself up out of it. Then she sat down on it again, and burst into a full smile. "Why, you're right, Perly Dunsmore," she said. "I never noticed it myself. But I can get out of this ever so much easier, and I can get into it without fallin' the last little way like I been doin' these past few years. It always jars me so." She got up and down again. "Well, I'll be," she said. "And you know, I think I can set here easier too. It don't tilt me back so much."

"Well, I have to hand it to you," Mim said to Perly, still thinking the new couch was not so pretty as the old one. "We none of us ever even noticed."

"Your own never do," Ma said.

Perly stood in the doorway with his arms folded and accepted their comments. "Sometimes a new set of eyes . . ." he said, and lit up with a beaming smile.

"Well, I do thank you, Perly," Ma said, in a glow with pleasure. He went over and took the hand she offered in both of his.

In silence, John helped Gore carry the couch down the front path to the truck. Gore wedged it securely into the end of the truck bed and padded it with a couple of tattered quilts.

"You got no new tales this week?" John said. "It's amazin'."

Gore leaned on the couch where it rested in the truck, its bright slipcover hidden now. He fished in his pocket for matches. "Come round to the house, you're lookin' for talk. You know there's always some of the old bunch around on a Sunday. But you never was one to come round much."

"Thought Perly'd got you all tied up these days," John said.

"Nope," Gore said. "Things're about the way they always been, exceptin' the auctions on Saturdays." He climbed out of the truck and glanced up at the attic window.

Dunsmore appeared in the doorway with the women. Even Ma had struggled to the door with her canes to say goodbye.

"Well, thank you," John said as he approached the truck. "That was nice of you."

"My pleasure," Perly said. "Your mother's quite a woman. She's really a symbol of what this country stands for. I can see that."

John stood with his arms folded, watching the auctioneer. Perly's motions were quick and easy, a little too quick and easy, John thought with a twinge of dislike.

Gore climbed into the truck. Perly opened the door on the passenger side and held out his hand to John. "See you next week," he said.

John placed his hand in the other man's momentarily. "What for?" he asked as the strong hand gripped his.

Perly cocked an eyebrow. "Well the auctions aren't over," he said. "Someone will be around."

"Like you said," Gore announced from his high seat. "We got enough cops for a circus now. Got to keep them busy."

Smiling, Perly pulled the door shut and Gore stepped hard on the accelerator.

"Hey!" John cried, but the truck was backing and turning, so that he had to move aside to let it pass.

Mim was mending overalls on the treadle sewing machine in the front room. From where she sat, she could watch Hildie on the lawn struggling to do cartwheels, tumbling over and over and over.

John and Ma sat with her, waiting for the seven o'clock news to begin.

"He has a way about him that makes you feel like gettin' up and doin' things, Perly does," Mim said. "I like to think it's not us that's left behind, but just the other way around."

"Well, I guess if it sets you to mendin', it can't be a total loss," John said.

"My but he was pleased with hisself about that couch," Ma said, running her hand over the worn red plush. "Didn't it seem to you that he was halfway settin' on hisself to keep from bustin' or dancin' a jig? It's partly that makes you feel like up and doin'."

"That child's goin' to break her neck," John said, frowning at Hildie through the window.

"Well, he was as good as his word," Ma said, "far's that Sunday School's concerned. Now there's one old-time value I'm sure was better than what we got today."

"But Hildie's a chip off me," John said, chuckling. "She don't take to Sunday School."

"That's because he told them about Abraham that was all ready to cut up poor little Isaac," Mim said. "I expect she's worried about what you'll be up to next time you get het up. Now that's one story no mother could ever understand."

"That's just because you got no faith you think that way," Ma said.

"You're the only one left around here as has much faith, Ma," John said. "Poor Hildie. God don't ask for things like that nowadays, and I'm hard put to think He ever did."

"No, it's just the little things He asks the likes of us," Ma said. "Like noticin' when an old woman needs a higher couch to ease a worn-out back."

"You think it's that he was noticin'? Or that Grandpa's old one is more like to catch a buyer's eye since Mim fixed it up so proper?"

"You never had no faith, son. You young people can't remember what old-time values was."

"Is it old-time values Gore's usin', then, when he says he needs a whole troop of deputies?" John asked. "What's he got in mind to use them for, I'd like to know? Is it old-time values tellin' me I got to keep on feedin' auctions every week? Before we know it, he's goin' to have every other man a deputy. God knows what he plans to use them for."

"Must be twenty towns in New Hampshire have an auction

every Saturday," Mim said, pushing the denim overalls under the needle and making the machine whir.

"And I been tellin' you all week," Ma said, "you can't blame Perly for Gore's prattlin'. Anything said by a Gore, you can put right out of your head. That was ever a topsy-turvy household. Weren't no one in it ever cared two whoops in thunder for the truth."

On Thursday, John was restless. After he had milked the cows and put them out to pasture, he lingered over breakfast, drinking cup after cup of coffee, casting around for chores to do in the house. At every long sigh of wind through the pines, he expected Perly and Bob to burst through into their yard.

He finished patching a hole in the screen door and turned to speak to Mim. She was blacking the stove, holding her body away from the stove to protect her clothes. Hildie, catching him idle, took his hands and started to climb him like a tree. He sat down by the table and bounced her on his knee, watching Mim.

Mim turned from the stove and stood at the sink to wash her hands. Afterwards, she took her brush from the shelf and started to brush her hair. She brushed it and brushed it, staring at her image in the small mirror over the sink that John used for shaving every second or third day. Her light hair sprang back from the brush into fuzzy curls. Usually she only brushed it like that when she washed it Saturday mornings. Hildie slid down John's legs and climbed up again. Mim put the brush down and leaned in closer to the mirror.

John pushed Hildie away. The heat rose slowly to his head. Ma's judgment rang in his ears: "She's a far sight too pretty to make a decent wife to a man."

Mim had been seventeen when he married her and so lovely he ached when he touched her. If anyone had asked him why he married her, he'd surely have said that was the reason. But he was pleased when, after a couple of years alone with the fields and the trees, with only his eyes and those of his parents, she forgot she was pretty and didn't bother with a mirror from the beginning of

42

the week to the end. It was all for him. And he remembered thinking, from time to time, in those first years—when she was running down the pasture in summer, or diving into the pond, or coming into the kitchen in winter, rosy with the cold—that it showed a man's worth to have a wife who looked like that.

He hadn't thought of such things for years, but now he saw that she was no longer young. Her slender hands on the hairbrush had grown as tough as his own. The good fair skin, which had once stretched so cleanly over the straight features that her face completely hid her thoughts, was faintly patterned now so that laughter, mockery, and her quick characteristic squint of doubt seemed always there, ready to break through. Still, her body had filled out and gained confidence without losing its grace, and her eyes remained the deep clear blue of a winter sky.

So she had not overlooked the auctioneer's eye for her. John got out of his chair and moved slowly toward her. She met his eyes in the mirror and stiffened with alarm. His two hands landed on her arms. She froze as she stood. He felt the power in his hands and closed his eyes to stop himself. She wouldn't struggle. She never struggled. She had let him have his way the first time he tried, when she was fifteen. Sometimes she had run away first, into the darkness under the trees, but if he sat still, very still, she had always come back and let him have his way.

She bore the bruising grip on her arms with perfect stillness until he himself was trembling. He shoved himself away from her so that she staggered against the sink. "Why you brushin' your hair?" he shouted.

Hildie screamed with surprise and ran to her grandmother in the front room, dodging between John and Mim.

Mim went pale beneath her freckles. "It's only right to look decent when company's comin'," she said. Without moving away, she started taking the dishes from the drainer and putting them away in the shelves overhead. "What are we goin' to give this week?" she asked—a question she'd already asked too often.

John stood in the middle of the room watching her, his green eyes half shut.

She glanced at him. Then, skirting him widely, she walked out

43

the back door of the kitchen, not stopping to pick up her jacket, though the day was chilly and spitting rain.

John sat down on a chair to wait, feeling the pulse at his temple subside and his breathing slow to normal.

"John?" called his mother.

He didn't answer. Hildie poked a head into the kitchen, then scuttled back to her grandmother. "He's there," she reported.

"Johnny?" Ma called again. "You got no call to treat her like that."

"I just asked her a simple question," he snapped.

They let him be and he sat waiting. She didn't come back until nearly three o'clock. When she did, she came in and went straight to the sink and continued emptying the dishes from the drainer, her blouse wet from the rain and sticking to her shoulders. "What are we goin' to give?" she asked again.

"Nothin'," he said without moving.

"Why should we stop?" she said. "There's the whole attic yet."

"Old Caleb Tuttle ain't allowed him so much as a broken chair for a month."

"Oh, Caleb Tuttle. Fanny says he meets them with a shotgun now. Can you just see it? Meetin' Perly Dunsmore and Bob Gore with a shotgun? Caleb was always spoilin' for a fight."

"I still say we done our share," John said.

"You wouldn't rather have some cash than that junk in the attic we never use? And it's a good cause. Don't you like to think we have a real police force? They'd come right away if we had a need."

"For what? For what would you ever need a cop when you'd have time to call one?"

Mim shrugged. "Well . . . you never know. The world's gettin' worse."

She went to the woodbox and picked out sticks of kindling to start a fire for supper. She lifted the lid of the stove and turned to John. "Say no if you like," she said. "But I for one like to be part of what he's doin' for the town."

"He's just in love with his own palaver," John said.

But when Dunsmore and Gore arrived as they had promised,

44

John and Hildie met them in the yard, led them to the attic, and let them take the painted-over rock maple chairs that needed gluing.

Monday, John came in to lunch with the mail. "The check for the chairs only comes to a dollar seventy-five," he said. "The note here from Perly don't say nothin' about that. Only says he was sorry he didn't have time to come in and say hello to you and Ma."

"Well that was just junk," Mim said.

Ma settled herself at the table. "I feel some better knowin' he sent a word to me," she said.

John washed his hands, then stuck his whole head under cold running water at the sink. The water pump started up underneath them and kept on churning after he turned off the water. He rubbed his head with a towel. "I don't know," he said. "I could do without the visits happy enough."

"I think you be a bit green, Johnny boy," said Ma. "There's a man can give you reason, too."

Mim turned toward the stove and hid her grin in the soup pot.

"I am thinkin' of some hard facts, Ma," John said. "Like why nobody's asked me to run the grader this year, not once, when the roads are graded all round by now."

"I keep tellin' you," Mim said. "You ought to go down to Jimmy Ward and ask him outright."

"You hintin' it could be an accident?" John asked. "An accident Ian James graded our road this year when ain't nobody but me or Frank Lovelace done it these fifteen years?"

"Most like," said Mim.

"I suppose you calculate what Gore said as accident too?"

"Bobby Gore?" Ma said. "Ain't nothin' but mush in his head. Just like his daddy."

"Old Toby's mean, Ma. Maybe Bobby takes after that too," John said.

"Mean he is," she agreed. "Chased his own flesh and blood off the place every one by the time they was fifteen and told them not to come back." She reached out to caress Hildie's arm, but

45

Hildie was absorbed in blowing bubbles in a glass of milk with a straw. "Serves old Toby right if he ends up on the dole."

"It's us endin' up on the dole worries me," John said.

The houses around the Parade were two-story colonials painted white with black or green blinds, most of them with a rambling series of tacked-on porches, ells, and outbuildings. Linden's store was tucked away in a corner, though not as inconspicuously as some residents might have wished. It had been a stable until a Linden two generations back boarded up the windows, filled the long flat interior with merchandise, and opened it up as a general store. In his time, Ike Linden had covered it with gray asbestos siding crisscrossed with dark lines supposed to make it look like granite. Except for the addition of a small plate glass window and a line of bare light bulbs hanging at intervals from the ceiling, the store looked pretty much the way it always had—not so much old-fashioned as just cluttered and dim. Outside it was identified by two Amoco pumps, a tired Coca-Cola sign, and a random display of outdated posters.

Nowadays, Harlowe people drove the seventeen miles down Route 37 to the shopping center when it was time to stock their shelves. Nevertheless, almost everyone in town had occasion to duck into Linden's two or three times a week. They came for milk and bread, treats for the children, tomato paste for a half-cooked supper, the right-sized screw, stove black, birthday candles, the newspaper, home-made banana bread, and gasoline—not to mention library books, insurance, hunting licenses, and tickets to the New Hampshire sweepstakes.

Part of old Ike Linden's genius as a storekeeper, and as a selectman too, was his ability to hear volumes and say practically nothing. This, combined with his mastery over such an abundance of material goods, gave him a reputation for knowing a great deal. People had always brought him their questions about income tax, etiquette, unruly wives, and new strains of apples. And Ike did his laconic best to satisfy them without giving any distinct answers. These days, the old man sat in the back room smoking and pondering over the store's accounts, and young Ike and his wife Fanny tended to the store.

"Father-in-law around?" John asked Fanny when he stepped into the store that afternoon, ostensibly to buy some razor blades. She jerked her head in the direction of the back room.

"I go in?" John asked.

"Best you wait," Fanny said. "He's got company."

So John went and stood awkwardly in front of the shelves where the fertilizers were stored, reading the labels, and glancing over his shoulder when the door opened to see who might come in. Presently, after a number of summer people had been in and out chattering loudly as if he and Fanny weren't there at all, Walter French shuffled in.

He stood in front of Fanny. "I want some sponges," he said.

"That aisle," she said, pointing.

"Can't find them," he said, without looking. So Fanny got down off her stool and went and fetched him a forty-nine-cent package of sponges.

French turned then and caught John's eye. John hadn't heard whether any new deputies had been appointed in the last few weeks. French had a hang-dog look built in and didn't seem the kind anyone would want for a deputy. For an awkward moment, John stood with his mouth open to speak. Then he reflected that a man like French, with his hungry brood of children, might serve Perly's purposes very well without being a deputy at all. He clamped his mouth shut, nodded distantly, and turned back to the fertilizers.

The bells jingled as the door swung shut behind French, and John turned to consider him again as he retreated. Through the jumble of items hanging in the window, he caught a single glimpse of a uniformed state trooper fitting his Stetson to his head as he strode away from Ike Linden's door. The deep smooth rumble of a car motor starting mixed with the cough of French's truck. It was a blue Oldsmobile with New Hampshire plates. John had noticed it when he came in.

Inadvertently, he turned to Fanny, the question in his face.

47

She stared back blankly. They were the only people left in the store.

"Go on in and see the old man if you like," she said.

Ike was a dark outline where he sat in front of the window. As John's eyes adjusted, he felt confused. The man he had planned to talk to was a strong man, but Ike was very old. He clutched a light blue sweater around his shoulders like a woman. His glasses hung on a chain around his neck, but he didn't bother to put them on to look at John.

"Trouble?" John asked, standing in the middle of the floor over the old man and nodding in the direction the trooper had taken.

"Friendly visit," Ike said, and rearranged the papers on the card table in front of him.

John continued to stand. He heard the bells jingle in the outer store. "I came to see how come I been shut out of runnin' the grader this year," he blurted out.

"Jimmy Ward runs the roads," Ike said.

"But Jimmy's a deputy," John said.

Now Ike put his glasses on to peer up at John. "Still runs the roads," he said.

"Thought maybe that was why I been let out," John said. "And you're a selectman too."

"I'm a tired old man," Ike said. "And I never was one for meddlin'."

John flushed and leaned his hands on the back of an easy chair that stood in front of him. "Just thought maybe you could help," he murmured.

"What's that?" shouted Ike, distinctly irritated.

"Thought maybe you could get me work," John said loudly.

"That's what I thought you said," Ike said, turning back to his papers. "Can't say's I ever heard a Moore beggin' before."

John clutched the chair, watching as the old man picked up a paper and brought it close to his eyes.

"I been gradin' roads for fifteen years," John said.

The old man made no motion to indicate that he had heard.

John turned and pushed through the curtain into the store and headed for the door.

"Your razor blades," Fanny said from the dimness.

John backed up, swept the package of blades off the counter, and continued toward the door.

"That'll be a dollar twenty-one," Fanny called after him.

John gulped on air and stopped. He reached into his pocket, pulled out two crumpled dollar bills, and presented them at the counter.

"Never mind," Fanny said as she picked his change out of the register. "He has all he can do to help hisself and us these days."

A lot of the stuff in the attic was disintegrating with heat and dust and age. The auctioneer took it away in great truckloads and the attic emptied out more quickly than they could have imagined. The only thing they got a decent check for was the trunkful of Mim's mother's letters and cards—thousands of them, gnawed at the corners by squirrels and sprinkled with the decaying lace from valentines. Mim's mother had belonged to a quilting club, a flower club, a postcard club, and a matchcover club, and she had corresponded with members from all over the country. Every letter started with a flat chronicle of failures, deaths, and ailments. The letters her mother wrote back, Mim thought, must have been almost indistinguishable from those she received. A large energetic woman, who believed every promise she ever heard, Mim's mother had chafed at reality right up until the day she died. Mim had been one more failure. She'd married young; she'd married a farmer; she'd turned her back on the promise of her young beauty —that beauty which, according to all her mother's dreams, should have won her a doctor or a senator or a prince. The letters made Mim uncomfortable. She half believed it was the complaining itself, the act of putting it on paper, that had kept her mother so unhappy. Herself, Mim never put pen to paper if she could find any way to get around it.

On June twenty-eighth, Perly and Gore took the three cartons of half-finished quilts, the only thing of any value left in the attic. After they left, John and Mim and Hildie climbed up and surveyed the debris: the gnawed bits of cardboard boxes, the rotted quilting scraps, the dust shoved up in scuffled ridges, the chewed corncobs of the red squirrels who lived up there all winter, and a heap of rusted smudge pots left over from the time John's father had tried to grow peaches. Mim went down for a broom, and they spent a hot and dusty afternoon cleaning the big room.

When they were finished, Mim folded her arms and watched Hildie run up and down on the wide loose boards. "Best spring cleaning we ever had," she said. "All that rummage was just an invitation to fire. I bet we never feel a need for one speck of it."

"And that's an end to it," John said. "An end to it once and for all."

Mim didn't answer until they were following Hildie down the path to the pond to bathe. Then she said, "Well, they got eyes in their head to see with. There's just no point to pesterin' us again."

John didn't answer.

"Do you think, John?" she asked.

"If you're so positive, why you askin' me?" demanded John.

·4·

ON THURSDAY, John and Mim were up in the garden picking the first of the peas and Hildie, squatting near the tangle of vines, was busy shelling and eating them. From time to time all day, in the course of their work, they had paused to listen. Gradually now the sound of a truck grew unmistakable, and one by one they all stood up and watched the road.

"It's just Cogswell," breathed John.

"Might be he needs a hand with a job," Mim said.

Cogswell jumped down from his battered green truck, waved, and started up the pasture to meet them. He was a tall rangy man with a looseness to the way he moved that was only partly related to his drinking. Like everyone who knew him, the Moores felt a kind of fond protectiveness for Cogswell, and at the same time a sense of awe, for he was a man who was always out of step.

Nevertheless, the Moores moved toward him slowly. They met in the meadow, where the rank grass was up to Hildie's shoulders, and faced each other as if they had met by accident.

"Will you look at Hildie?" Cogswell said at last. "She's spindled since I seen her. Pretty near big enough to milk a cow."

The child clung to the pocket of Mim's jeans.

Cogswell fished in the pocket of his shirt and pulled out a wad of tissue paper. "For you," he said and held it out to Hildie.

Hildie took the offering and unwrapped it. It was a small green plastic marine kneeling behind a gun. Hildie gave Cogswell a dazzling smile. "A hunter," she said.

"That's mighty nice, Mick," Mim said.

"One of the kids dropped it in the truck. Benjie got a whole bagful for his birthday." Cogswell put his hands in his pockets and looked around at the pond and the house and the cows further up in the pasture. "Appears the crows got a fair amount of your corn," he said.

"Always do, the beggars," John said, and they turned together and headed down toward the bridge over the stream. "What's the occasion, Mickey?" John asked. "You ain't been down since your separator broke after that big snow."

"Well, it's the Fourth of July auction this time," he said. "They had a meetin' and Perly there convinced the firemen to split the profits from this here auction fifty-fifty with the police, instead of havin' their own affair. You know, they voted, and it was the firemen that's deputies against them that ain't."

They moved through the stile between the barn and the shed. In the dooryard they stopped and Cogswell looked down over the pond.

John stood with his arms folded.

"Well, I think they already took the last scrap we care to part with," Mim said.

"Mighty nice place to be situated," Cogswell said. "Always did think that. Right smack on Coon Pond like this. My kids think this is livin'. Set them loose here for a summer and I calculate they'd all turn into pickerel. I been takin' them over to Decker's Pond, but the water ain't half so sweet."

"Is this a good thing to be mixed into, Mick?" John asked.

"You ought to sign up," Cogswell said. "They're still takin' on deputies."

"How many big shots we got these days, Mick?" John asked.

Mickey dug his hands into his pockets, then took them out and let them dangle at his sides. "Well, I'm not sure," he said.

"Not sure!" John said.

"Well, they ain't advertisin' any more. It's only us first ones left hangin' out there for everyone to see."

"The rest'd rather hide in their closet," John said. "Can't say I blame them. The whole thing's beginnin' to give off a bad smell."

"Still," Cogswell said, folding his arms, "I have it on Gore's sayso they're still takin' on men. Course it's got to end somewhere, and I think soon, but if I talk to them . . ."

"We'll take our chances," Moore said.

Cogswell leaned over them. They could smell the whiskey on his breath. "Listen," he said. "I could get you off the hook maybe."

"Off the hook!" Mim said. "First I heard we was on it."

"But why you, Mickey?" John pressed.

Cogswell shrugged and forced a chuckle. "Well, at first I liked the sound of what he said. Still do, I guess. But lately I been sayin' to myself, 'If you can't lick 'em, better join 'em.' Think about it, Johnny."

"Not me," John said. "I can't say as I feel no needs in that direction. Nor no attractions neither."

"Well, I ain't sayin' I can come back with the same chance later," Cogswell said. He felt restlessly for the steel flask in his back pocket. "But maybe I'm shootin' off my mouth again. None of my business, eh?"

John folded his arms and didn't answer.

"I hear your mother's doin' poorly," Cogswell said.

"Not so poorly," John said, and they stood in silence midway between the house and the truck. Hildie was off across the road aiming her hunter at brown and yellow butterflies.

"Well, they sent me here," Cogswell said. "They'd be mighty glad if you could give just this once again. You don't want to be the only holdout."

"There's always Pa's big chiffonier," Mim said softly. "It's not like we used it so much now he's gone. Only to look at."

And, because it was Cogswell, John led the way upstairs and helped him carry out the heavy old piece. When he was ready to go, Cogswell stood by the open door of the truck, working the door handle up and down, looking at the door and not at John.

"Hear about Caleb Tuttle?" he said. "A heart attack got him just as he was headin' into the barn to do the milkin'. Somethin' must've startled him. The coroner over to Powlton says it seems he took a fall."

"I heard," Moore said. But he hadn't.

Cogswell wiped his forehead with his sleeve. "A man just does what he has to do," he said, mostly to Mim, but she was staring at him as if he were a stranger.

After the truck had rattled out of sight, John and Mim stood where they were. Then, in a rare gesture, John put his hand on his wife's back and turned her around to see the pond flattening out to a mirror now in the calm that preceded evening.

Ma was fretting because Cogswell hadn't come in to see her. "He was the sweetest, funniest one of the lot of you," she said. "And he always had ideas in his head. Nobody likes to let Mick Cogswell get away without a word."

"He asked after you, Ma," Mim said.

"He say why he ain't been down this long time?" she asked. Cogswell's land abutted Moore's on the high side and they were neighbors in the summer when the old fire road between their farms was open. Cogswell had thirty-five acres of blueberries, some stock, and a fair-to-middling skill as a mason, depending on how sober he was.

"Too busy bein' a deputy," John said.

"He'd been hittin' the cider," Mim said.

"The more's the pity," Ma said. "Though there ain't three men in Harlowe can drink and still work as staunch as Mickey Cogswell. He have a job for you, Johnny?"

"No."

"Well what was he here for then?"

"He was sayin' that to his mind it's a pretty good idea to be a deputy."

"Him and his schemes," Ma said. "He's goin' to be the death of Agnes and those kids. How many times have they had potatoes and milk gravy for supper because he was off squanderin' their

54

cash on some fool scheme? What was it he done that time up to the blueberry field?"

"He was goin' to make an airport of it," Mim said.

"How about the pond for raisin' ducks?" John said.

"It breeds dandy mosquitoes," Mim said. "They're head and shoulders worse up there than they ever used to be."

"After all that money," said Ma. "What a crazy man. If he'd just stick to buildin' his chimneys, him and you'd do just fine. What'd you show him up there overhead? Thought maybe you was lookin' at our chimney."

"He was collectin' for the auction, Ma," John said.

"Collectin' for the auction?" Ma said. "Thought that attic was plumb empty."

Nobody answered. Mim was peeling carrots at the sink. Hildie was still outside. John was standing at the back door peering up into the pasture.

Suddenly Ma banged her cane on the floor. "What'd you give that man from up in my room, without so much as a by your leave?" she cried.

"Pa's chiffonier, Ma," John said, whirling to his mother, the temper piled up and heavy in his stance.

Ma leaned to him over the table as if to plead with him. "Pa's chiffonier?" she said in a small voice.

"Must be others gettin' low on patience," Mim said the following Thursday as they did the morning milking. "We don't need to be the ones to start a fuss. And we can spare another piece or two. Must be some who can't."

"Oh, we still have enough to spare," John said, slapping a big cow on the flank, "providin' the garden comes in good, and Sunshine here stands by us."

"So you'll give them something," Mim said. "My dressin' table, maybe?"

John filled a pail and leaned into the rhythm of filling a new one. "I don't know," he said. "Sparin' it's not what hurts."

But the day remained peaceful until almost five o'clock. Mim was shelling peas in the kitchen, Ma was watching her programs in the front room, and John, who was making butter, had just begun to whistle to the rhythm of the churn.

When the truck pulled into the yard, Hildie and Lassie burst out the screen door followed by John and Mim. This week Dunsmore himself came, driving a big yellow van, the doors and the big flat sides stenciled in tidy red and black: *Perly's Auction Company, Inc.*

Perly swooped down and caught Hildie as she ran to him, swinging her high so that she squealed with delight. "How's my plump little goody?" he asked. He held Hildie in front of him where he could look at her.

John pulled Hildie out of the auctioneer's arms and held her himself.

"That was a fine piece you gave last week," said Perly, leaning slightly toward the Moores and looking from one to the other.

Gore was making a pile of pebbles in the road with the toe of his boot. "You know the firemen came off with more money than they ever did on their own?" he said.

"We're goin' to keep Harlowe a wonderful place to live," Perly said, "thanks to generous souls like you."

Bob Gore stood with his thumbs hooked in his belt. "What have you got this week?" he asked.

John stood, Hildie still in his arms, and did not answer. Gore was wearing a small leather holster strapped onto his belt, and the gun. John looked at him. He had gone to school with Gore, only two years ahead of him, in the one-room schoolhouse up at Four Corners where a bunch of hippies lived now. They had had their moments together. "How many of them fancy leather holsters you pay for?" he asked.

"People was good enough to buy their own," Gore said.

"Which people, exactly?" John asked.

"We got a terrific special," Perly said, and his face opened up in a grin that showed his straight white teeth. "It's like having a genie, the way doors open to us around here." Balanced lightly on the toes of his boots, Perly stood perfectly still like an axis around which pasture, pond, and woods—even the other three adults—revolved.

"That how you see it?" John asked.

Without moving, Perly shifted his gaze to John, his dark face settled in easy contemplation. The silence stretched. John took a breath and kicked at the hubcap of the truck.

Mim touched the auctioneer's sleeve. "Upstairs," she said softly.

John turned on Mim, his face coloring deeply. Then, quite suddenly, he turned to Perly and shouted so sharply that a slight echo came back from over the pond, "We got nothin' for you!"

The auctioneer seemed not to hear. He smiled down at Mim and nodded just slightly.

Mim stood paralyzed, watching as John lurched away from them and marched into the barn, slamming his open hand against the doorpost as he entered. When his form disappeared in the shadows, she looked up at the auctioneer.

"Where?" he asked gently.

She stood still, undecided, her clear eyes studying the auctioneer's face.

He gave her a quick smile that embarrassed her, then turned and walked up to the front door, opened it, and bowed to usher her in. She paused, then obeyed, brushing past him in the doorway and leading the way up the stairs. She could hear Perly's light tread behind her and Gore's heavy one in back of him.

She turned into their bedroom and indicated the dressing table without a word. It was walnut with a pattern of flowers and leaves stenciled in fading colors on the delicate curved drawers. When he saw it, Perly said, "That's fine, just fine." He turned and leaned over Mim, tense and sober. "You're a very giving woman."

Gore lifted the dressing table himself and stood in the doorway trying to maneuver it through. Perly and Mim were trapped in the room.

"This is not for me, you know," Perly said, the strong beat of his voice held down to a murmur. "It's for the town. For all the things I know you want as much as I do."

The blood rose to Mim's face. "I don't want you to have it," she said. "It's special to me."

He leaned closer to her and spread his broad palm to touch her face, then arrested it an inch away, as if to catch her warmth.

"You know, I'm really sorry Hildie didn't come to Sunday School again. Now is the time for teaching her right and wrong. You know right well—a woman like you—the day comes when the blood gets high and you can hardly help yourself." Perly's eyes gleamed like polished mahogany, and Mim couldn't stop searching for her reflection in them.

"You frightened her," she said unsteadily.

"I never frightened anyone," Perly said, as if reciting something from the very center of his stillness.

"And what about Caleb Tuttle?" Mim whispered.

"Tuttle?" Perly said, without letting her eyes go. He sat down on the bed and made room for her beside him.

Mim didn't move.

"Was he a friend of yours?" he asked. "Are you grieving for him? I'm so sorry." He reached out and gripped Mim's waist in his big hand. "Why do you say this to me? Is there something you want me to do for you?"

Mim whirled and ran down the stairs, practically stumbling over Gore, who was still lumbering down the last few steps, carrying the cumbersome dressing table ahead of him.

As Perly helped Gore lift the dressing table into the van, Mim walked back through the house and stood watching from the kitchen door. Then, while Gore padded the table with the old quilts and tied it securely, Perly walked back up the stone path toward Mim. He opened the screen door and walked in, forcing Mim to retreat. He looked around the kitchen. "I thought I'd say hello to Mrs. Moore," he announced. "She's something of a favorite of mine."

"She's not up to company," Mim said loudly.

"Mim," he said. She stood with her back to the wall, and he planted himself before her, leaning slightly so that she could feel his coiled tension like the heat waves rising from the pasture in summer. "Does it mean so much to you? I know the pleasures of a dressing table to a good-looking woman. But there are other things—better schools for Hildie, year-round church, more ready cash, more comforts . . . I know what I want."

Mim could not move without flailing out at the man and making him back off, and she trembled from the effort of suppressing her need to do so.

"Comfort," he said almost fiercely. "You've never known much comfort, have you, Mim?"

Mim raised her eyes to Perly's, blue and defiant.

Perly dropped his gaze to Mim's hands, pressed flat and angry against the wall behind her. Slowly he raised his eyes to Mim's again, his face curling into lines of pleasure, perhaps of triumph. "You and I will have to get together someday, Mim," he said. "I admire a woman with grit." Then, with his own glittering stillness, he held Mim motionless against the wall while the clock in the kitchen chimed over and over again. When she dropped her eyes, he moved quietly away.

After the truck began to move, Mim slammed the kitchen door and leaned against it, the chipped enamel on the panels cool against her face.

Gradually, she began to hear Ma's calls, and realized that they had started even before Perly left.

She came to life abruptly and lunged into the living room. "Where's John?" she shouted at Ma. "Where is he?"

Ma was standing up halfway across the room. She had abandoned the chattering television set and begun the journey toward the kitchen. "What right had you, you fresh miss?" she hissed. "What right had you? This is my house and I had things to say to that man."

"What can you want to say to him?" Mim asked. "What can a body say? He don't care—"

"No. That's what," Ma said. "No. No. No. Not the pair of you together can muster an ounce of gumption. Give the man a chance. You never said a word to hint you wasn't just as happy to give away your dressin' table. You never—"

"It's not the dressin' table, Ma," Mim screamed. "I don't give a hoot about the dressin' table." She turned abruptly and sat down on the piano bench with her back to Ma, staring at the dusty keys that no one knew how to play any more.

Ma sighed. "Miriam dear," she said. She turned and hobbled back to her couch. She settled herself with a cushion against the small of her back and her bad leg up on the stool. Then she said, "Was a weddin' present from your mother, if I remember right."

Mim nodded.

"Such a pretty thing you was," Ma said. "A dressin' table she gave you. This was a mean place for the likes of you."

"It was not," Mim said crossly, standing up and walking to the window so that she looked out over the green lawn, the stretch of garden yellow with the first marigolds and zinnias, the ribbon of field where they used to pasture the work horses, and then the pond, blue beneath the summer sky. "My mother never had a scrap of sense."

"Perly ain't the kind would of gone off with it, child, if you'd let him know."

"He knows, Ma," Mim said, her voice rising. "He knows. John told him. I told him. You just wait. He won't stop." She started out the front door, but banged back in to say, "All you can do is run, Ma. There are people like that. Either you give in or you run."

Mim ran out and up the path to the garden to face John. He stopped work and stood grasping the shaft of the hoe tightly with both hands. He watched Mim come and thought about catching her at the waist and shaking her until her waywardness came loose like chaff. But when she was near, running the tips of her fingers over Hildie's face and hair, watching him warily, he took his hoe to the soil again. He would have touched her then, for his comfort and hers, but it seemed a difficult thing to do.

Alone in the house, Ma sighed. "It's that crazy streak comin' straight down the line from her ma." She settled back to catch the last wisps of her program. She had missed the whole scene where the doctor told Angela that Dirk had leukemia. And now, in the last few minutes, Angela was staring wildly, balling up a handkerchief, screaming, "No! Oh, no, no, no!"

"You'll pay worse if you try to say no," Mim said, scraping her chair back from the supper table and stamping to the sink.

"If I'd spent my life doin' what other people had in mind for me, I wouldn't be settin' here right now and neither would you," Ma said. "Ain't nobody goin' to tell me to give away nothin' I prize."

"He's not tellin' you, Ma. He's makin' you."

"He's just doin' his job. There's never any harm in askin'. But you needn't keep answerin' the call. If you was a real Moore, you wouldn't be so eager to give away our belongin's."

"I'm a Moore as much as you," Mim said. "It's you that's on his side, refusin' to see what he is."

All week the women wrangled, while John sat, sometimes with his head buried in his arms. When he could stand it no longer he shouted and they sulked in silence.

At night, after they were alone in bed, he pressed himself on Mim. "What happened with him? What did he do?"

"It's not the table, Johnny," Mim said. "And it's not the fact he took it. It's what he is all through. He just made that clear as clear."

"We'll tell him no," John said, "both of us—no bickerin' this time to let him get his way."

"You can't, Johnny," Mim said. "You can't just tell him no. He'll bring a world of trouble down on us."

"I can tell him what I please."

"Johnny, give him something. For me. Give him something. Hold him off. It can't go on for long."

"Funny how it's all gone sour," John said. "Even his way with Hildie. I hate it when he swings her up like that."

"Just give him something, John. The extra bed in Hildie's room. Promise me. Just one thing every week to hold him off. Promise me."

But John made no promises. He touched his wife and when she clasped him harshly to her, hiding her face against his neck, the excitement rose in him quicker than his habits said it should. And nothing was clarified.

On Thursday, John checked the guns—the shotgun and the .30-'06—and the square steel box of ammunition. Dull with dust, they lay side by side in plain sight on the top shelf in the pantry back of the kitchen. He didn't jar them. They looked as comfortable and natural as the tall glass jars of flour, sugar, corn meal, and dried beans. He turned away and went upstairs. From the doorway of Hildie's room, he pondered the extra bed. It was a rather plain but pretty rock maple bed exactly like Hildie's. The two beds used to belong to his parents. He must have been conceived on one of them.

Finally he went out to the barn and started the tractor. Up in the cornfield, he ran it back and forth cultivating between the rows under the hot morning sun until he was bathed in sweat. The hours of work had not helped him to any decisions when he saw Hildie race down the path from the back door and stand by the road watching.

It was not the bright yellow truck that he had expected that rolled down the hill and into the yard, but Cogswell's dusty old Chevy pickup. John covered the field in long strides and joined Hildie.

Cogswell got out of the driver's side and faced John without a smile or a word. Red Mudgett climbed out of the other side and came around to join the pair of neighbors. Mudgett was wearing the gun again.

Before any of them spoke, the front door opened and Ma appeared. Leaning on both canes, she began to struggle down the rough stone steps.

"I ain't a goin' to let you get away this time, Mickey Cogswell," she called.

Cogswell and John jumped to help Ma out to the single wooden chair sitting in the middle of the lawn.

Hildie danced with delight to see her grandmother outside, and Mim came slowly down the path from the kitchen and stood by John.

"Now, Mickey," Ma said. "You set right down here in front of me. Me and you's goin' to have a talk."

Cogswell hesitated a moment, glanced at Red Mudgett, then grinned at Ma and folded his long body up like an Indian on the lawn at Ma's feet.

"And you, Red," Ma said to Mudgett. "You set too. You make me nervous jerkin' around like that. Just as antsy now as you was at eight."

Mudgett laughed quickly, then squatted on his haunches. He was small and wiry. He watched the old woman with small black eyes that seemed to have no need to blink.

"Now just suppose you tell me, Mickey, what you're doin' here," Ma said.

"Collectin' for the auction, ma'am," he said.

She shook her head. "You been involved in some hare-brained schemes in your day, Mickey," she said. "I keep expectin' you to make good, everybody's favorite like you be. How come you keep doin' such crazy things?"

"That's what my wife keeps askin'," Mickey said. "Must be I was born under the wrong star."

"What if I was to tell you we got nary a stick left we care to part with?"

"I wouldn't do that, ma'am, if I was you. You can give a little somethin' this week, a little maybe next week." Mickey picked up a stone and tossed it into the road, then looked up at Ma.

"If this is Perly Dunsmore's little project, how come he ain't here hisself?"

Mickey shrugged. "It'll all be over pretty soon, Mrs. Moore. Why make trouble?"

"Trouble," Ma said. "It's you that's makin' trouble."

"I think I been a decent neighbor," Mickey said, pulling at the grass between his knees. "I wouldn't tell you what I didn't think was right."

"Right!" cried Ma.

"Well, smart then," Mickey said.

"Smart," Ma said, making room for Hildie beside her in the broad chair. "You tryin' to tell me it's smart to give away what's mine? It ain't even natural. And as for you, Red Mudgett, you was always playactin' at somethin'. Now tell me is it cowboys and Indians or cops and robbers with that gun—"

"Mickey," Mim said, stepping closer. "Take the extra bed in Hildie's room."

63

Mudgett jumped up like a released jack-in-the-box. "Where's that?" he asked.

Cogswell followed more slowly. "That'll make another week chalked off," he said to Mim, nodding gravely.

John turned abruptly and went into the barn, leaving Ma to watch the two men load the bed frame and spring into the back of Cogswell's truck. They left the mattress behind, explaining that it was illegal to sell mattresses. Cogswell left Mudgett tying the bed into the truck, and went over to Ma. "Everything will work itself out, Mrs. Moore," he said, touching her hand.

"That's the last thing," she said, clutching the arms of the chair. "The very tail end of it. You hear me, Mickey Cogswell?"

"Maybe," Mickey said. "Try not to fret." He turned away from Ma and went into the barn. John was sitting on a sawhorse in the corridor between the stalls.

Cogswell said nothing. He stood waiting for John to turn.

Finally John looked up and said, "I didn't know you was so thick with Red."

Cogswell shrugged. "You think I take to it? It's me has to ride around with him all day." Cogswell kicked at a post as if to test it, then leaned against it, tipping his head back wearily. "Never mind," he said, pulling the flask from his back pocket and offering it to John. "They're goin' to round us up one of these days real soon and put a bullet through our heads."

John shook his head. "Who is?"

Cogswell shrugged again. "I don't know, exactly," he said. "If I knew I might just liquor up a bit and turn myself in. Oughta be the state troopers, but I don't know. There was a trooper I didn't know at Mudgett's when I picked him up this morning. And that same one and another one was comin' out of the old Fawkes place, I think it was last Tuesday. Makes you wonder. There's some money kickin' around in this, and I for one ain't seein' all that much of it."

"Old Ike Linden, he in on it?" John asked.

"Who knows?" said Mickey. "I don't collect from him myself. But Perly has this big thing about privacy. We ain't supposed to say who gave what, or even who we asked. I think there's some he

64

even leaves alone. Like Ike, maybe. He's not one you'd want against you. But I can't see him gettin' into the kind of pickle I'm in neither." Cogswell shook the liquor around in his flask. It was nearly empty. "It can't go on. Somebody—some head guy somewhere's bound to catch on and put the lid on the whole thing."

John studied the flask in Cogswell's hand. "The thing is," he said slowly, "who?"

"I wish I knew," Cogswell said, his voice unsteady. "All I know is every blessed plan I get myself roped into turns out dumber than the last. This one's like to be the end of me."

"Me too," John said with a short laugh. "I can't even get together with Mim on this one."

Cogswell cocked an eyebrow. "She's smart," he said. "Always was."

"What if I just tell you and Mudgett to get the hell off my property?"

"Well," said Cogswell, "if that snake out there don't get you now, then . . ." He turned and started out of the barn. "Oh hell."

"Then what?" asked John, starting up after him.

Cogswell stopped but didn't turn. "Emily Carroll went out of control on Route 37 night before last," he mumbled.

"She had an accident?" John reached for Cogswell's shoulder to hold him. "Bad?"

"She's on the danger list," he said, turning. "Her back or something."

"Emily Carroll! She's got four kids—"

"Five," Cogswell said. He pulled out a handkerchief and wiped his face.

John watched. "But these things happen," he said quickly. "You make it out an accident, don't you?"

"I just wish it was someone . . . not Emmie," Cogswell said. "She's just about Agnes' best friend. The steering bust."

"She alone in the car?"

Cogswell nodded. "Thing is, Carroll quit us two weeks ago. Let everybody know it too. And when they sent me and Mudgett round to collect from him last week, he said nothin' doin'."

It was an hour and a half before John could bring himself to face the women. When he did enter the kitchen, Mim whirled from the sink to face him, her normally soft features set hard in rebellion. "I don't care," she said. "You got to give it to him. You're just wrong to think you can . . ." She stopped. "Oh my God, John," she said. "What happened? Hildie . . ." But Hildie was sitting at the kitchen table facing her father, her dark blue eyes round with fear.

"Somebody's goin' to kill him," John muttered. "Somebody's goin' to kill him."

Mim caught her lower lip in her teeth and unconsciously grasped Hildie by the shoulders. "What did he do?" she whispered.

·5·

Now that regulations made it too complicated to sell milk, John churned what Hildie didn't drink and sold the butter to Dr. and Mrs. Hastings. The doctor and his wife had only been in Harlowe since a little before Hildie was born. But they were educated people and came from the outside, facts which might, John thought, help them know how to deal with the situation.

The doctor was a short bald man who wore glasses that magnified his eyes in such a way that he seemed to listen with them. He gave his patients—and everyone in town was his patient—the impression that he saw everything and probably understood it too, though he never said a word more than necessary. He asked what questions he had to, but never gave people any names for what was wrong with them. And when he wrote out an illegible prescription, he never said what it was for, only repeated the directions, usually the same ones: "Three times a day now, after breakfast, lunch, and supper, till the pills are gone."

The doctor had delivered Hildie, but John himself had never had any reason to go to him for help, and when he took the butter down, the doctor only glanced at it, blinked at John nearsightedly, and paid him. Nevertheless, John was determined somehow to break through and talk to him.

Thus, when he rang the back bell on Friday morning, he was

distinctly disappointed when it was Mrs. Hastings and not the doctor who answered the door. She'd been to college, as everybody knew, and had friends up from the city almost every weekend. Her children, all but the youngest, went to boarding school. She talked enough to make up for the doctor's silences. In fact, she was always as nice as could be, if anything a little too jolly, as if she were restraining an impulse to slap John's flanks and cry, "Off with you, Bossy!"

He waited on the far side of the kitchen table while she stood at the counter and weighed the butter on her scales.

"Doctor home?" John asked.

Mrs. Hastings looked up sharply. "You sick?" she asked.

"No," John said. "No, not me."

"Your children?"

"No, Hildie's well."

"Then what do you want to see the doctor for?"

"Something I wanted to talk to him about."

"The doctor doesn't handle emotional problems, you know. He's far too busy. If you just want to talk, his nurse will refer you to a psychiatrist in Concord."

John raised his shoulders and thrust his hands into his pockets. The butter, he noticed, weighed over. He took a breath. "Been attendin' the auctions?" he asked.

"A few," she said, turning to face him. Her features were large, pointed, and subtly pockmarked. "Where on earth are they getting all that beautiful stuff week after week?"

John paused. "People like me," he said.

"That so?" she said and laughed, her chest heaving. "Well, isn't that generous of you. I, for one, wouldn't care to part with my furniture."

"No," John said slowly. "You wouldn't."

She raised her chin suspiciously, no longer smiling. "Well, why do you do it?" she asked almost angrily.

John flushed with embarrassment and didn't move. He couldn't go because she hadn't given him his money. Everyone knew that Mrs. Hastings hated Harlowe and Harlowe people and, for that matter, everything about the country. Harlowe and Mrs. Hastings, in fact, tolerated each other only for the sake of the doctor. Clearly, she must find the auctioneer classier than the people she bought butter from. And, if she did, probably the doctor did too.

"Well, why do you?" she repeated, her black eyes full of accusation. She reached over to the counter, picked up a half-empty wine glass, and drank.

John took a step back, watching her. Then he held out a callused hand for the bills and change she had counted out for him.

She plunked the money down on the table where he would have to reach for it. "I'll just never understand you people," she said.

John tried to scoop the change off the edge of the table into his hand, but the three dimes stuck at the chrome edging.

The doctor's wife drank from her glass again, holding it gracefully, looking down her long nose at John's hands as they fumbled after the dimes.

When he was three steps down the outside walk, the back door slammed so hard the house shuddered. He paused, momentarily paralyzed by a flashing impulse to go back and tell the woman she was worthless. But the pause was no more than a hitch in his gait as he walked back to his truck and climbed in. The butter money was their only cash at the moment.

It was full summer now. The borers drilled new rows of holes around the trunks and branches of the apple trees, and the coons and woodchucks, grown fat by now, moved slowly down the high pasture toward the garden every evening at dusk. Beetles turned the leaves on the tomato plants to lace despite a weekly dusting, and clusters of black-eyed susans showed where weeds had taken root even in the newly seeded hay. John and Mim accepted the signs of high summer the way they accepted the first warning cricket. There always ended up being enough hay for the cows, enough apples and corn and tomatoes for the family.

And now, for weeks, they accepted the Thursday visitations. At first Ma fussed. She screamed the week that Mim pitched in to help Cogswell and Mudgett take the piano. But, by the time they took the rug from the front room and the good dishes Mim had packed, she said very little.

John let Mim choose what should go, but he went to elaborate

69

lengths not to mention the things that were gone. And every Thursday and Friday after the visits, he worked long hours in the fields, going back even after supper, until he could fall into bed exhausted.

One week, Cogswell lingered by the door of his truck to speak to Mim. "Listen," he said, swaying slightly so that she was engulfed in a mist of alcohol fumes. "Agnes says to tell you she'd be mighty pleased if you and Hildie should see fit to visit. The raspberries are at their best this week up to the blueberry fields. And she ain't been pickin' once. She says it makes her nervous now, them big fields ringed all around with woods." He stared at Mim, then past her at the pond until he started to list toward it as if drawn. He caught at the mirror on the truck to steady himself. "Oh, Mim," he said, "makes me nervous too, her and the kids up there . . ."

Mim stood with her arms folded over her denim shirt. Mudgett leaned on the hood of the truck watching her.

"Not that I'm tellin' you you have to or anythin'. It's just that generally you do. And Agnes is half crazy frettin' over Emily. They was in the same year all through—"

"How is Emily?" Mim murmured, glancing at Mudgett and turning away immediately from his baleful attention.

"She's paralyzed," Cogswell answered, pushing the button in and out that worked the door of the truck. "She'll be in the hospital for a long time, maybe always." He met Mim's eyes. "Makes a man feel so helpless," he said softly, "a woman struck like that."

He climbed into the truck. Mudgett moved quickly around the front of the truck.

Mim put a hand in the open window of the truck. "Drive careful, Mick," she said. "You don't seem strictly sober."

Cogswell leaned down and said, "They been takin' things off Carroll like his place was a public dump."

The next morning Mim took the butter into town and stopped at Linden's. After lunch, when John and Hildie went up to work in the garden, she stayed in, working on the doors with a drill and screwdriver. John came back to see where she was and found locks on two of the five doors, and Mim working on the third.

"The only people locks keep out's your friends," he said.

Mim dropped the screwdriver and hasp with a clatter. "Where's Hildie?" she asked.

"Up to the garden still."

Mim got up and rushed to the door to check.

John came up behind her and they stood together at the back kitchen door looking up past the stream and the bridge to the garden, where, poking up between two rows of green, they could just see Hildie's bright head catching the sunshine in the calm of midday. John touched Mim's short hair and a tendril caught at his finger.

"I'd a good deal rather do without," she said.

"We ought to meet them with a gun. They're makin' slaves of us," he said.

"John," Mim said.

"That's all well and good for you," he said. "You're not a man."

But after Mim went up to get the child, John walked around the house and examined the locks, tightening the screws as he went, thinking that paying for them must have taken all the butter money and then some. Afterwards, carefully and methodically, he installed the remaining two locks on the shed and cellar doors.

They gave the china cabinet, now that it was empty, then their own bureau, then Hildie's. By the first week in August, it was hard to see what to give next.

Ma had fallen into silence on the subject of the auctions, and on most other things as well. When she wasn't watching her programs or playing with Hildie, she sat on her couch for long periods, her thin arms folded across her limp housecoat, looking out the window. She barely answered when she was spoken to, and for weeks she didn't tell a story. Uneasy, John and Mim spoke, even to one another, only behind her back. The gloom at the supper table was such that Hildie put up a battle every night about sitting down.

In town it wasn't much better. When John or Mim ran into people they had known for decades, they smiled and chatted about the weather or the cost of living or the orneriness of machines. They talked exactly the way they always had, except that now the familiar conversations seemed to be built on a silence as deep as the one that prevailed at home.

It was Mim's idea that John go to the auction. "Just one man alone, John," she said. "They won't hardly notice you. Could be you'll learn somethin'."

There were cars pulled up on the town hall lawn, on the church green, all around the firehouse. They were parked on Mill Street all the way down over the bridge and up around the corner again.

Mudgett was selling balloons again. Next to him, a strange girl in a maternity smock sat on a bright beach towel moving nervously to the rhythm of a transistor radio. She was very young and her hair was long and dark and tangled as if it had not been combed. Something about the way she watched the people moving toward her to buy balloons made John think that she was hungry.

There wasn't a woman or a child Moore knew. Ward was there —Speare, Pulver, Janus, Stone, and a few others he knew. That didn't mean they were all deputies, of course. They sat quietly here and there, distributed evenly among the crowd, sprawled on chairs, the edge of the bandstand, or the backs of trucks. John reflected that most of them were probably wondering whether he was a deputy. James and Cogswell, in denim overalls, were arranging the things to be auctioned off. Ezra Stone was selling popcorn, and Sonny Pike was selling Coke and beer.

And there were people—plenty of them—people he didn't know. They'd brought coolers and blankets to spread behind and beside the wooden chairs. They hailed their summer neighbors and the people they'd met the week before.

Moore wandered uneasily up toward the things for sale. A hard slender middle-aged woman in faded yellow jeans was saying to another in a white slack suit, "Isn't it marvelous? Some of the stuff I've bought is so good I've taken it back to Weston. Can you just

72

imagine what this stuff would sell for on Beacon Hill? Where do you suppose they get it week after week?"

"Isn't it splendid?" said her friend. "I've been to auctions and auctions in seven summers up here, but never a set like these. Take a look at the rosewood highboy over there."

They were right. It was clearly no benefit auction. There wasn't a thing to go into surprise packages to start at a quarter a lot. There were oversized wing chairs, hand-carved beds, solid cherry tables, walnut dressers, a big roll-top desk. Moore ran his hand across the top of Hildie's low pine dresser—it had been his sister's, and old then—and tried to remember where he'd seen the stenciled buffet.

A man in a bulging Hawaiian shirt, Bermuda shorts, and slippers was saying, "Lotta good wood here."

And his wife was complaining, "But what I specially want is a butter churn for the rubber plant."

There was a long table surrounded by boxes of produce. They were selling tomatoes by the crate. Further on, there were two chain saws, a water pump, a milking machine, and four power mowers. And, almost hidden behind the bandstand, a tractor. Tractors have personalities, and this was a dark green John Deere made in the thirties sometime. Moore tried hard to think where he had seen it before. It could have been at Rouse's, but he wasn't sure.

The auctioneer appeared, moving light and erect toward the bandstand, his dark head bare and gleaming in the sun. Dixie trotted obediently at his left heel.

"Quite a character, that Dunsmore fellow, wouldn't you say, Moore?" It was Tad Oakes. He had two greenhouses full of geraniums at the far corner of the Parade, and nowadays he did a bit of landscaping for the newcomers. He was also the chief of the volunteer fire department. "You helping?" he asked.

"Not me," Moore said.

"Good," Oakes said. "Me neither. Nothing from the old Oakes place up there this week either."

"How'd you manage that?"

"Just said, 'Sorry, boys, haven't got a thing left.' They said,

'You're sure?' and I said, 'Sure as shooting.' And that was that. They took off without a word. First little thing that happens I call in the troopers."

"Cogswell figures the troopers must be in on it."

Oakes paused. "Hell. I'll go to Concord. I'll go to the goddamn President if I have to. This is ridiculous."

Moore nodded. He knew all about Tad Oakes, of course, but he didn't know the man particularly, any more than he knew anybody who actually lived in town. But now he said, surprised to hear himself, "There's a three-day calf up to our place. And the water's nice enough if you ever happen to be round our way with your boys."

"Thanks," Oakes said, clearly pleased. "I'll make a point of it."

Perly was starting the auction, talking in that deep singsong voice he saved for auctions.

"It can't go on like this," Oakes said, "do you think?"

Moore shook his head. "Two hundred years my people been on that land. They weathered shenanigans before."

"That's what I say," Oakes said grimly. "What's a few auctions? I didn't half mind getting the barn and cellar cleaned out. It's just that you have to draw a line."

Moore looked up and Oakes followed his glance. From under the trees, Mudgett was staring at them, unblinking as a fish. Without another word, the two men turned away from each other.

That week Mudgett arrived on Thursday driving a brand new Crew Cab International pickup truck, the kind every man in Harlowe admired whenever he passed Tucker's new showroom up on Route 37.

"What you got for us, Moore?" he asked, fixing John with his flat eyes, while Cogswell shambled around the truck.

"What color's yours?" John asked Cogswell.

Cogswell shrugged. "There's them as gets and them as don't," he said. "The big boy says I got to swear off the bottle first. He's after makin' preachers of us all."

"He dropped a bureau the other day, with me underneath,"

74

Mudgett said. "Damn near killed me. Never mind the way he drives."

Cogswell laughed loosely. "You tell him, John," he said. "Ain't no use tryin' to reform me. Agnes been tryin' all these years. I keep tellin' him if he'd just join me in a daily bottle for a while, he might grow a head or two."

"He's goin' to get himself tossed out, if he ain't careful," Mudgett said. "His tongue gets to flappin' round in the breeze about this time of day."

John and Mim looked at Cogswell with alarm.

"Well, what have you got?" Mudgett asked.

"How long you plannin' to keep this up?" John asked.

Mudgett shrugged. "Have to ask the boss about that," he said. "By the by, saw you talkin' to Tad Oakes Saturday. You a special buddy of his?"

"Just passin' the time of day," Moore said. "Any law against that?"

"You hear he sold out and moved to Manchester? Left yesterday."

"So quick?" Moore said.

"You know that old dead elm, the one he should have took down some years back? Well, it fell over his two greenhouses and smashed them up pretty good. They was lucky, you ask me. Whole damn family was up to Concord at the time. But I guess Oakes got to feelin' pretty discouraged."

"He sell his place already?"

"Dunsmore gave him cash on the barrelhead."

"How much?"

"How should I know? You know how people clam up when it comes to money."

John dug his hands into his overall pockets. "Whatever brought you back to Harlowe anyway, Red?" he asked.

Mudgett shook himself with annoyance. "It's all unreal out there," he said. "Whole shitty world."

"So you came round to Harlowe."

"Naw," said Mudgett. "I just hate the place more, that's all. Good a reason's any for comin' back." He grinned and John saw that his front teeth, leaning together as they always had, had been broken to sharp points.

"You're no favorite round here either," John said.

Mudgett continued to grin. "Never was," he said. "Never want to be."

That night while Hildie sang herself to sleep, John and Mim sat down in front of Ma's quiz program.

The M.C. asked a man in a dark turtleneck what year the Cheerleaders' Association of America was formed. Ma waited until he answered—in the twenties sometime—then she said, "Some things you got no right to. And my bureau's one of them. And Pa's chiffonier is another."

Mim and John looked at each other and the M.C. awarded two hundred dollars to a girl in leopard-skin tights who must have given a better answer.

"A handout here and there, all right," Ma went on. "But you don't go givin' up every stick you own. Your father would have chased them rascals off the place with a whip, I tell you. Your great-great-grandfather cleared that whole high pasture and then some, when the woods was still filled with Indians too—riddled with them."

"You got no use for that bureau, Ma," John said.

"You tellin' me my time has come?"

"Course not," Mim said. "It's just that maybe the bureau will fetch us through without an accident."

"Accidents," Ma said. "You should hear the accidents used to happen in the old days. Look what happened to Pa. How about the accidents in the news? Hundreds of people in one fell—"

"That don't help if you happen to be one of the hundreds," John said.

"I got a feelin' it's Red Mudgett underneath all this," Ma said. "Never had a speck of faith, least not in somethin' so simple as right and wrong. It all comes from bein' too bloomin' smart. Pipsqueak as he was, he was always too big for his britches. Every year he won the prize for memorizin' the most scripture. Did it out of sheer spite because it come easier to him than to others. One year he got hisself elected president of his Sunday School class. I never did cotton on to how he did that. But it's certain he found some wrong way or other, cause he never had a bona-fide friend. It galled me just to think about it. And the worst of it was, afterwards he'd be all over me, pullin' at my sleeve like a little gypsy. 'Ain't you glad I won the prize, Mrs. Moore? Ain't you glad I got elected?' Must of come of not enough home trainin'. Plain and simple, I never took to him. Weren't nobody I know of did. He was too smart. Nothin' ever good enough for him. He never liked the Bible stories and he never liked the singin'. Why he even resisted bein' a angel in the Christmas pageant."

Now the M.C. was making all the contestants twirl a baton, and a young woman in a sequined dress had just dropped the baton on her foot and was jumping up and down on the other.

"What would you have us do, Ma?" Mim asked. "It's not as if me and John was all that partial to givin' our comforts away."

"I'd have you tell him where his business lies. That it ain't here."

John exploded out of his chair. He glared at his mother. "There's only just one way to get that message across, Ma," he said. He paced the room from stove to window and back. Then he turned toward his mother again, grabbing the steel trim on the cold stove behind him and hanging on. "And the only thing keepin' me from that, Ma, is I got three women on my hands."

Piece by piece they let the furniture go—the overstuffed chairs and the rocker from the front room, the old dropleaf table in the dining room, even the pine kitchen chairs. One week Cogswell settled for three crates of shell beans.

Meanwhile, as if their decision to let the furniture go had bought some time, the Moores settled into the end of summer. The corn, what the crows had left, was ripe. And the cucumbers and tomatoes and squash and beans were in full season. They took Hildie swimming in the pond every day and tried to teach her to climb without stepping on loose stones or dead branches that might give way beneath her. They mowed and raked the hay, pitched it up into the old hayrack with forks, then pulled the hayrack to the barn with the tractor and unloaded the hay through the upper doors of the barn. Together in the late afternoons, complaining of the heat and listening to the crickets, they put up tomatoes and squash. It was a wonderful year for blackberries, and after supper John and Mim and Hildie roamed the edges of the pond in the last light picking blackberries and sometimes high-bush blueberries, eating what they could, and collecting more to can.

The days grew shorter as their supply of furniture dwindled. While the weather was still nice, they would carry Ma out at meal-times and settle her in the big wooden lawn chair with a tray, spreading their own plates and glasses out on the granite stoop. Afterwards they milked, squirting milk into Hildie's mouth to make her laugh, then they scrubbed the bright steel pails in the kitchen with soap and water heated on the stove. Twice a week John churned butter. At lunchtime when the stoop was warm with sunshine, they drank the chilled buttermilk and watched for the first red stains to mark the swamp maples by the pond.

They never mentioned the missing objects, but their lives changed. They did things they had never done before. They carried a picnic supper up to the top of the pasture. One still day at dusk, they loaded Ma onto the truck and took her down as close as they could get to the pond so that she could see the fish jump. John drove up to the gravel pit and got a load of sand to dump by the side of the barn so Hildie would not dig in the dirt of the road. One day, Mim, pulling carrots in the garden, leaned her elbows on her knees, looked out over the house toward the pond, and said, "Funny, I feel like it's my own relations been here those genera-tions back. I feel attached." She sighed. "It *is* the prettiest place."

John did not stop working, but he glanced at her and at his child throwing a stick for the dog behind the house, then running to fetch it herself because the dog was too lazy. "We never sprayed the ivy," he said. "It's bad luck."

It seemed clear to Mim that Fanny Linden's perch behind the counter of the store gave her a uniquely unobstructed view of the complex situation in the town. Despite her stinginess, Fanny was not unkind, and so, John's experience with old Ike notwithstanding, Mim continued to hope that Fanny somehow knew what should be done and would let her know too.

Thus, whenever she went into the store, she lingered, talking weather, labor pains, and ailments with Fanny the way she always had. Fanny went on and on, her voice as flat as the cheese she made, but Mim could glean few clues. Neither Fanny nor the store seemed changed in any way. She did learn that Collins up on the ridge had fallen under his bulldozer and had to have a leg amputated.

"Course that don't slow Jane down none," Fanny said. "She's in here just as often as ever, all gussied up like she thought we was New York."

"How could he fall under his own bulldozer?" Mim asked, wishing she could find out where the Collinses stood with the auctioneer.

"Takes talent, don't it?" Fanny said. "This has been one bad year for accidents."

Mim frowned.

"Course there's one good thing come of it."

"What's that?" Mim asked cautiously.

"You mean you ain't heard about the ambulance? Why I thought everybody'd heard by now. They broadcast it loud enough. That happened last Tuesday after Collins got hurt. Some of the money came from the police budget. Guess they got some extra now on account of the auctions. Then Perly Dunsmore donated what was missin'. He went hisself, Perly did, up to Boston and come back with a brand new ambulance. Everything the very best. They was showin' it out there on the Parade all day Wednesday. Next time someone gets hurt, it's nothin' but twentieth-century care for them. That's how Perly puts it."

"You think Perly had to donate much?"

"He says so," Fanny said. "Soft-like he says it, but plenty loud enough to hear."

"The auctions must be rakin' in a pretty penny. Young Ike helpin' with them?" Mim said, trembling at her bluntness.

"Store's open Saturdays," Fanny said. "Always was. But we keep an eye on things from here. Don't hurt our business none, all that flock of outsiders landin' on our doorstep every Saturday—and all in a spendin' mood too."

"Oh," said Mim, abashed. "I don't suppose. Do you . . . have you been donatin' much?"

"Nothin'," Fanny said, sitting unnaturally still, even for her. "They ain't asked and we ain't volunteered."

Harlowe shared a preacher with eleven other towns. She spent one quarter in each area, preaching in three different towns every Sunday. It wasn't a job with much appeal for men with families, and so for eight years they'd had a woman—Janet Solossen. Once a year she called on the Moores, rattling in over their road in an old Willys Jeep, always just when they least expected her. She wore men's work boots and covered her large uncorseted frame any which way, usually with blue jeans and dark turtleneck sweaters. Before she came in, she always stood and talked cows and tractors with John in the yard, running nicotine-stained fingers through her cropped yellow-gray hair. In the front room, she smoked and talked babies with Mim, and quilts and television with Ma. Nobody thought she was particularly smart, since she always talked about what they knew, but they noticed that she usually had good answers when problems came up, and they had long since concluded that, woman or not, she had a line to God in the proper way of preachers. People had stopped calling her "that lady preacher." She was just "the preacher" generally, and "Reverend Solossen" to her face. Except for the newcomers and the French Canadians, most of the people in Harlowe still got married and buried out of the Union Church, but there weren't as many as there used to be who paid attention to it on any regular basis.

"The first Sunday of the preacher's quarter here's comin' up," Mim said. "I don't rightly see how she can come by and not notice."

"And when she asks," John mocked, "I suppose you'll say you gave it all away because an old man took a stroke, and an elm tree fell on a greenhouse?"

"I expect the preacher could sit patient for the whole long tale."

"And if we tell her and she thinks it's us is wrong and passes on our tellin'?"

"I'm goin' to tell her anyhow."

Sunday was cold and bright, etched with the fresh hard energy of autumn. Ma was pleased to be going to church. Looking strange and fragile in her navy blue gabardine suit, she sat between Hildie and John on the hard seat of the pickup truck. After Pa died, John had taken her to church until she gave it up of her own accord. "It ain't the same," she said, "with you a twistin' and turnin' in the pew like a cat in a trap."

John and Mim said nothing as they drove slowly past the church with its half-finished steeple. John passed the four shiny new Crew Cab trucks in front, then pulled to a stop by the post office.

"Don't stop," Mim said. "No point to goin' now. We seen enough already."

"Not go!" Ma said. "Just on account of them trucks? They got as much right to the church as you. More. It would a been fittin' when you took a Harlowe man if you'd a took his church as well. But you was always strong in your ways when it was any but Johnny doin' the pushin'."

"Get out, get out," sang Hildie, absorbed in the delight of wearing her party dress. "I want to twirl my twirly skirt."

"And the child's as wild as a Chinese," added Ma. "You send her to Sunday School once. Then she says no and you let her be."

"Look who's teachin' it, Ma," Mim said.

"Well Sunday School's Sunday School. And anyway, I say it's Mudgett's behind all this."

John let the truck idle, staring out at the church. Ma reached over and patted Mim's knee. "Not that I blame you," she said. "It's just you mustn't let them stop you when you got a plan."

In the foyer of the church, the greeters lined up—first Sonny and Theresa Pike, then Mickey Cogswell looking overstuffed and florid in a suitcoat and tie. The Moores shook hands unsmiling with the Pikes and passed on to Cogswell.

81

"Where's Agnes?" Mim asked.

"Not up to comin'," he said. He looked down at Hildie and had no greeting for her. "You heard the preacher's gone?" he said.

"Gone!" Mim said.

But Cogswell motioned to the Moores to move on. "You'll see," he muttered.

Mim caught the child up and carried her down the aisle, while John supported Ma on his arm and followed Ezra Stone as he ushered them to a pew in the middle of the church.

In the sanctuary, Fanny Linden was playing the organ the way she always had, and sunshine poured past yellow maples through the high clear windows. The church was never more than a quarter full even on Christmas, yet as soon as the Moores sat down, they felt another couple move in directly behind them. Glancing back, John saw the Jameses. Ian James was a deputy, one of the first. John pulled Hildie close to him.

Ma picked out her friends among the old people, and noted with pleasure that there were more of what she called "young folk" than usual. But then, there always were on the first Sunday of the preacher's quarter. It was like a special town holy day. John looked around marking which men were there, wondering whether they were all deputies, or whether some were there for the same reasons he was. Mim listened to the solemn music and longed for the rough boards of her own kitchen beneath her feet.

With a decisive series of chords, Fanny moved into the Processional. The choir—six people in maroon surplices—shuffled into the back of the church. Mim turned to look, just in time to see Perly crowding Dixie into a back pew. He caught her eye and nodded at her as if, in all that congregation, she were his special friend. Then he sat and bowed his head.

Everyone stood up and the singing began, discordant and somewhat unsure—"A mighty fortress is our God, a bulwark never failing." Mim followed the words in the hymnal with her finger, too shy to sing.

Suddenly, Ma clutched at her arm. "Good God in heaven," she said.

From a side door, a figure was approaching the pulpit wearing

Janet Solossen's black robe with the red hood. He climbed slowly up into the high central pulpit and stood silent during the singing, looking out over the congregation with blank black eyes. It was Mudgett.

After the singing was over and the organ fell silent, Mudgett read the Psalm: "My heart was hot within me; while I was musing the fire burned . . ." His voice was high and tense and slow. He seemed more a preacher than the preacher herself. When he lifted his head and prayed, Mim raised her eyes from her bowed head and watched, struck cold by her feeling, despite all she knew, that Mudgett had received a call and turned himself into a spokesman for God.

After the prayer, he looked out over the congregation until everyone began to squirm. It seemed a practiced gesture, one that brought the pressure of conscience to bear on them.

"I have a letter here from the Reverend Solossen," he said at last. "It's dated yesterday.

> *My dear friends:*
>
> *As you all know so well, I have for years taken as my special missionary concern the plight of the orphans of Vietnam. Now a wonderful opportunity to serve God has come to me, and indirectly to you. Three days ago I received an invitation to serve on a delegation of clergy to the government of Vietnam to discuss facilitating the care of these needy children. Then, today, even as I was considering whether I was meant to leave my own parishioners, and whether I could afford the plane fare, a ticket was slipped under my door for the midnight flight to Hong Kong, where I can connect with a flight to Saigon. This anonymous donation from one or more of you came to me like the answer to my prayers and like an assurance that my participation in this delegation is meant to be.*
>
> *Although I know that this probably means that Harlowe will not have a preacher at all this year, I hope that you will feel that through me you are all helping to save the lives of these poor children—the victims, in part, of America's tragic involvement in Southeast Asia. May your prayers go with me, as mine are with you.*
>
> *Janet Solossen*

The service went on—the Lesson, the Responsive Reading, the Anthem. It seemed a normal service, and it was hard to realize that the man in the robes was Mudgett. Jimmy Ward preached the sermon, taking for his text "Suffer the little children to come unto me." Much to Mim's relief, he seemed exactly like Jimmy Ward, stumbling and apologizing and getting tangled in his words.

Afterwards, Mudgett made the announcements: coffee after the service, a fellowship dinner on Thursday, a meeting of the Women's Overseas Mission group to sort clothing for the Vietnamese orphans. "We plan," he said, "to continue church services on a regular basis while the preacher's gone. Anyone who wants to help should speak to Mr. Ward or myself after the service."

"That's not even the way Red Mudgett talks," Mim said on the way home.

"He was ever a weasel, that one," Ma said. "Ain't nothin' he could do would surprise me."

·6·

THE WEEK CAME when there were no nonessentials left. They couldn't let Ma's couch go, and not even Perly could have raised any cash for the kitchen table and benches John had put together from some old planks in the barn. As if he sensed their difficulty, the auctioneer came himself with Gore.

Dixie ran up the path to meet Lassie, her silky tail waving. John watched from the doorway as the two men approached. When they stood on the stoop facing him, he opened the storm door and stepped out to join them.

"There's nothin' left, Perly," he said, his body firmly planted between Perly and his door. "There's no point you stickin' round. You can't squeeze blood from a turnip."

The auctioneer looked down on John, his brown eyes heavy with concern. "You've been very generous," he said slowly. He stood so close that John inched back until he could feel the glass of the door against his shoulder blades.

Gore leaned on the cornerpost of the house, turning the handle of a rake around and around in his hands, not meeting John's eyes. Finally he put the rake down and said, "It don't matter, Johnny. All we want's your guns."

"My guns!"

Perly stooped to pick a sprig of mint growing near the door. He put it in his mouth and chewed it. "With hunting season coming up, we thought a special firearms auction might be a good idea."

"So it's come to disarmin' us," John said, standing solidly before his door.

Perly threw back his dark head and laughed. "If you're working for law and order," he said, "you have to admit it's not a bad idea."

"It happens I need my gun," John said.

"What for?" Perly said. "Town records show you haven't taken out a hunting license for ten years."

"A farmer needs a gun," John said.

"Don't suppose you've got an old muzzle-loader?" Perly asked, glancing through the door into the kitchen. "Those are fetching a pretty price these days."

Gore was kicking at the mudscraper by the door. "He keeps them in the pantry, Perly," he mumbled without looking up.

Perly raised his brows. "If you'll excuse me . . ." he said to John.

John stood his ground and Perly waited to pass. Gore watched, his hand hovering near his gun. Hildie was chirping inside, happy to see the auctioneer.

Perly raised his brows. "Have you considered, John, whether you're in a position to bar the door?" he asked. He cast a glittering eye over Mim and Ma and Hildie, then seemed about to turn away.

Finally, his face flushing deeply beneath his sunburn, John thrust his hands deep into his overall pockets and stepped slowly off the back step. He paused, then moved away toward the barn.

Perly nodded politely at John's receding back. Then he opened the door and waited for Gore to lead the way.

But Gore stood scowling and didn't move until Perly said pleasantly, "Well, Bob?" Then the policeman moved heavily into the kitchen and, without stopping to greet Mim or Ma, strode directly into the pantry.

Perly entered with a smile for Mim and squatted before Hildie where she stood with Mim in front of the sink. "Hi there, sweetie," he said, holding out his arms. "Come say hello to your old friend."

Hildie smiled, but hesitated. As she headed toward Perly, Mim caught the elastic at the back of her jeans and pulled her roughly back, so that she howled in outrage.

86

Perly stood up. He looked down into Mim's face with a different kind of smile. Dixie whined at the door to come in but he ignored her. "So sorry," he murmured, but Mim was looking past him at Gore who was carrying the shotgun and the .30-'06, one in each hand, his eyes fixed and sullen on the floor in front of him.

Perly turned to him. "Did you get the ammunition?" he asked.

"God damn it, Perly," Gore muttered and did not turn.

Perly turned back to Mim. "Where is it?" he asked.

Mim stood still, pressing Hildie's shoulders against her thighs, her face gone white.

Perly shook his head and grinned. "Guess you just can't please all the people all the time," he said, and brushed Mim's cold cheek with his fingertips.

Then, with one step, he moved into the pantry and, without searching at all, reached up and swung the red steel box of ammunition off the top shelf.

Mim watched from the kitchen, Ma from the front room, and John from the barn as Perly followed Gore down the path and the two men sprang up into the cab of the truck and drove away.

The following Thursday, under a scudding sky, heavy with rain, Perly and Gore came again.

John came out of the barn and stood in the doorway, his feet spread wide and his arms folded. "There's nothin'," he said.

Perly gazed cheerfully around the yard, his face darker than ever after a summer in the sun.

Gore leaned against the truck watching. "We're takin' cows," he said.

"Cows!"

"Just a couple," Perly said and winked at Mim who was standing behind the glass in the door looking out. "Figure that's two fewer to milk. Or if you've got a couple that aren't milking at the moment, we'll settle for those."

John glanced up at the pasture where the seven red Jerseys were bunched together under the white ash by the gate, their udders swollen, waiting for him to come and bring them in.

Perly stood with his arms folded in a graceful parody of John. His eyes reflected the rainy sky. "We'll take two," he said.

"The hell you will," John muttered. Then he said, forcing the words out slowly, "Get off my land."

John turned and headed up the path toward the back door and his family. His body seemed numb and each step was an effort. He felt he was pushing not only through his fear of the gun in Gore's holster, but through walls of confounding anger as well.

He didn't hear the steps behind him or the rustle of clothing. Without a sound of warning or the slightest appearance of haste, Perly slid between John and the door he was approaching.

"Did you want to consult your wife?" Perly asked. He opened the kitchen door and caught Mim tightly by the shoulder as she stepped away. He smiled down on her. She raised her eyes to his and the two were caught in the posture of young sweethearts.

John stopped.

Holding Mim by the arm, lightly now, Perly led her toward her husband.

John saw Mim, pale and unfamiliar, walking obediently toward him in the crook of the strange man's arm, her body brushing his. Fear had blanked out all expression on her face.

Catching his breath, John turned quickly away toward the pasture and the cows, his anger and the heaviness of the humid afternoon combining to stifle him. He moved toward the path between the barn and the woodshed that led up into the pasture. Dixie darted out ahead of him and Lassie yapped along behind.

He moved up and up into his land. He could hear Gore puffing behind him, but he could only sense Perly's silent tread. Under the ash, a flat sharp stone, as big around as a milking pail, had fallen from the wall. It grew and changed in his sight as he approached, becoming a weapon.

When he got to the barbed wire section that opened to release the cows, he stopped until Gore and Perly came up behind him and he could feel their breath swirling around his head. The stone was six feet ahead of them. He would wait until they were through the barbed wire. Perly came first, moving through as silent and effortless as a cat. Gore watched John as he went past, his small eyes cautious.

John noticed the empty holster first. Then he saw the gun. Gore wasn't pointing it, just dangling it at his side, half hidden behind his broad thigh.

"Well," said the auctioneer, "which of your pretty lasses will you part with?"

John stood staring down at the stone. If he bent to pick it up now, next week's news would be that John Moore had had an accident cleaning up his guns for hunting season—never mind the fact the guns were gone.

And then the three women would be alone.

John held the fence post and looked past the men to the weathered house below to steady himself. It looked small with distance on the gray day. And in the yard, diminished too by distance, Mim stood where they had left her.

"Which ones did you say?" asked Perly.

Silently, John pointed to Moon. He leaned on the post for support as the auctioneer himself moved toward Moon, slapped her on the flank, and started her ambling easy down the field.

Gore kept watch, his feet planted wide apart, his gun tight in his hand, and his mouth half open, gasping for breath.

After that, Mudgett and Cogswell came again for a while. Mudgett led the way and Cogswell ambled after him like an enormous awkward pet. He was drinking heavily and had to be spoken to sometimes two or three times before he responded. They made two trips one week to take the entire crop of squash, and then they took the churn and separator and, finally, the rest of the cows, always a pair at a time. John and Mim worried about Hildie without the milk, but she went on thriving. They still had good vegetables, and they started eating the chickens as fast as they could, one or even two a day. "Guess they can't take what's already et," Ma said.

They picked the last of the green tomatoes and hid them under the floorboards in their bedroom, then pulled up the bean and tomato stakes. They picked pumpkins and what few squash were late to ripen. They picked bushels of wormy apples. The cider press was gone, so Mim cut them up and made apple sauce from some and hung the others on strings from the rafters in the attic to dry. They put plastic over the windows of the front room and the kitchen. And every day they went into their woods and cut a load of firewood. John got up on the roof with a burlap sack full of bricks on the end of a rope and cleaned the chimneys, and together they emptied the traps behind the stoves.

It was too cold now to bathe in the pond. Instead, on Saturday afternoons, they heated three big kettles full of water and poured them into the galvanized tub. Ma got the first bath, than Hildie, and finally Mim and John. Mim heated a bowl of water and, scolding and coaxing, washed Hildie's bright thin hair.

The leaves began to fall from the trees and everything seemed to move closer to the house—the pond, and the pines where the road opened up, and the edges of the pasture. Mim brought the old wooden lawn chair into the kitchen so that Ma could sit in the kitchen comfortably.

John went and told the doctor's wife he didn't have the cows any more.

"Why is everyone giving up cows?" Mrs. Hastings asked. "I see Lovelace and Rouse don't have theirs any more either. I hear they're being sold at the auctions. You must be getting a fine price."

John stood before her thinking of the check for five dollars he'd gotten the week before for two good milkers.

"Well, I guess it wasn't that much we paid you," she said with a touch of irritation. "It was good butter, I'll say, but I guess it just isn't worthwhile any more."

"The doctor," John said, "he must know what's going on. All the . . ."

"What?" said Mrs. Hastings. "Inflation? If it's Harlowe and this auction business you mean, I have to tell you right out we never could understand what makes you people tick. How can anybody hope to understand people who won't raise a finger to better themselves? It's just like the butter problem. Nobody even wants to do an honest day's work any more."

The tall woman opened the back door and stood brooding at John, waiting for him to leave.

John paused in the doorway, meeting the contempt in her gaze.

"Ma'am," he said, "for all your fancy schoolin', ain't much you do understand."

After Hildie was in bed, John poured the money out of the crockery jar over the sink and counted it, as he did at least once a week. "A hundred seventy-three," he said. "And a hundred in the bank."

They had never been so low going into winter. "Six dollars a month for a phone what never rings," he said. "Don't suppose they'll be askin' me to run the snowplow neither."

"What if there's an accident?" Mim said.

"A phone ain't that much help," Ma said. "We got along without a phone happy enough when Johnny was a boy. Some things we can do without."

There was an unaccustomed peace in the house. Ma had stopped complaining. She lived on her couch as if it were an island. She slept there at night near the warm stove, and in the mornings she made room for Hildie and the two of them played "Let's pretend," or told stories about when Grandma was a little girl—stories Hildie could soon tell as well as her grandmother. They cut up ten-year-old magazines from the barn and pasted them together in new ways with flour and water paste. Sometimes they watched *Sesame Street* together, and for a week Ma worked with her stiff hands sewing together two puppets from quilting scraps the auctioneer had overlooked.

"I 'most wish she'd start in to meddlin' again," Mim said.

"Makes her seem old, don't it?" John said. "To take it all so peaceable like it's nothin' to do with her. But she was always that way. It struck home with her, his pullin' a gun on me. Time will tell how peaceable she is at heart."

Hildie was not always so cooperative. She hated to leave her warm corner to go with John and Mim into the woods for firewood. She whined and complained until Mim screamed at her and she threw herself on the floor and cried. Each morning they headed into the woods in silence, John carrying Hildie on his shoulders, still pouting and working hard to shiver.

John would notch a tree with the chain saw. Mim would set

91

Hildie firmly out of the way. Then, while John sawed through the heavy trunk, Mim put pressure on the wedge to make sure the tree fell where they intended. The trees seemed incredibly long stretched out on the ground. Mim limbed them with the ax, and John, measuring with a pole, sawed them into nine-foot lengths. Together they lifted them onto the wood sledge. And when they had a load, they hitched up the tractor and dragged it back to the woodshed. After the snow came and there was little else they could do, they would split the big sections, then cut the green wood into eighteen-inch lengths and pile it in the woodshed, in a separate pile from last year's dry wood.

"Best we saw it up this week," Mim said one Tuesday. "You wait. He'll be after the saws this time."

"Not the saws," John said. "I draw the line at the saws."

"When you didn't for the cows?" Mim asked.

The next day, without splitting the logs first as they usually did, and without discussing what they were doing, they spent a long day, each using one of the chain saws, cutting the wood to lengths. And on Thursday John let the saws go with barely a glance. After that there was no point to going into the woods, so they spent the week splitting the wood and piling it.

John climbed up and put a patch on the tin roof where it was rusted through, and Mim dug a barrel of potatoes from the icy soil, packed them in straw, and rearranged the cellar to hide them behind an empty set of shelves. They continued to cook and can the last late pumpkins and some chard. They drew Ma's couch up closer to the parlor stove, and kept a fire going in the kitchen range all day. Hildie drew patterns in the first frost on the windows, and they all kept a lookout for the first snow.

Hunting season started on a Tuesday. Cars lined the road, some of them with out-of-state plates. Hildie stood on a box at the window watching the silent red figures moving in and out of the woods. Hildie was not allowed out of the dooryard, and the grown-ups stayed in, occasionally answering the summons of a stranger asking if he could park in the yard. From time to time, they heard the hard flat report of a single shot in the woods.

On Wednesday night, they woke to rifle shots nearby—a dozen of them and so close together they had to be made by several guns. Hildie came into her parents' room, dragging her blanket. "Mama," she whispered. "Do the hunters come at night?"

"Sometimes, Hildie. If they want to shoot a deer too scared to run," Mim said, straining her ears toward the dark woods. "There, lovey, don't you be frightened," she added, but she wasn't sure whether it was she or the child who was shaking. The shots had broken open a dream in which she was being hunted down. She pulled Hildie in under the covers.

But it was John who gathered the child to him and buried his face in her hair. Hildie fell back into a heavy sleep in the comfort of his arms, but he lay planning the moves he would have made if he had had his guns still, craving the shotgun very specifically. He hadn't touched it from one year to the next; yet, as if he had carried it with him always, he could conjure up the precise heft and balance of it in his hand, the chill of the inky barrel, the smoothness of the stock.

When it became clear that John was not going to get up, Mim folded back the blankets and crept out of bed. Touching the cold plaster walls and the banister with her fingertips, and feeling for the chipped edges of the stairs with her toes, she made her way downstairs in the dark. At the door to the front room she could hear Ma's breathing, heavy and uninterrupted and weary.

Mim stood at the foot of the stairs looking out through the glass in the front door. The sky glittered with stars and the pond was outlined like a dull pewter plate. But the land was so heavily swathed in dark that she could not see the road. They could be standing in her very yard, fooling with their jacklights and their guns, moving in that slow silent way of hunters, so as not to frighten her away from the doorway before they had a chance to paralyze her with the light and the dozen gunsights.

She crept into bed and lay with her teeth clenched to keep them from chattering, sensing in the perfect silence John's wide eyes. She clasped his fingers where they were cupped around Hildie's back, but he made no response. "John?" she whispered, but he made no answer. "John?" she said. "Tomorrow, can we bring Hildie's mattress in here close to ours?"

The next day Mudgett came with Gore.

"Where's Cogswell?" John asked as he met them in the dooryard.

"Hits the cider a mite too hard," Mudgett said. "Makes him sentimental."

"Can't have no drunks on the police force," Gore said. "It ain't like I got a grudge or anythin' against Mickey. But the way Perly figures it, maybe if we bust him down a bit now, we can—"

"How come," John said, "if you're so smart, you can't keep the hunters in line?"

"You got any complaints?" Gore asked. He shut his heavy lips tight on whatever else he might have said and kept John well centered in the range of his small eyes. His hand fluttered restlessly near the butt of his gun in its holster.

"They was jackin' deer up here last night," John said.

The lines bracketing Mudgett's thin mouth deepened and he said, "Feelin' tender for the deer, Johnny boy?"

Moore shrugged. "Last I heard there was a law," he said.

"I'll see what I can do," Gore said, straightening up with interest. "You got no idea who it was?"

"You got good reason to be nervous," Mudgett said. He folded a stick of gum and shoved it into his mouth, dropping the wrapper to the ground. "Sam Parry got a stray shot in the shoulder walkin' to his barn. Just missed his heart."

John turned to Mudgett. Mudgett's face was as grizzled and dark from outdoor living as his own. Face to face like that, John still felt the authority of Mudgett's five-year advantage, and of his cleverness with sums. "Real sharpshooter," he said under his breath.

Mudgett considered, chewing his gum as if it were a form of contemplation. Finally, his face cracked into a flat-eyed grin. "You got to admit," he said, "Harlowe ain't half so borin' as it used to be."

94

Mudgett was in high spirits. He toured the entire house and shed, taking his time, loading Gore with every last screwdriver and pair of pliers he could find, as well as the ax, the mallet and wedges, the whetstone, the scythes, the rakes and hoes. Every once in a while he stopped and laughed out loud. "Real sharpshooter, eh?"

Gore, incapacitated by his armload, kept a wary eye on John and never turned his back.

While Gore was loading the tools into the truck, Mudgett took John's big wooden toolbox from the kitchen and practically danced into the front room. "A cuckoo clock!" he exclaimed and lifted it off the wall as Ma watched from the couch. Gore reappeared empty-handed in the doorway.

"I would just like you to know, Red Mudgett," Ma said, struggling to stand between her canes, "that when my time comes, I am goin' to rise up and haunt you the longest day you ever lived."

Mudgett chuckled. "Will you look at her?" he said to Gore. "Some Sunday School teacher. Nothin' I could ever do was good enough for her. You should a seen her." He puffed out his chest, pulled in his chin and intoned in a falsetto not unlike Ma's, "You children just ain't a goin' to come to no good." He nodded with satisfaction.

"I remember," Gore said, making no commitments.

"And many's the Saturday night, Bob Gore," Ma said, "you shared Johnny's bed with him and ate at my table—your own pa too drunk to abide you. And just you keep in mind, young man, it's sorry luck to bite a hand that's fed you."

"Ain't my idea," Gore muttered, but Mudgett was already rushing down the front lawn to put the clock and toolbox in the truck. Gore turned to follow him, but, before he could escape, he bumped into Mudgett returning.

"All we got's a load of scrap," Mudgett said. "Not one decent piece."

"Tools sell good, Red," Gore said.

Mudgett stood in the front doorway snapping his gum. Ma's program rattled on unheeded. Suddenly Mudgett's dark eyes came into focus. He swept across the room and unplugged the television

95

set so that the picture of Dr. Rebus and Susan shrank to a point and disappeared. "Grab an end, Bob," he said.

Gore side-stepped warily around the room, keeping John within his sights, and picked up one end of the console.

"Just hold on half a minute," Ma cried, struggling across the room to block the door.

Gore put his end of the console down, which forced Mudgett to put his down as well.

"Ain't nobody goin' to just walk off with my TV set like that," Ma said.

"Want to put money on it?" Mudgett asked.

"I'll put money on it," John roared. He lunged for Mudgett, but Mim caught him and stopped him momentarily.

Gore backed into a corner and, fumbling, unsnapped his holster and pulled out his gun. John shook himself free of Mim, but stood where he was, watching Gore.

Mudgett sneered, leaned over, and picked up the console himself. He was a small man and the set was so big it gave him the look of an ant struggling beneath an enormous crumb. He staggered toward the doorway where Ma stood.

"Oh no you don't," said Ma, but even as she spoke, the corner of the set caught her in the shoulder. She grabbed at her cane for balance, but the cane slid out sideways on the floor and tangled in Mudgett's legs. Ma, her weight on the cane, fell headlong to the floor. Mudgett struggled, his feet encumbered by the cane and Ma's housecoat. The television set swayed precariously. Finally, he freed a foot and groped for the floor ahead of him. When he stepped, he landed on a pile of Hildie's marbles. His foot flew up in front of him, the television set leaped from his arms and smashed against the stairway, and Mudgett fell swearing into the debris.

"Jesus, Red," Gore gasped, still standing in his corner watching as John lifted his mother and led her to the couch.

Mudgett picked himself up and kicked at the wreck of the television set. The glass was smashed and the cabinet broken open, revealing a tangle of transistors and tiny colored wires. Mudgett had cut his forehead and a slow trickle of blood started down beside his eye. "I'll get you for this," he said to John.

Suddenly Mim came running at him. "Get out," she screamed. "Get out of here." Mudgett stepped back to avoid her fists and sidled out the front door. "You too," she screamed at Gore. "Get out. I just can't stand it."

Gore backed around the room past John and his mother and hurried down the path after Mudgett.

Mim leaned against the wall and sobbed. "I can't stand it," she moaned. "I just can't stand it." Hildie clung to her legs, crying loudly.

John looked up from his mother, his face fierce. "Then why'd you grab me when I went for him?"

Lassie came in and started to whimper.

Ma patted her hair into place as John rearranged her on the couch. "Stop that," she said coldly, sitting bolt upright on the couch. "You stop that wailin' this minute, the lot of you. If there's one thing I won't have in my house, it's hysterical women."

Mim and Hildie looked up, startled into silence.

"I'm quite all right, and so are you," Ma said, smoothing her housecoat over her knees. "Quite all right."

But that was not the end of it. For three days, Mim looked after the remnants of the household and tried to create a sense of normalcy for Hildie in the midst of a silence as unnatural as that which precedes a hunter through the woods. John sat before the kitchen range and Ma sat on her couch near the parlor stove and neither said a word.

On Sunday, John brought in a load of wood and dumped it in the woodbox behind the kitchen stove. He chose two sticks, lifted the lid on the range with the handle, and added them to the fire. Then he sat down and leaned silently into the heat once more.

Hildie was building a village in the corner with kindling chips and didn't look up, but John and Mim heard Ma coming. She moved slowly, thumping the floor with her two canes and dragging her feet in their felt-soled slippers. She stopped in the doorway and leaned on her canes. Her gray hair stood out around her head in stiff curlicues and the rope around her flannel dressing gown was tied in a knot at the waist.

Mim brushed past her and came back with her pillows and blankets which she arranged in the lawn chair. But Ma did not take the arm she offered. She stood steadfast where she was. "I expect I can do without my television set, son," she said, "if you can do without your ax."

Mim glanced at John, but he watched Hildie as though his mother had never spoken.

"What's your plan now?" Ma went on. "You figurin' to cut down the forest with your teeth?"

Hildie came over and leaned against her father. He took her into his lap and stared at the front of the stove.

"We had bears and Indians and winters that lasted all summer. We had dry spells and floods and wicked men before too. But I don't recall as our people ever run away before."

"You see me runnin', Ma?" John asked, jolting to his feet so that Hildie slid to the floor.

"Like a jack rabbit, boy," said Ma, her hands white on the knots of her canes. "Where you think it's goin' to get you to?"

"Next time I'll stand up and let him shoot me," John shouted. "Then where'll you be?" He yanked the door open.

Ma took a step toward him. "And that's just another way of runnin'," she shouted back.

He slammed out the back door of the kitchen, and Hildie, thrust to one side in his rush, began to cry. Painfully, Ma turned herself and started on the journey back to the couch.

"Stay with us, Ma," Mim said. "You still got us."

"We still got plenty of wood too," Ma said, refusing Mim's help. "And I'd as soon sit by myself. That way I'm sure of where I'm at."

Mim came back to the kitchen and took Hildie into her arms to rock. Through the window over the sink she could see John climbing quickly up the dry brown pasture in the dusk. She worried about hunters.

·7·

THE CLOCKS WERE GONE and the old Moore place was silent, but
every human motion seemed to mark off an interval in their in-
exorable approach to Thursday. The usual list of autumn chores
dissolved. There were no cows to care for, no spare dollars to
buy paint, no tools to gather wood or mend furniture. Even the
endless knickknacks for dusting and polishing were gone. Now
that the television set was gone, the Moores had the electricity
turned off to conserve cash. Their routines took on a primitive
rhythm which would soon have acquired a comfort of its own,
had it not been jarred anew with every Thursday visitation.

Their best moments were the sleepy ones first thing in the
morning when they lay on their mattress with Hildie cuddled between them, letting some time pass before they got up and ran
barefoot down the icy stairs to stoke the stoves and dress, to eat
oatmeal without milk, and wait for something to happen. There
had always been times after the snow came when they had a few
hours a day to sit by the stove and let the flurry of summertime
wear off. On stormy afternoons of other years, Mim and John
and Ma had played hearts in between trips to the barn. But this
was different. John sat on the bench in overalls and a sweatshirt
faded to pink and shrunk so that it pulled halfway up his back
when he rested his elbows on the table behind him and his feet

on the fender of the stove, examining day after day the dust settled into the cast iron leaves and flowers. He spent hours scraping and digging with a hunting knife at a stick of maple from the woodbox. Uneasy at his furious silences, the women avoided conversation themselves, and whole hours went by broken only by Hildie's fantasy chatter, the settling of the fire in the stove, and the rough scratching of John's whittling.

It was Mim who disconnected the water pump, now that they had no electricity to drive it. And Mim who went out to the bell pump behind the barn and brought in milk pails full of water, two a day for the kitchen and two to flush the toilet. And Mim who cleaned the kerosene lamp each morning. Even so, by ten o'clock most days, she could find nothing more to do. She dressed Hildie in red and led her out protesting into the cold sunshine. She sought out dandelions and dug them for the roots and drying leaves. She gathered the tubers of day lilies and dug through the garden for the last small carrots and beets. She dug chicory and gathered black birch twigs for tea. There were still chrysanthemums in the garden but she didn't bother to cut them. "All the mums in Harlowe won't make one decent soup," she said.

On Sunday Hildie climbed into her father's lap and wouldn't budge. "I want to stay in where it's warm," she said, "like Pa."

"Tell her to come," Mim said to John when she was dressed and ready to go out. "Not healthy for a child to sit all day and watch you brood." But John looked at her as if he had not heard and kept his arm crooked protectively around the child. "Can't you do anythin' but set?" Mim cried. "Day after day like you lost all your yeast?"

There was a silence while John rocked Hildie and Ma watched Mim from her chair at the table.

Finally Ma said, "You needn't act like it wasn't you first begged him to give it all away. It was you went and gave your ma's dressin' table, as I recall, right when John was up for sayin' no."

"And what if he had, Ma?" Mim shouted. "What if he had said no? You think we'd be better off?"

Mim moved up the pasture alone, working back tears and the vision of the three sets of Moore eyes accusing her—Ma's and John's the color of storm clouds, John's only more bruised.

The poison ivy in the cemetery was a deep shiny red. It lay like a flood halfway up the grave markers and sent out tentacles from under the stone wall into the pasture. It climbed around and around the trunks of the old cherry tree and coiled its way out along the branches, like snakes moving toward robins' nests. There hadn't been any ivy there at all when they buried Pa seven years ago. John had dug a proper grave six feet deep so the ground could never heave the coffin back. Afterward, they had taken Ma up in the tractor once a week and she had tried to get Mayflowers and sheep laurel growing on the new raw place. She knew as well as they that Mayflowers would never bloom in that high dry place, but it was a labor they could not talk her out of, as if she hoped that Pa, wherever he was, could breathe life into the flowers he had loved the best.

When, in the spring, they took Ma up to see if the Mayflowers were in bloom, they found that what had taken root was poison ivy. Ma never asked to go up again.

John didn't care for poison ivy and wouldn't take the scythe in there, the way Pa always had, to keep down the growth. And so the ivy and everything else ran free. Black clumps of juniper began for it to climb on, and poplar saplings took root the next spring and mixed their sticky gray-green leaves with the chartreuse of the spring ivy.

Mim had a sudden image of a new-dug grave with the ivy filling it like water in a muddy footprint. Filling it to overflowing so there was no room for the coffin. "Ma's gettin' old," she murmured, but what she saw was the kind of small flat stone that said simply, "Child."

She whirled around and examined the black verges of the forest that surrounded her on three sides. The woods on the edge of a pasture are like a window, easier to see out of than into, and she could only feel the presence of the hunters stalking silently, invisible within the dimness. High in the woods, near Cogswell's field, there was a sheltered place between a huge seed hemlock

and the flat face of a cliff, and every year the hunters left a
bushel basket full of beer bottles under it. Sometimes too, working in the woods the following autumn, she and John would find
a beer bottle upright on a rock, half full of rain water as if a
hunter had put it down suddenly to lift the gun from across his
knees and take his deer. Mim let her eyes fall down over the
empty pasture toward the house and listened to the sweep of
wind across the gray sky.

Then she turned and sank her gloved hands into the fiery sea
of ivy, grasped all she could, and pulled it free. It snapped quite
suddenly and sprang back around her body. She stepped away,
leaving the ungainly mass in a heap outside the wall, and went
back for more. She tore at the ivy, pulling tendrils of it sometimes
twelve feet long. She pulled up the junipers and kicked at the
poplars till they were bent and stripped of leaves. She worked
until the ground around the gravestones was trampled and brown.
Then, in three trips, she carried the pile of ivy over and dumped
it in the woods. She stood over the broken brown twigs showing
in the dirt. In spring they would send up wild new growth. The
pruning would be like a tonic to the ivy. She stood over the
cemetery too tired now to cry. All her effort, she knew full well,
might ease her anger now, but it would all grow back in fresh red
shoots in the renewal of spring.

Back at the house, she brought in four pails of extra water.
Adding boiling water from the kettles, she washed her gloves,
her wool shirt, her jeans, her socks, her jersey, and finally, with
harsh yellow soap, herself.

By Thursday, when Mudgett and Gore came, the poison ivy
was raging all over her arms and face. They took the water pump
and roamed around looking for something more. Gore found the
old wooden barrel of potatoes where Mim had hidden it in the
cellar, heaved it onto his shoulder, and carried it out to the truck.

After they left, Mim stood at the sink with her back to the
others in the room and indulged in the painful luxury of scratching at her face with her fingernails. Then she scrubbed her hands

yet again with the yellow soap and a plastic brush. She was afraid to touch Hildie for fear of starting the plague on her, and John would not touch her even in their bed.

Finally Ma said, "Well, and just what do you plan for Christmas dinner now, missy?"

Mim turned. "There are more potatoes in the earth," she snapped.

John sat with his feet on the fender of the stove as if the women weren't there. The shavings he peeled from the stick fell to the floor beneath his feet. There was a long silence.

Mim stood at the sink scraping carrots. "Could we get ourselves on welfare, do you think?" she asked. "It's hardly even shameful nowadays."

"Since when?" Ma said. "Maybe not for folks who ain't got sense enough to hang on to what's theirs."

"No one goin' to put us on the dole when we got a stand of pine like that one east of the pasture," John said.

"But what good is that?" Mim said. "Soon's we make it movable, they'll cart it off."

"If you let them," Ma said.

"Well, what would you do? You with all the answers," Mim asked Ma. Then she turned on John, rubbing her face again. "And you?"

John didn't look up. He had whittled the stick in his hands to a point like an enormous pencil, and now he kept on peeling away at it, sharpening it more and more so that, like a pencil, it diminished as the pile of shavings on the floor accumulated.

Mim stood in the middle of the room, their silence swelling around her in stifling clouds.

Suddenly Hildie flung herself into her grandmother's lap, away from Mim.

Mim smashed out the swinging kitchen door so that it rocked on its hinges as she pounded up the stairs.

Their room was cold, and the mattresses on the floor smelled of damp. She grabbed John's brown sweater off a hook and crushed it against her face, rubbing and rubbing until she started tiny flecks of blood.

The next day Mim announced that she was going up to Cogs-well's to see Agnes before the road was snowed in. "I've a mind to borrow some calamine," she said.

John went over to the cookie jar over the sink and brought back a dollar bill which he laid out on the board tabletop.

Mim rubbed her cheeks, looking at the dollar. "It's really that I want to see Agnes," she said.

He shrugged and she put the money in her jacket. Hildie was following Mim so closely that every time Mim moved she nearly tripped over the child. "You're not comin'," she said. "So just get your big self out of my way!"

John scooped up the child and held her like a vise while she howled to be free.

The road over Constance Hill that connected Moore's place and Cogswell's had once been the main post road, two carefully leveled lanes terraced into the steep grade of the hill. But now the lower lane was grown up in trees already a foot thick, and the upper lane, the one they used, was deeply rutted from the rushes of spring storms. Thus, in summer it was less than a mile over the hill to Cogswell's, whereas in winter, when the snow cut off the road, they had to travel seven miles around the foot of the hill. Mim drove carefully, one wheel up on the high center hump and the other way up on the edge so that the saplings crowding the road scraped the panels of the truck with a sound like finger-nails on slate. At the crest of the hill, she looked past the stone wall into Cogswell's blueberries. They spread in a scrubby growth around boulders and burned stumps, skipping bald patches of ledge and clusters of raspberry canes, and stopping only where the hill dipped down and vanished into forest. Unlike Moore's pasture, which looked down on the pond and the flat green stretch of Freedom Ridge to the south, Cogswell's field faced north and, on a clear day, the view stretched past the Heskett Hills to the mountains. It was the first time in fourteen years that Mim hadn't been up to glean what berries were left after the rakers were finished.

It would have been easier to call when Cogswell had asked her to. Now she turned over excuses in her mind. She had come empty-handed. It was the season for pumpkin bread, but she could hardly afford the butter and sugar. It didn't make sense to rattle over the hill to borrow something that only cost a dollar. She should have brought some chrysanthemums. They weren't worth anything now that Mudgett ran the church.

Cogswell's house, which would have been a center-entrance colonial if the windows on one side hadn't been slightly askew, had new sash and a new coat of gray paint. The lawn had been let go toward the end of the season, so there were wilted dandelions and daisies mixed in with the battered green growth.

Two Doberman pinschers came bounding out and leaped against the doors of the truck, their paws scratching at the windows. As if they fed on neighbors, Mim thought and made sure the doors were firmly fastened. She waited in the truck for someone to come out and rescue her.

The inside front door opened and Cogswell's oldest child, thirteen-year-old Jerry, stood behind the storm door cradling a heavy shotgun in his arms.

Mim waved to him and waited. He continued to watch her warily over the din of the dogs.

Finally she rolled down her window a little and the dogs leaped up eagerly as if in hopes of a finger or two. "It's just me, Miriam," she shouted. "Can I see your ma?"

The boy kicked open the door ahead of him and came toward her, still pointing the gun. "Put your hands up on your head so I can see them," he called.

Mim put her hands on her head with a sense that this was play. Before Hildie was born, she used to come over sometimes, especially in the summer, to spell Agnes. She felt that this was not the first time she had responded to a command from small imperious Jerry to "Stick 'em up."

"Dad said once to let you in, but that was a while back," the boy said. "You after somethin'?"

"I heard your ma's feelin' mean," Mim said. "And I always did come callin' every year."

"She's okay," Jerry said, standing by the door of the truck with his gun pointed at Mim, considering. Mim sat very still, aware

105

that her face itched and she didn't dare move to scratch it.

"I guess you can come on in," he said. "Down, Rex. Here, Duke. Shut up now."

The dogs cringed growling at his feet and Mim, moving very gingerly, climbed out of the truck and walked in at the rarely used front door ahead of the boy. Just inside the door, the five other children clustered on the bottom of the stairs. Mim tried to smile at them. She knew them all. She remembered sitting at the picnic table in the shade of the maples, letting them tumble around her. They would talk and talk, even the littlest ones— they got that talking streak from both sides—and whoop, running out onto the lawn to show her backwards somersaults and lop-sided cartwheels. Now they were silent, and she looked at them in alarm. In the fading afternoon light of the front hall, it seemed to her they were peaked, and the youngest, Jonathan, a year older than Hildie, was sucking his thumb. They looked wary, the way Hildie did when she had just kicked over a pail of milk and expected to get a whack—five pairs of sky-blue eyes waiting for her to strike, and another behind her attached to the heavy shotgun. She didn't ask them why they weren't in school. She could tell by looking that they wouldn't answer.

But Jerry had at least put the gun down in the corner. He nodded in the direction of the front room, and Mim opened the door and went in.

Agnes was a tall woman with big bones, who had grown blowzy with the birth of her children. She never had been quite in control —of her big body, of her sprawling house, of the garden Mick planted and left for her to tend, of her six children, of her affections or her tears. She reminded Mim of the peach trees Pa had planted that fell beneath the weight of their own fruit when they weren't pruned. Agnes could never keep anything in place, least of all her tongue.

Leaning on the arm of a new maple rocker upholstered in a pattern of golden eagles and flatirons, she faced the door, waiting for Mim. Mim was startled at the way she looked. She had gained a lot more weight, and all of it showed in the blue jersey pant-suit she was wearing. The jacket was a mass of stains down the front as if she spilled everything she touched. And she had cut her gray-brown hair short and possibly given it a permanent, for now it stood on her head in an almost solid mat of tangles.

Mim put her hand to her face. "You're looking a bit pale, Agnes," she said. "Kids too. You been ailin'? And winter not come on yet?"

"Ain't nothin' I can do for the child," Agnes said, her surprisingly high-pitched voice screwed down tight on the words. "I can't think why you come to me." She got up and walked heavily across the room. Her toe picked up a corner of the new hooked rug and she stooped to lay it down again. Then she went to the back window and stood with her back against it, and Mim noticed that she was leaning on a radiator.

"Central heat!" she said. "You sure done a lot with this room."

"It's bad luck," Agnes said. "So don't bother bein' green. I got six to count every hour. I get up at night and count them."

Agnes hugged herself as if for warmth, but Mim felt a prickly heat spreading from her wool jacket, making her face itch.

She giggled, ashamed that Agnes should think her jealous, embarrassed at Agnes' strangeness. "You know, Agnes," she said, "the foolish trick I pulled? You know the poison ivy's been growin' in on Pa's grave these seven years now he's gone?"

Agnes backed up and sat on the radiator. "He still sucks his thumb," she said. "At night it makes a clickin' sound. You hear it all over the house so you know he's there. But Benjamin, there ain't no way to tell about him, short of goin' in there and feelin' his head for warmth."

"Well, I went up there," Mim went on uneasily. "I was all in a flap, and I yanked it out by the roots, all that ivy. It kept jumpin' back at me as if to say you shouldn't tackle anythin' head on like that. Now I'm all over ivy, worse than measles. Look at my poor face."

"It ain't so terrible," Agnes said, examining Mim's face. "They pay. They pay. Better that than what happened to Molly Tucker's boy."

Mim rubbed her face. Agnes had always talked a mile a minute and only half made sense—her words, like her feet, tripping over

107

each other. She would have filled her house with company if there'd been anyone interested. Usually she had an oversized laugh she couldn't hold in. And she loved to do favors as long as they didn't require organization or too much money. Slowly and a bit too loudly, as if she were talking to someone who was deaf, Mim asked, "I was just wonderin', could I borrow some calamine?"

"They'll go to good homes. That's what he says. 'Good homes.' Anyone willin' to buy them must really want them. Mostly they can't have them." Agnes laughed. "Think of that. And here I am. Half buried in them. But you'd never be bothered countin' someone else's all night long. You couldn't care like that but for your flesh and blood. Not when the floors get cold. And you wouldn't put up with the clickin'. It ain't regular like a clock and it always catches you the hardest when you want to sleep."

"Agnes?" Mim asked, rubbing her hand across the back of the new rock maple sofa. The colors were all very bright, though the blinds were down and the room was in shadow. Then, as if she weren't thinking right herself, she found she had no words for the question pressing on her throat. She said instead, "The room is done over real nice. Did you fix it yourself?"

"This ain't such a bed of roses that I can see," Agnes said, her big jaw drooping. "Now there's Jimmy Ward. He just up and left. Mick don't know I know, but I heard it from my Joanie. Joan's the only one tells me what's goin' on. She says he just up and went. Not all that deputy business and bein' a selectman and a deacon both at once could keep him."

"You don't mean he left Liza after all this time?"

"No, no. All of them in the truck, with what all they could carry. Not a soul knew they was gone till next day when one of the Pulvers noticed the cows bellowin' in the field near crazy. Seventeen he'd got too, with the extras, though he never took much interest in stock."

"Where'd they go?" Mim asked.

"They ain't leavin' tracks." Agnes paced across the room to the front window, fitted one eye to a small hole in the shade, and looked out. "He was pickup man for Carroll and Carroll's pretty itchy. You can't hardly blame him. Then his boy, Ward's boy, took a bullet in the leg up huntin', and Ward, he don't think it was no accident. He must have got to thinkin' the way I been thinkin'. There's two ways most anythin' can fly."

"Jimmy Ward's boy took a bullet in his leg?" Mim asked. She was still standing just inside the door in her coat, leaning on the wall.

Suddenly Agnes straightened up again and came toward her. Her eyes were wide and her face blotched with color. Mim straightened up, expecting the weight of the other woman to land on her. "Where's Hildie?" cried Agnes. "Oh my God, where's little Hildie?"

"She's home," Mim said.

Agnes retreated. "You hadn't ought to leave her out of sight. You got to hang on for dear life. Mick's never gone a minute I don't expect him back in a coffin. And then what? Ain't like I could drive. You're real smart the way you can do for yourself. And I always thought you was so queer."

Mim rubbed her face and the backs of her hands on the rough wool of her jacket. She felt as though everything had frozen in place, and the question had to come up from somewhere very, very far away. "What happened to Tucker's boy?"

"If I had my way," Agnes said, "we'd pile the kids in the truck just like Ward done, and load in what we can take, cash out whatever . . . Jimmy Ward's nobody's fool. But Mick . . . He's never been a tight man except when it comes to his land. Like there was some kind of spell on those particular acres."

"What happened to Molly Tucker's boy?" Mim asked again, her voice grown hoarse.

"The land. Never a speck of sense, my Mick. Now it's the land. I left the land all right where I was reared. Never a backward glance. He says, 'You don't do that. Up and leave your land.' And I say, 'You'll get killed, all for the sake of your precious land.' And he says, 'Six kids, Agnes. Six kids.' And I say, 'You think they love that piece of rock and sand—that never grew nothin' right but weeds and berries? You think that's better than a livin' breathin' father?'" Suddenly Agnes was gulping on big sobs, haphazardly.

109

"The land, Mim. Why the land?" She stopped. "Shhh," she said and crossed the room again to look out of the hole in the shade. "They're listenin'."

"I guess you got your own problems," Mim murmured and she walked toward Agnes, thinking to kiss her goodbye, forgetting the poison ivy.

But Agnes turned and screamed as she approached. "What are you after?" She stumbled across the room out of Mim's reach. "Get your hands away from me."

Mim turned, frightened, and collided with Jerry as he opened the door with the shotgun in his arms again. "Good Lord, be careful," Mim said, backing off and sidling past him as he motioned to her.

In the hall, she reached out to touch Joan, who was as big as Jerry now, but Joan eluded her with an angry flip of her shoulder.

"Joanie," Mim whispered. "Tell me what happened to Molly Tucker's boy."

"He drownded in the well," said the child, with a hard frightened stare. "The little one."

"But why?" Mim asked.

The four smaller children huddled behind Joan ready to skitter away like beetles if Mim moved. Jonathan sucked his thumb and Mim could hear the clicking sound.

She stumbled out to the truck in front of Jerry's gun, rubbing her face. The thin dogs crouched growling on either side of the door, ready to leap if she should decide to come back.

There was a new brown Crew Cab pickup in front of Linden's. It turned out to be Ezra Stone's. The jangle of bells when Mim opened the door made Ezra look up from the fishing tackle at the back of the store, and she met his yellow eyes full on across the shoulder-high rack of cupcakes and potato chips. Without greeting her, he went back to fiddling with the boxes of fishing hooks.

"Where's Hildie?" Fanny asked, and Mim turned to find her sleepy blue eyes uncharacteristically awake.

"Home with Ma and John," Mim answered.

"Oh," said Fanny, and her eyes went back to sleep. "What'd you get into?"

"Poison ivy up to the top of the pasture by the gravestones," she said.

"All by yourself?"

"All by myself," Mim said. "Some people ain't got the sense they was born with. I need some calamine."

Fanny opened a glass cabinet over her head and rummaged.

"You got any bottles smaller than a dollar?"

"Nope," Fanny said.

Mim hesitated, fingering the dollar bill in her pocket. "Been to any auctions lately?" she asked softly.

"Oh they're still goin' strong," Fanny said. "They move them into Perly's barn when the weather's foul, is all." Mim thought her eyes flickered at Stone in the back of the store. "But me, I mind my own business. Run the store the way I always done and mind my own business." She plunked the bottle of chalky pink liquid down on the counter. "That'll be a dollar."

Mim stood at the counter. She didn't want to go. "Any news?" she asked. "I ain't been to town in ages."

"Yeah, thought maybe you was gone, too," Fanny said.

"Too?"

"Lot of people movin'," Fanny said. "Guess maybe it's the times." But she took a big bag and put a *Boston Globe* in along with the calamine.

Mim opened her mouth, but Fanny said softly, "Yesterday's. We been all through it. You was askin' after news."

John took the paper immediately and went to work on it, starting at page one. He read laboriously, shaping his lips around the words and rereading each sentence. When it got dark, he spread the paper out on the table, brought the kerosene lamp up close, and went on reading. Ma had them pull her chair up to the table so that she could work on the back half of the paper. John told Mim about anything that interested him as she moved around him, tending to the fire, chopping onions and potatoes for the

111

soup, admiring the fragile edifices Hildie was erecting with the kindling.

"You know that lot of forest fires in California?" he asked. "It says here, 'Over eight hundred homeless. The American Red Cross, with the aid of the citizens of nearby communities, is providing food, clothing, and temporary shelter. Three hundred fully equipped mobile homes are being transported to the area.'" He stopped with his finger under the last word. "They just give them to them?"

"Anybody give you one, son," said Ma, "you'd be givin' it away again the followin' Thursday. 'Sure. Sure. Help yourself. Take it away. Me? My child? My wife? My old Ma? The silver linin's all we need.'"

Still holding his place with his finger, John looked up at his mother. The lamplight under his chin deepened the lines in his face and seemed to bend them grimly downward. "You got complaints, Ma?" he said. "You got complaints about the way I been keepin' you these ten years?"

She said nothing more. She bent over the classified pages with her magnifying glass, commenting occasionally on the outrageous price that someone wanted for a used upright piano, or a pickup truck with a plow on it. Eventually it was she who found an ad with a Harlowe telephone number.

Under *Machinery, New and Used:*

> Secondhand Farm Machinery to be auctioned off Saturday in Central N.H. Call 603-579-3485.

But when Mim leaned over her shoulder to look, what caught her eye immediately was the big ad. "Listen to this," she cried, taking the paper from Ma. "Says 'Harlowe, New Hampshire,' right here."

> Perly Acres. Rolling hills, high ledge, views, fields, pasture, trout streams—preserved in all their rustic natural beauty. Enjoy the beauties of the country, the comforts of your own home, and the luxuries of the finest resort. To be developed

next summer: guest lodge, ball-room, community center, movie house, pond for sailing and swimming, trails for snowmobiling and horseback riding, ski lifts, tennis courts, golf course, even an indoor gymnasium for those "rainy days in the country." Central caretaking services to protect your property and rent it for you summer or winter when you can't be in residence. Expert advice and contractors available for building. Complete financing on excellent terms. Get in on the ground floor at ground floor prices. First parcels to be auctioned off this Saturday. One acre. Five acres. Twenty-five acres. Or be the aristocrats of the development and buy one of the first two authentic antique farmhouses to go up for sale. For information and a tour of the properties available, call 603-579-3485.

"And then all along the bottom like a border, it says 'First Ad. First Ad. First Ad. First Ad.'"

John took the paper from her and read it again. "Which houses? Ward's maybe and who else's?" he said.

"A pond?" Mim said. "And a hill for skiing?"

That night, after Ma and Hildie were asleep, John and Mim lay on separate edges of their mattress. A full moon over the pond threw a bright ell of light down the wall and across the floor. The dim blue light outlined the underwear folded in piles on a new shelf, and the jeans and shirts hanging on hooks along one wall. Mim's face and hands and arms, a flat bright pink with calamine, glowed in the half light.

"We got ourselves, John," she said. "And the truck and money in the jar still. All the smart ones are gettin' out."

"Where do you think the likes of us could go? Ain't like we had relatives."

113

"Maine, maybe? Canada?"

"How do you make out we could live without the land?"

"Get jobs. Lots of people never had no land."

"Anyplace but here we'd be outsiders."

"I could work with flowers or cook. You're a good farmer. You're real good with stock. You know how to run the snowplow and the grader."

John snorted. "So does every jackass farmer's kid in Maine," he said. "You don't see the jobs in Harlowe goin' to some poor slob's just showed up from nowhere without a penny in his pocket. Without the land, we're nothin'. Tramps. Gypsies. They'd think we was runnin' scared. They'd guess in a minute we was runnin' from the law." The thought gave John a certain sardonic pleasure. "Not far off the mark either," he said.

"There's the city," Mim said. "I bet they're not so close with jobs in the city. Can't be where everyone's strangers."

"What do we know about the city?" John asked. "And they'd see right off we wasn't onto their way of livin'. Pick our pocket, hit us over the head, stick a knife in our back. You want to bring up Hildie in the city?"

"But how will we live here?" Mim cried. "He's got in mind to turn all Harlowe to his ends."

"The land, Mim," John said, reaching to touch her in spite of the ivy. "The land is all we got. And what would it do to Ma to tear her loose of it?"

"Not all your talk can change things, John. What can we do but go?" Mim sat up and her voice rose over John's head. "They give you choices, John—your blessed land or . . ." and her voice fell to a whisper. "Think what happened to Tuckers' boy. And them with so much more than us."

"Mim, Mim," John said, pulling her down under the covers. "Things is things. But they can't take your flesh and blood. And they can't take the land, because we're on it."

"Words, John," Mim said. "That's not stoppin' them. What is it they been doin' all this summer and fall?"

"This is still America, Mim. They can't. There's limits."

"John, think. All the land that's city now was farms one time. And somehow they made the farmers go."

"But, Mim," he said. "Jimmy Ward just up and left and so did Oakes. Fanny says there's others. They're willin' to oblige. But ain't nobody can sell the land out from under us. We got a deed up to Hampton says they can't."

"Agnes counts her children all night long," Mim said. "And she's on the side that's supposed to be safe. And even Fanny's askin' after Hildie."

John held Mim. The house banged and creaked and clattered as if it were full of secret footsteps. The November wind outside blew over the pond and the pasture and the stand of heavy white pine. It pulled at the shingles of the empty barn and rattled the loose sash, searching out the couple who lay in each other's arms listening to the warm breath of the child on the floor beside them.

·8·

"I'M GOIN' TOO," Mim said.

"I'll tell you just how it is," John argued.

"You won't. You're set to stick to the land. You'll hold back the worst."

"It's no day for Ma to be outside. Listen to the wind."

Ma listened silently, to her thoughts or to the wind wasn't clear.

"Nor is it any place to bring a child," he went on. "Think of the guns. Too many guns with tempers runnin' high."

"And it's you wants to say that all is well," mocked Mim.

"It's no place for women," John said.

"Nor for men either, but for the ones that's in on it, or strangers," Mim said.

"If not for Ma, then you should stay for Hildie."

Mim shook her head. "I have to go," she said. "You stay."

"Let her go," Ma said. "And you go too. There's not a thing that we can any of us do if they should come with their mind set otherwise."

So Mim took Hildie by the hand and showed her the hay and the old quilts in the horse stall in the barn. "Show me how you'll hide yourself when you hear a truck," she said. "Hide good and don't come out no matter who should call. Even if Ma should call. Not even if it's your friends. Most especially, you hide good if it's

116

your friends." She could not bring herself to mention in particular the auctioneer. "And keep a sharp ear out all day. Your grandma don't hear as good as you."

It was a gray day, the Saturday before Thanksgiving. The last leaves were browning in the gutter and the post office had a sheaf of Indian corn hanging on the door. There weren't nearly as many people at the auction as there had been in high summer. No children at all. No balloons or sneakers with stars, and nothing resembling a red wagon. The people waiting were mostly leathery men in overalls, smoking, each alone.

"They're comin' from all over the state for that machinery," Mim said.

Near the bandstand were three tractors, a small house trailer, three pickup trucks, four old station wagons, and a Volkswagen.

John took Mim's arm just above the elbow and steered her where he wanted her to go, holding on a bit too tight. They passed two milking machines, three wood ranges, their own water pump, an oil furnace, four chain saws, and finally, neatly loaded in a sagging hayrack, a winter's supply of firewood.

"Wood," Mim said.

"Maybe they got heat," John said.

Mim shook her head. "Stoves must be gone," she said.

There was a haphazard but distinguishable circle of Harlowe men roaming like sheepdogs around the area of the auction. They moved tensely and startled easily. Most of them kept their hands in their pockets near the guns Mim knew were hidden under their jackets. John and Mim never caught anyone's eye head on, but often they caught a deftly shifting glance.

"They're on the squeamish side, the lot of them," Mim said, rubbing at her raw face. "They want us home."

"It's a public auction," John said.

"Wouldn't you think," Mim murmured, "everyone would see that somethin's mighty queer?"

"They see all right. You think they come all alone and stand so quiet because they find it comfortable? But the stuff is cheap.

They know it's cheap and cheap because there's somethin' not quite right." John looked at the strangers so like himself. "They figure it couldn't smell all that bad or the state would step in to stop it. It will too. It's damn well got to."

"Wish it'd hurry up," Mim said.

The door to the old Fawkes place opened behind the high chain link fence Perly had erected. The auctioneer strode out of his gate and across the green with Dixie, followed at a tactful distance by Gore and Mudgett. He took the steps to the bandstand two at a time, then leaned over the railing of the bandstand sizing up the people spread out below him. Mim shuddered as the dark eyes raked across the place where they stood and followed through to where the deputies roamed at the edges of the crowd.

The wooden chairs were out, of course, but only a few couples sat down, some of them summer people Mim recognized. Most of the men stood around the edges, as if their presence there were tentative, or only incidental.

Perly climbed to his place and rapped his gavel. Dixie traced two circles near him and plopped herself down with a sigh. This was no crowd for banter or joviality. Perly read off the specifications in a grave voice and offered short-term guarantees on almost everything. He did not hurry. Nor did the farmers hurry. The auction moved at a subdued and orderly pace, even cautiously, without excitement. Ezra Stone and Ian James followed up each sale, negotiating with the new owners about papers and signatures and checks. By eleven-thirty, everything was sold except the oil furnace. "That's it," he said. "Though I am going to feel a personal sense of failure if I can't interest a single soul in this prize oil furnace. What with all the craze round here for antiques, I can't rightly figure why no one wants this genuine ancient article." There was a ripple of laughter through the crowd. Perly looked out over them and smiled. "Thank you all for coming," he said and walked quickly down the stairs and into the crowd, where he was immediately flanked by Gore and Mudgett.

He headed, at a leisurely pace, toward his house, allowing himself to be stopped by various people who had bought things. When he passed the Moores, who were staring at him as if they themselves were invisible, he stopped so abruptly that Gore walked right into him.

"Nice to see you folks out," he said. "Haven't seen you in a dog's age. How's your mother?"

"Good's can be expected," John said, glancing sideways at Perly.

Mim stepped back a pace and looked down past Dixie to the hard ground, her face flooding uncontrollably with color.

"Maybe I'll be by next week to see for myself," Perly said, waiting for Mim to glance up. When she did, he nodded seriously as if to confirm some carefully negotiated bargain. "Yes," he said, "I've missed my friend Hildie. An old bachelor like me gets very attached to little girls."

John and Mim waited in the truck. Even before the people from the morning auction had packed up their machinery and driven off, a new set of cars was pulling in around the green—foreign sports cars this time, polished hard-top convertibles, and family-sized station wagons. A big Travelall pulled up in front of the Moores' truck. All four doors opened at once and four boys went tearing across the green toward the bandstand. A paunchy father trudged along after them, hugging a football to his chest and scowling at the sky.

At one o'clock exactly, by the clock on the half-finished church steeple, Perly reappeared on the porch of his house, paused to look over the situation, then headed across the empty Parade. He was wearing a black suit and a metallic gray tie that caught the wind and blew over his shoulder as he moved easily toward the bandstand. Gore ambled after him wearing a hunting jacket over his usual denims, and carrying a square black briefcase.

The cars began to empty out with a slamming of doors, and people filled up the green—families and older couples mostly, with a few clusters of young people in faded blue jeans and long hair. The strangers, many of them carrying blankets against the chill of the day, sat obediently on the chairs set out for them. Perly stood at the base of the bandstand watching until a fair crowd was

119

assembled, then he climbed up onto the bandstand, opened the briefcase on the railing in front of him, and once again squinted out over the heads of the people as if searching the distance—for whales on the horizon, perhaps, or enemy ships, or help.

Then, as if he had found what he was looking for, he broke into a broad smile that swallowed up the disconcerting eyes and turned him into any big well-put-together deeply tanned American businessman. "This is one very special group," he said, his voice deep and restrained. "A mighty fine-looking group of people. Take a look around you, my friends. See that couple next to you? That handsome happy well-heeled couple? Well, if you buy land today, your son may marry their daughter. Makes you stop and think, doesn't it?"

Perly's voice began to rise and fall in singsong cadences, and people stared at him, compelled, as if, before their very eyes, the strange dark man were taking on a gloss and brightness that they dared not turn away from. "I can see it," he went on. "This crowd here has got the makings of a community you'll be proud to be a part of. I can see it." He paused and each person watching felt his own gaze reflected in the speaker's eyes. "You, *you* are the first," he said. "The very beginning. The pioneers. The bold ones. The grain of mustard seed from which the kingdom shall arise. And, within a year, I promise you, there will be a kingdom."

Perly threw back his head on his strong neck and laughed. The crowd spread out on the green stirred as if with bad conscience. "Perly Acres is going to be known from Maine to Florida as the most desirable, the most exquisitely preserved, the best-regulated, the safest, the most-coveted little piece of paradise on the east coast of these United States of America."

Perly took a breath and continued in a lower, more matter-of-fact voice. "Now I hope that each and every one of you was chalking up the mileage and measuring out the minutes it took you to get up here today. Why, we're so close to Boston, you can just meander on up here for a swim and an hour or two of that friendly country feeling if a Sunday afternoon is all the freedom you allow yourself in a week. If you want to, you can leave the wife and kids up here for a week or a month or all year long.

You're a free man. You'll know they're safe and healthy and well looked after in the country. And we're so close you can check in any time you feel the need.

"I promise you. One year from today you'll be toasting yourselves with champagne for being the first to get here. For being at the head of the line. For being the ones to cash in on the good old American way: first come, first served. In a year you'll be laughing when the fat cats offer you twice what you pay today. Everyone knows there's no investment like land. Any land. But this here is special land, Perly land. I promise you. The world will be your oyster. They're going to put Perly Acres on the map and embroider it in gold.

"Now a lot of you are already chomping at the bit to buy—the ones who've been around with my agents to see the parcels. But, let me warn you. Don't you buy unless you're head over heels in love. Because, if you don't fall in love this week, we promise you, you will next week, or the week after that. Because that's the first thing we're offering—though it's only the beginning—a piece of land so sweet, so seductive, it'll do things for you your first sweetheart wouldn't."

Again Perly stopped and centered himself on his toes, then began again in a deeper, more sober register. "If you want to see the site of the recreational facilities before you lay out cash, come back in a month. By that time, the present owners should be gone and the land freed up for us. But, believe me, my word is gold. And that is the prettiest piece of land of all. That's why we're saving it—so the entire community can partake of it together. It's better than bread and wine. It's right on a pond with a barn that's going to make a dandy recreation center, a steep pasture behind will make you swoon if you're a skier, and acres and acres of woods for snowmobiling and cross-country skiing. It's even got an enchanted forest—pines big enough to keep you hidden if you want to see the fairies dance. In a few weeks too, we'll have the roads bulldozed through all the parcels, and you'll be able to drive right up to every single lot.

"But just keep this one hard fact in mind. The whole world is already waking up. Millions of people are realizing that they lost something priceless when they left the countryside. And they're coming back in droves. Land around here has quadrupled in value in the last ten years. When people see what we're up to here, when they smell that air, feel those rolling fields swelling beneath them, they're going to quadruple the value again in as many weeks. If you wait, you may find yourself in a duel to the death with someone who's fallen as hard as you have for that little homestead of your dreams. If you buy now, you're just paying for the land. All the frills—the recreational facilities, the true old country community—they'll all come along to you as a free bonus, a bonus because you were the ones who had the vision to be pioneers.

"And let me tell you something about what made our forefathers great. Until you've pioneered on a piece of land of your own, you don't know what life is. You don't know the rush of sap in the veins that comes of having roots. You don't know the sense of power that comes from making your own mark. And when I say land, I don't mean a naked quarter acre in suburbia. I mean wild land—land without a human mark, land where you still hear the fox's mating call, land where you lose yourself without a compass, land that's dark at noon. That's land where anything can still happen—anything at all. Until you've taken up an ax and bent your back to marking the wilderness with your own name and labor, you don't know what it feels like to be a man. And you don't begin to understand what made America great. We have out here in the country a quality of life, something that money can't buy, something more important than a new automobile or a new TV or something you're trying to get for your house. Something we call freedom. We call it opportunity. And it's a spirit we've had from the beginning." Perly finished with his head thrown back and a high half smile on his face. He ran his hand through his dark hair and bowed his head a moment, collecting himself. The crowd barely stirred.

"And then there's financing," he said quietly. "Forget the bank. If you've tried to buy land, you know you can't get a penny from the bank, not for land, and only a pittance for a second home. There's one thing past for good, traded in for all our speed and luxury, and that's the right to a homestead just for the working of it. But here's what we're offering you right here today—the chance to buy land, and even a ready-made house if you want, for just thirty percent down."

Perly raised his right hand and brought his palm down on the railing of the bandstand with a thump that made the whole fragile edifice shudder. "And now for Parcel Number One," he cried. "Are you ready? Who is it going to be? Number One. Numero Uno, the very first, the Christopher Columbus of Perly Acres. The beginning of a whole new way of life."

He looked down into his briefcase. "Now this house—and I know some of you have already been up to look at it—is the quaint gabled authentic nineteenth-century house up on what we call Gable Ridge Road. The very road is named after the house that can be yours."

"It's Ward's all right," John said.

Perly looked up. "Now this comes complete with twenty-five acres, most of it in open fields and woods, alive all summer long with wild flowers and butterflies, so pretty it'll take your breath away. This is a house that'll do it. This is a house that'll set your head to spinning like it hasn't since your eighteenth birthday. If you want to spend all your time outdoors, this is for you. Unlike most of what we'll be offering, this house is completely furnished. The living room and kitchen done over just this year. The owner had a hunch he was going to sell and wanted to get the best possible price. So now, folks, who's it going to be?"

Bidding began. It moved slowly. Couples consulted with each other between bids, and several men had out pencils and paper. The contest narrowed, rather quickly, down to a swarthy young man in a checkered overcoat and muddy patent leather shoes, and a lean and nervous gray-haired couple.

The auctioneer paused to examine the two bidders, then he swung his eyes out over the crowd, looking for others. "The ones who buy the antique houses on the big old estates," he said, "will be the aristocrats of Perly Acres. The lords of the manor. The squires. The true gentlemen. Once these houses are a part of our development, they'll become a symbol—a symbol of the old-time values we're all working for."

Finally, the young man gave up and the couple got the place

for $53,500. The man whooped and hugged his wife, and the wind caught his soft felt hat and blew it across the green. Ezra Stone caught it and brought it back to him, along with a sheaf of documents.

Perly held an arm out to the man as he pulled a pair of plain rimmed glasses from his pocket to examine the papers. "Before you sign, maybe you want to bid on this too. I have a ten-acre parcel adjacent to what you just bought. It starts at the first stone wall below your pasture and runs down past the brook. Fine trout in that brook too. If you don't want it, there's others will. A level place up near the road is just made for a home site, or a person could run a road in and build with complete seclusion and a view of the brook.

"Now, for those who are worried about how to go about building a house, we have six different models you can contract with us to build for you. They run from ten to fifty thousand dollars. Or you can design and build yourself. Or you can cut down your own trees and do it the way our ancestors did."

The young man in the checkered overcoat started bidding again and the man who had just bought Ward's house looked distinctly uncomfortable. More people took part in the bidding now. The crowd had swelled to fifty or sixty people. The land sold finally for $5,800 to a young couple in blue jeans who looked very sober when their bid turned out to be the winning one. The new owner of Ward's house instantly left Ezra Stone and made his way around the chairs to speak to them, while his wife stayed where she was, eying her husband's conversation nervously.

"Five thousand dollars for ten acres," murmured Mim.

"Five thousand, eight hundred," corrected John.

The auctioneer sold one other ten-acre piece and then a number of smaller ones. Even the one-acre plots went for over a thousand dollars each. When he came to the other house, he said, "Now this has some features you won't find again in a hurry. It has the real old central chimney with four—I repeat, four—fireplaces. The one in the parlor has a priceless hand-carved mantel and hand-painted tiles. Somebody lavished a lot of love on that fireplace. Somebody knew that the hearth is the keystone that makes a strong family. And then there are some stone animal pens —a real curiosity. Wasn't every farmer, even in those good old days, who bothered to keep his pigs and sheep in stone pens. But, here's the best thing of all, for today's recreation-minded families. There's a watering hole for the cattle there—small to be sure—but plenty big enough to make a dandy swimming hole."

"Prescott's," John said. "First I heard he was gone. He always cursed that chimney. Said it took up half the house."

The auction went on. There were twenty-eight parcels sold from what were once two farms.

"Some of them must be swamp," John said when they got to the lower parts of Prescott's property.

"How will they know, this time of year?" Mim said.

Presently, Perly checked his papers and wound up the proceedings. "Well, now we're all in this together, folks," he said and looked slowly around at the intent crowd. Then, suddenly, he laughed, spreading out his arms to include the people before him. "You're in the most exclusive company," he cried. "I love you all and I congratulate you. Believe me, this town is going to be the biggest double-barreled front-page gilded rooster of a place you ever set foot in."

John and Mim moved slowly in the babbling crowd back toward their truck. The wind had picked up and grown colder, so damp now that patches of water darkened the blacktop on the road. A dozen or so people surrounded the auctioneer in a chattering group as he moved toward his house. Dixie trotted at his left heel, shouldering people's knees to keep her place, her tail waving just slightly in a suggestion of friendliness. Gore moved behind the group, squinting and nervous, his right hand poised near his hip pocket.

"They got a wicked surprise comin'," John said, watching from the truck.

"Maybe it's them and maybe it's us'll get a surprise," Mim said. "For my money, Prescott and Jimmy Ward did a smart thing. We ought to clear out too."

"Folks with cash to buy a farm or a hunk of land just to play games with, like it was a kid's red wagon . . . It must take quite a dent to make them hurt."

"They bought that land and now it's theirs," Mim said. "He's not goin' to stand for Prescott comin' back and makin' any claims."

"I just know that nobody but a Moore's goin' to do with that authentic antique farm on the pond with the steep pasture up behind. He may think it, but he's wrong."

"He got the Wards to go," Mim said, "for all they were such a big deal in town."

"Ward's a fool," John said. He started the truck, then sat over the steering wheel watching the Parade ground empty out. "He may think the Moores are nobody, but he's goin' to find out different."

Sunday morning was icy cold and still, a fragile day. The last oak leaves clinging to their twigs were like blown glass, jingling and shattering at a touch.

"Snow's late," Mim said.

John sat on the bench in front of the stove. He had shaved a maple kindling stick away to the size of a scallion, then chopped it into quarter-inch slices as if to add it to the soup. Finally he shoved aside the last shards of maple and his knife, and now he simply sat, his elbows on his knees and his face in his hands, staring through his fingers at his boots and the fender of the stove. Occasionally he rubbed his scalp until his thick gray-brown hair stood out from his head, reminding Mim that he needed a haircut.

In the front room, Ma sat alone on her couch. Now that the room was bare, it seemed wrapped in wallpaper. The paper had once been yellow behind some sort of bluish vine that had never existed, at least not in New Hampshire. Ma had chosen it because it was springlike, and John had approved because it was cheap. Now it was almost black behind the big parlor stove where fingers of smoke stroked it all winter. It was still a startling canary yellow in patches where the piano and sewing machine had stood, and where the pictures had hung, but everywhere else it had faded to a brownish cream. Mim had potted geraniums from the garden to fill the windowsills, and washed the windows, worrying that the putty was so far gone that even with the plastic they would rattle and perhaps crack in the winter wind. But today sunshine streamed in through the small rippled panes and marked out a warm gridwork on the unvarnished pine floor. Catching the tips of Ma's gray hair, the light made them shine like milkweed as she sat—perfectly still and years away as she gazed out on the quiet day.

But Hildie had few memories and could not be still. She raced from the front room to the kitchen, and back to the front room, shaking the house with footsteps and jarring the air with shouts. Mim shook out Ma's pillows, swept the floors, dusted the hot stoves, and fussed after Hildie. Finally she stopped in back of John, with Hildie still whirling around her.

"They'll take the tractor this week, sure," she said.

John neither moved nor answered, so Mim repeated her statement in a louder voice. This time John turned his head and looked up at her. She saw that he was trembling with anger.

She turned without a word and grabbed Hildie's sweater and her own jacket from the hooks by the back door. She caught up the child and whisked her outside. Hildie huddled and held on to her hand, complaining of the cold.

"This is just a taste of what we'll get before we're through," Mim said, but she took comfort in the child's closeness. They walked across the yard and stood behind the truck. The bed of the truck seemed pitifully small. Mim pulled open the sliding door to the barn and stepped into its dank interior. She could hear rats scuttling. She kicked at the heap of old boards under the stairway. A lot of them were rotting. The problem of building a house on the truck seemed too immense for her. Hildie shivered and pulled at her hand to go outside again.

In the yard the sun was almost warm and she walked with the child down to the road and across it to the flower garden without glancing again at the truck. The last chrysanthemums lay trampled on the ground by the cold, but still pink and rust and yellow. The leaves on the rose bushes, a dusty green, were curled and dry on their thorny stalks. Mim stood idly in the middle of the garden. Hildie let go of her hand and marched up one row and down the next until she had worked over the entire garden. Then she climbed on top of the overturned wheelbarrow and jumped up and down. The dark pond beyond the scrubby growth of laurel and huckleberries reflected the puffs of clouds suspended over it. Mim thought she could detect a crinkled rim of ice around the edges. The year was turning. One storm would do it now.

"Off with you," Mim said. "I'll ride you to the barn."

Hildie jumped down and Mim righted the wheelbarrow. They bumped over the field, stalling on stones, backing up and trying again.

Hildie laughed. "Giddap, Sunshine," she cried, holding tight to the sides of the bucking wheelbarrow.

In the dark barn, they loaded the wheelbarrow up with hay to bank the roses. Mim was surprised to find that they had everything they needed to do this chore. Mudgett had overlooked the wheelbarrow because, in her carelessness, she had left it overturned in the flower garden. "Nothin's changed at all for the roses," she said to Hildie. "Come spring, they'll green up like nothin' was changed at all."

When they heard the truck coming, they were still in the garden. Mim hesitated, then took Hildie's hand and turned to watch the opening in the trees. It was Cogswell, alone.

John came out the back door. Mim approached slowly as the two men greeted each other, Hildie pulling at her to hurry.

Cogswell glanced at John, and then smiled faintly at Hildie. He fished in the pocket of his faded blue sweatshirt and got out his cigarettes. He cupped the match against the weather, his hands shaking so he could hardly bring the match to meet the cigarette. Then he drew on the cigarette and flipped the match to the ground. He was a tall narrow man, with long hands covered with reddish hairs like electric wires.

"Still got the same old truck," John said.

"I'll drive to my grave in it," Cogswell said.

John raised his brows and waited for whatever news was coming.

"Good of you to call on Agnes," Cogswell said to Mim.

Mim held tight to Hildie who was squirming to be free. "She's not right," she said.

Cogswell shook his head, then looked down at them with a crooked smile. "Who is?" he asked.

John stood before him, his hands sunk deep into the pockets of his overalls, his shoulders drawn up against the cold.

"Your ma all right?" Cogswell asked him.

"She's not her old self," John said. "But she'll weather winter all right, if she don't starve."

Cogswell shook the ash off his cigarette onto the ground and spread it carefully over the earth with the toe of his shoe.

"Hear you done over your house," John said. He took his hands out of his pockets and folded his arms, the muscles between his jaw and his ear working.

"At too much cost," Mickey said.

"If there weren't nobody jumpin' to be deputies, Dunsmore wouldn't a got so far."

"Ain't nobody jumpin' now," Cogswell said. "Not anyway since last night."

"You mean the auction?" Mim said.

"That and Sonny Pike gettin' shot."

"Pike?" John said and lifted a corner of his thin mouth.

Mickey shook his head. "He's all of a piece, I expect. But he's got a good hole in his shoulder."

"Shakes you up a bit, don't it, Mick?" John said.

Cogswell put his free hand in his pocket and leaned back against the cab of his truck.

"It's not so much you, Mickey," Mim said. "It's just the auction and what he said."

Cogswell turned to her and spoke quickly. "He sent you this," he said, pulling a roll of bills from his pocket. "To get you off the

129

land. Three hundred ain't enough, I know. But it's enough for you to set up in your truck and go."

John looked past Cogswell to the pond. Then he spit on the ground. "Never mind, Mickey," he said, but he wasn't angry any more. "You got your own brood to fret over."

"John," Mim said and John turned on her too quickly. "If we could go . . ." she said, ignoring the rising anger in his green eyes.

"It's time, John," Cogswell said. "He's got his eye peeled right on you."

"It don't seem like you're about to scamper," John said.

"It's gettin' to that point," Cogswell said. "He's bankin' on it. After you, then us."

"Keep your money," John said. "I ain't movin'." He turned and started back toward the house.

Cogswell took a step after him. "John, you're a fool," he said. "You always was that proud you'd cut your nose off before you'd give an inch."

John stopped and turned. "You're okay, Mickey," he said. "I don't forget a turn like this." His face colored up as his eyes locked with his neighbor's. "It's just that I aim to stay."

Cogswell held out the money. "You got it comin' from one cow alone," he said.

John looked at it. Mim held her breath. "Guess my land's still firm enough to carry us," he said and walked slowly into the house. Mim noticed that his body was bent with age and work and care. He walked as if he were very heavy.

She turned back to Cogswell, eying the roll of bills in his hand, her desire tangible.

He turned to her. "You're a good woman, Mim," he said. "You keep tight to your sense of things. Make him see sense too." He thrust the bills into her hand and clouded her with the thick smell of soured whiskey.

Feeling them against her palm, warm still from his, she felt the relief flood over her and longed to fall into his arms. She let her eyes fall into his. Weak with gratitude and the sweetness of the man, she said, "I'm real sorry about her, Mickey."

130

He watched her tears come up for him and turned abruptly away. He walked around the truck, got in, and started it with a burst.

Then he got out and came slowly back. "Mim," he said, his head nodding loosely, "if you can't get him to see sense no other way, take him to the auction Tuesday at three." Mickey ran a hand over his face. "Oh Christ," he said, as if he had forgotten where he was. Then he straightened up and focused fiercely in on Mim. "But mind you don't let on how you heard about it."

He got back into the truck and headed up the road over Constance Hill. Mim watched the back of his head through the rear window of his cab. He tipped it back and drank from his flask as the truck swayed precariously up the bad road and out of sight.

Hildie reached for the money in her mother's hand, jumping up and down to see it. Mim held it high and, standing where she was, counted it twice. Fifteen twenty-dollar bills. Then she turned to the house to face John.

He was standing in the doorway waiting for her. "Give it to me," he said, his face white and deeply lined.

She gave it to him, feeling the fear that was almost desire touch her fingertips as they brushed his palm. He turned and, in a motion so quick she hardly felt what he was doing, crossed the room, lifted the lid on the range, and dropped in the roll of bills.

Instinctively, Mim dove for the stove. He caught her. One hand tangled in her hair; the other tightened on her arm. She screamed and he shook her.

She felt the world turning around her, the familiar piles of dishes on the shelf over the sink, the board bench and table, Hildie's frightened face by the door. She screamed and struggled toward the stove. Vaguely, she knew that Ma had hobbled to the doorway and stood leaning on her canes, with Hildie pressing her face to her dressing gown.

"The money, Ma," she sobbed. "Get the money."

Finally John flung her loose of him, and even as she fell she yearned toward the stove. Her head hit the fender with a bump she heard more than felt. John slammed the back door so that the kitchen shook. Mim struggled to her feet and opened the stove. A tuft of smoke rose in her face. Inside she saw a jumble of red coals and one bright lick of flame.

Mim crumpled on the edge of the bench, buried her head in her arms against the table, and sobbed. She did not hear the hard thumps of Ma's canes approaching, but she felt the crooked hand catch in her hair.

"Now, now, Miriam," she said. "Don't carry on so. You'll give the child a fright."

Mim looked up. Hildie was leaning over the bench on the other side of the table, whimpering. She held out her arms, and the child came into her lap and cried with her.

"It don't mean he don't love you, Miriam," Ma said, stroking Mim's head.

"Ma," Mim said. "He's off the deep end, just like Agnes. He just burned up three hundred dollars."

Ma's hand left Mim's shoulder and clutched the side of the table. "Three hundred dollars," she said.

"You see him, Ma," Mim said. "He just sets and does nothin'. Nothin' but snap and growl. He's not himself at all. It's the auction yesterday's the last straw."

"Well," said Ma, "well." And painfully she took herself back to her chair and settled into it. "It don't run in our family, bein' crazy. But then it don't run in our family, givin' everythin' in sight away, neither." She shook her head. Mim and Hildie were swallowing their sobs, watching Ma. It seemed as if, from the wisdom of her age, she were about to pronounce an answer that would shake the house on its foundations, shake it into order. But all she said was, "With a little luck, it's the one and not the other. With a little luck, he's just a gettin' stirred up."

"He was ever stirred up over somethin'," Mim said.

"A bit of temper shows a man's got feelin'," Ma said. "And self-respect. It's high time now he got hisself stirred up and movin'."

"You mean you see we have to go?" Mim asked in a small voice.

"No!" Ma cried. "That ain't what I mean at all. I mean it's time and then some he moved hisself to put a stop to all this."

Mim started to sob again. "It's you is crazy, Ma," she said.

"No one's stoppin' you, girl. I see you jumpin' up and down you're so antsy. Well go, if go you must."

"Oh, Ma," Mim said, and turned her face to the stove, rocking over Hildie.

"Just leave me the shotgun," Ma said, watching Mim, her eyes stormy underneath the spray of pale hair. "This land's been Moore land since before the likes of us was born and it'll go on bein' Moore land after the likes of us is gone. John's grandfather and his great-grandfather and his great-great-grandfather, they didn't fight for this here land just to have—"

Mim lifted her head and shouted through her sobs at Ma. "Big talk, Ma. The shotgun's gone."

John did not come back until Hildie was in bed. When he appeared at the door, Mim left the room. His supper was on the table, though everything else was cleared, as if life had made its sweep and left him out. Ma watched him without speaking. He ate the cold pea soup and the baked potato, troubled by her silent attention. When he finished, he took his dishes to the sink, scooped up a dipper of water from the pail under the sink, and rinsed them. "Well?" he asked.

"She's fearin' for your mind," Ma said. "With good reason, I say."

John moved to the back door and looked at his reflection in the dark glass.

"That was a bad mistake about the money," Ma said. "You got to feed a child somethin' more than pea soup and potatoes."

John leaned his forehead against the door and looked up through the dark toward the pasture. In the stove, the fire settled and a green stick gave a long high whistle of complaint as it hit the coals and burned.

"I'll give you a hand to your couch, Ma," he said.

"Take the lamp yourself," Ma said. "I'll manage. You go make your peace with her."

133

In the bedroom, John felt Mim's presence on the mattress, although she was so still he could not hear the rise and fall of her breath. But the sheets, when he moved between them, were warm with the heat of her body in the chill room. He lay beside her for a moment, hoping she would speak.

Then he said, the words piling high on each other with the difficulty of saying them, with the horror of having done it, "It was a bad mistake, burnin' Mickey's money."

And his wife turned to him sobbing very suddenly, as though she had been crying all along and he had not been able to hear it.

·9·

ON TUESDAY at two-thirty, the Parade was deserted except for Cogswell and James, sitting on the edge of the bandstand smoking, with their feet dangling over the edge. Cogswell did not seem to notice John and Mim sitting in their truck, though James eyed them soberly. James had a thermos of something steaming. They passed the plastic cup back and forth and stared out over the empty green toward the post office. Cogswell drank from his flask and offered it to James who shook his head.

A red Mustang and an Oldsmobile were parked in front of the Moores' truck, near the small church at the edge of the green. In each, a couple the Moores had never seen before sat waiting. After a few minutes, a station wagon with yet another couple pulled in behind them.

"Remember how we planned?" John said. "A flock of children, another barn for all the stock, more pasture clear, maybe a serious orchard. Pa would never listen."

"There's no need to do such things," Mim said. "We're all right the way we are."

"You know your weddin' dress?" John asked. "With the yellow flowers you embroidered on? You embroidered since?"

Mim shook her head. "Guess I'd rather be outdoors."

"I'd like to live that long to see Hildie married in that dress,"

135

John said. "Seemed so simple before the auctions started."

"Not likely she'd want to wear my dress," Mim said. "Anyhow, it was in the trunk—the one that was my mother's. They took it with the others."

"You just let it go?"

"It was me said let them take the attic stuff. And then to make a fuss . . ."

Three cars and station wagons at once pulled in around the Parade. In each, a man and a woman sat moving their lips in conversations silenced by rolled-up windows. They stared curiously at the post office and the houses ringing the Parade, and passed their muted judgment on to one another.

"Who are they, John?" Mim asked, somehow fighting tears. She had a need that was physical to touch her child and feel her land beneath her feet—as if she'd traveled a thousand miles and couldn't get back. "What can be worse than Saturday?"

As it approached three, pickup trucks and dusty old American sedans began to join the newer cars of the strangers, bringing the Harlowe men who had been at the Saturday auctions—deputies most of them, without a doubt. James and Cogswell sat on the bandstand silently now, watching. A foreign station wagon pulled up. The door opened and let out a man in horn-rimmed glasses and a tweed topcoat. He walked around the car and opened the other door for his wife. As he did so, he perceived the dozens of eyes on him and looked up startled. His wife stepped out, a small woman in a beige cloth coat and a tidy felt hat. He said something to her and she glanced quickly at the other cars, then motioned to the church. The man put his hand on the small of her back and hurried her toward the church, hunching his shoulders against the gaze of the people in the cars. He pulled at the door, then leaned back against the knob and pulled harder. It was locked. For a long moment he and his wife stood staring at the blank door before them. Then slowly the man turned again toward the unlikely collection of people watching him.

But even as he hesitated, the door opened inward and Pulver

136

and Stone stepped out and ushered the couple into the church.

Then, as if at a signal, the deputies and the strange couples got out of their cars and trucks with a great slamming of doors and moved toward the open door of the church—the deputies abruptly, looking straight ahead, and the couples tentative and clinging to each other.

Rather suddenly, Perly's big yellow van backed out of his driveway, turned, bumped a hundred yards along the road, and backed into the church driveway, up to the side door of the church. Gore got out of the driver's seat and climbed into the back of the van.

"It gives me a creepy feelin'," Mim said, "havin' to go inside walls with the likes of them."

"With all that pile of outsiders," John said, "what can happen?"

So John and Mim climbed slowly down out of their truck and followed the couples up the walk toward the church. A woman in front of them was so fat she moved by rocking from side to side like a mechanical toy. She dropped a cigarette, still lit, and John stepped, out of habit, to grind it out, though it wouldn't have set fire to anything there. The woman tapped another out of her purse, and her husband, who was only somewhat less fat, stopped and turned to cup a match against the wind. John and Mim passed them as they struggled to light the cigarette.

"We shouldn't have come, Billy. I don't think so."

"What're you goin' to do?" the man said. "The agencies said no, didn't they?"

"It's not goin' to be to his taste, findin' us here," Mim whispered.

"I can't tell no more what's meant to be," John said. "Could be he planned on us comin'."

Inside the wide church doors, Pulver and Stone sat at the table like ticket takers at a church supper, asking the names of the people as they filed in, checking each couple off on a list, then letting them by. John and Mim simply walked by them. Tom Pulver's eyes followed their progress across the foyer to the swinging doors that led to the sanctuary, but he said nothing.

There were no greeters and there was no organ, only the nervous shifting of the silent people on the horsehair cushions in the pews. The couples were scattered around the church, and evenly dispersed among them were the deputies. John and Mim took a pew near the back, and Ian James moved in immediately behind them with a stealth that set Mim's scalp to prickling.

They sat for what seemed hours. Afraid to turn and look, they listened to the strangers rustling behind them, and focused with sharp-edged intensity on the slow motions of those in front of them.

At last the side door at the front of the church opened, and Perly began walking slowly toward the high central pulpit. His crisp black hair was combed back so tightly it barely curled, and the silver cuff links at his wrists glittered as he gestured to the crowd. Except for the gentle golden dog at his heels, he looked like the chairman of some important board of directors, or possibly a middle-of-the-road evangelist. He stepped into the high pulpit and Dixie disappeared behind its balustrade.

Perly scanned the assembled people, reducing them to perfect stillness. Mim thought his gaze caught on hers momentarily and had to pull away as if snagged. Without moving, she let the heat of embarrassment and anger wash over her and fade.

When Perly finally spoke, it was in the deepest range of his voice, a soft rumble like thunder that spread through the sanctuary and bound people together as if against a distant storm. "We will start with a moment of silent prayer," he said, "asking God's guidance and seeking God's love that we may spread it to these innocent children. Let us pray."

Mim's hand tightened on John's knee. Around them the strangers bowed their heads. Perly raised his eyes toward the rose window at the back of the church and the red and yellow bands of light stained his face. The deputies did not pray, but looked around them like errant boys. The woodwork in the old church snapped and clicked as if to mark off the passing seconds.

"Amen," Perly said, releasing the people before him to stir and gaze back at him.

Perly shifted his weight and leaned forward on his elbows to look down on the people. "I'm Perly Dunsmore," he said. "I've talked to a good many of you on the telephone. For the others, let me explain. I am, by profession, an auctioneer and environment designer. In addition, I think it would be fair to say that I make a hobby of philanthropy. Altogether, I guess I'm one of Harlowe's more noticeable businessmen, and as such, the town has approached me to serve as trustee and guardian for these children.

"Now I've been pondering the problem of these children. Clearly, as an old bachelor, I can't look after them myself. Now the traditional way to handle a problem in a small New England town it to get all the interested parties together and start thrashing out a solution.

"The exact problem in this instance is that we must provide the best possible homes for these children. Luckily for them, the world today seems to be full of wonderful folks like you who are willing and eager to open their hearts to homeless orphans. So now that we've brought you all together, our task boils down to the problem of choosing which of you will take the children."

There was a long silence. A bare branch rasped back and forth against a windowpane in the wind.

"We have two children this week," Perly went on.

The group in the church rustled as if a gust of wind had caught briefly in their vocal cords.

"As I've told most of you, they come with complete adoption papers. After a year, you can go to the court in Concord and finalize the adoption. The children are in perfect health. If you're worried on that score, rest assured. They are happy healthy rosy white pure-bred all-American children. Their only problem is that they need someone to love. If, within a month, you find anything medically wrong with them, you can bring them back to me and I will, of course, return every penny of the fees.

"Naturally, our social worker will have to come and look into your home a bit before the adoption is finalized. I'm sure that this will present no problem. Under normal circumstances, we'd want to have the home study completed before entrusting the child to you at all. But if we put the children into foster homes now, we'll only have to move them again into their permanent homes. And that kind of double readjustment for the child seems more cruel than kind. So, since the children are available now, and since most of you are potentially very loving parents or you wouldn't have come, we're prepared to let you take the children home just as soon as all the fees are paid."

Cogswell, sitting diagonally in front of the Moores, watching the fat couple who sat in front of him, leaned his elbows on his knees and covered his face with his hands.

"We have a three-year-old boy today and a newborn baby girl, just ten days old. Born a week ago Thursday."

The people stirred. For the first time, wives turned to their husbands and whispered.

"We're going to offer the baby girl first. Now I don't want to commit any indiscretions here, but I know you want to know what kind of genes she has and why she's up for adoption. It's the usual story. Her mother's a lovely little woman only fifteen years old. Her blood was a little too strong, you might say."

There was a pained silence in the church.

"Nobody's supposed to know who the father is, but there's some pretty good speculation it's a doctor's son," Perly went on. "A kid who stuck around just long enough to give the valedictory address at his boarding school graduation, then got hustled off to Europe to see the world. This whole affair could have turned out to be a tragedy for the young parents as well as for the child herself. When you adopt her, you're giving the parents, as well as the child herself, a running chance at life. Believe you me, this child has the very best of genes. I know. And, as for her parents, I'm sure they've learned their lesson.

"Now I know you want to see her, but she's awfully little, so if you could just quietly look and be fairly quick . . ."

Mudgett came through the side door, carrying a car bed. Perly leaned over and picked up the pink bundle as expertly as any practiced father.

The wooden pews creaked as people strained to see, and a few couples pushed their heads close together to whisper.

Perly moved up the center aisle, holding the baby out on one side, then on the other, like an usher with a collection plate. Each couple leaned in toward him and examined the baby. When he came to the Moores, he carefully showed them too. The child was wide awake, staring solemnly up at them from the folds of a pink sleeper, a pacifier stuck in her mouth. She had the deep blue eyes and wrinkled face of any newborn baby and could have belonged to almost anyone.

Perly stood over them until Mim glanced up at him. His eyes were as glittering and impersonal as diamonds.

He returned the child to the car bed and she began to whimper. He leaned over her and she quieted down. Mudgett took the car bed away.

Perly returned to the high pulpit. "God's ways seem dark," he said softly, "to deprive this perfect child of home and natural kin." Perly looked out over the people, his eyes gone flat and accusing, as if it were they who had abandoned the child. Finally he leaned back on his heels and smiled. "I'd keep this little beauty for myself, if I could find me a wife," he said. He shuffled a sheaf of papers before him on the pulpit.

Perly went on, reciting almost in a monotone. "Adoption is a very expensive procedure. In this particular case, we had to pay a good sum to the child's grandparents to keep for the child's mother. As it all works out, we can't let this baby go for under ten thousand dollars."

There was a gasp from the crowd.

"Now keep in mind," Perly went on, his voice rising, "this is a white child with the very best racial antecedents. Her mother is part German and part Swedish and her father is English. She promises to be your perfect blond blue-eyed child. If you've tried to adopt a white infant elsewhere, you know you have to wait four years or so, and even then, if you have other children, it's virtually impossible. Independent adoptions like this one are entirely legal, but they're hard to find—very hard to find—especially if you want your perfect white brand-new baby."

Perly stopped. He stared at the back of the sanctuary and ran his eyes over every person there, as if he were privately making his choice among them then and there.

When he finally broke the uncomfortable silence, it was in a hard staccato voice. "This baby is available now. Today," he said. "So unless you want your grandchildren to have slanty eyes or nappy hair, here's your chance. The fact is that you get what you pay for in this world."

A couple two pews in front of the Moores exchanged a look. The woman nodded. She was slim and good-looking, but not young.

The man, who had crew-cut salt-and-pepper hair, raised his shoulders slightly and turned back to Dunsmore.

"Now the most economical way to settle the thorny problem of who takes the child is to offer her by the time-honored New England methods of the auction." Perly banged his fist on the pulpit like a preacher making his point. "So," he said, "do I hear ten thousand?"

The crowd shifted and made no bids.

"Now I know you feel shy and uncomfortable," Perly soothed. "It's an uncomfortable business. But I know you want to be parents or you wouldn't be here. I wish there were some easier way, both for these children and for you. But remember, even the usual way costs money, with hospitals the way they are. This is a mighty painless way to go home with a brand-new baby. No red tape. No labor pains. No racial problems forever after. So let's hear some bids. Ten thousand. Do I hear ten thousand for a start?"

This time the woman in front of them looked over at her husband and he raised his hand.

"Ten thousand?" Perly asked, almost as if he were surprised himself.

The man nodded.

"Good. Now do I hear twelve?"

"Eleven," said a woman in the front row. She was tall and dark with the high cheekbones of a gypsy, and an expensive dark brown coat and matching turban.

"Twelve thousand," said the man in front of them.

Then a voice on one side said, "Twelve five." There was a long pause in the bidding. People stared at the man who had offered $12,500. He was standing on the pew in order to be high enough to see. His legs were as tiny as a five-year-old's, though his head was perhaps even bigger than normal and puffed out further by a generous crop of black curls.

"Come on," Perly coaxed. "Let's hear how badly you want to be parents."

The man in front of the Moores upped the bid to thirteen thousand dollars.

The child finally sold for fifteen thousand dollars to the gypsy woman in the front row, who sat with her head bowed when it was clear that she had won. Her husband, a pale man with cream-colored hair and a white shirt, continued to puff on his pipe as if nothing had happened at all.

Perly leaned down over the edge of the pulpit. "Congratulations," he said, beaming. "I'm so happy for you." The woman looked up idly but did not smile and the man continued to contemplate the auctioneer as though he were an insect under a microscope.

Perly grinned at the crowd as if to apologize for the couple. "It's enough to stun an elephant," he said. "To find yourselves parents as suddenly as all that.

"But I know you're eager to know about the next child," Perly went on. "This is a little boy named Michael. He has a smattering of freckles and a wonderful laugh, though these are pretty hard times for him. His mother was in a tragic accident and lost the use of her legs. She's going to be in the hospital probably for the better part of a year and she'll always be in a wheelchair. Since she has four older children, she feels that the best thing for Michael is to find him a home with loving parents who are capable of giving him the care and attention he really needs. She's especially worried about Michael because of his really extraordinary intelligence. He's only three and already he knows the alphabet and can count to twenty forwards and then count back to one again. He really needs a good nursery school, or maybe first grade. With a little help, he could be reading in a month. Because they knew that they couldn't give their child what they wanted for him, his parents have signed him over completely, and the adoption can be final in a year. If you doubt whether he's had the very best of loving, just think what it means to sign away your child in his own best interests. What's more, this is not an illegitimate child. This is a child begotten in a marriage bed and brought up, to date, in a proper loving family.

"Now I'll bring him out for you to look at. But, mind you, if he looks a bit down at the mouth, remember this is pretty tough for little Michael. You take him home and cuddle him a bit, feed him a hamburger and a Coke, and put a baseball bat in his hands.

He'll be laughing in no time—and hitting homers for the Little League besides."

Perly himself went out the side door. He was gone so long the door seemed to go in and out of focus under the intensity of Mim's stare. Finally it opened and Perly appeared carrying a small fair-haired boy sucking on a lollipop. When the child saw all the people in the church, he put his arms around the auctioneer's neck and hid his face against his neck.

"You see how eager he is to love someone." Perly smiled. "Come on, Michael. Look at the nice people. See how they're smiling? And all for you."

Perly waited, and presently Michael peeked out. He was clearly a Carroll, the down-sloping brown eyes unmistakable.

"Emily had an older brother Michael," John murmured. "Killed in the war."

Michael rested his head against Perly's chest, but allowed himself to be carried slowly down the aisle so that people could get a good look at him.

The bidding this time started at five thousand dollars. Couples conferred with each other frequently, and there was a murmur underlying the whole procedure. Except for the dwarf, the group that bid this time was a different one. It narrowed down, eventually, to the dwarf and a middle-aged couple in back of the Moores. They bid angrily and quickly toward the end and finally the middle-aged couple quit. The dwarf and his rather faded but perfectly normal blond wife had won for $9,800. The little man stood up on the pew and made a victory sign to the people while his wife burst noisily into tears.

The auctioneer laughed and said, "All power to you." The deputies stirred, but the people stayed put.

"Now don't be discouraged if you aren't one of the lucky sets of parents," Perly said. "We'll be having another adoption session sometime in the next few weeks. We'll mail you a notice. I know of at least two other children who are coming available—one not yet born and an exquisite four-year-old girl—cornsilk hair and royal blue eyes—prettiest thing you ever saw." He paused as if he were waiting for people to go, but nobody moved.

"And now," he said, "I think it would be appropriate if we all bowed our heads in prayer again for the newly formed families in our midst."

Again people bowed their heads. Finally Perly said, "Amen. Now if the happy new parents would like to be my guests over at my house, I'll have the children brought in so you can meet them in the comfort of my parlor. And we can take care of the formalities as well."

Perly stepped down from the pulpit. Dixie stood up and stretched, then trotted to his side as he held out his hands toward the couple who had bought the little girl. They stood and waited obediently to follow him, nodding distantly to his questions. The dwarf, in his turn, stood wringing Perly's hand on and on, his other arm stretched up to circle his wife's waist as she stood laughing now and red-faced.

People stood up and side-stepped out through the pews slowly and absent-mindedly, completely absorbed in staring at the cluster of people around the auctioneer, straining toward the side door for yet another glimpse of Michael and the baby girl.

Mim and John said little as they drove home. The buff gravel road blurred in the last afternoon light and the trees closed darkly overhead. Mim gripped the edge of her seat and planned in detail how they would fix up the back of the truck for the family to sleep in. They would sleep with Hildie clasped between them. John pictured the pasture the way it had been that morning, pale gray with frost, the rank witch grass near the stream crunchy underfoot, Hildie in the big orange hand-me-down sweater and a green stocking cap running and sliding, running and sliding down the hill.

Mim jumped out before the truck was quite stopped. "Where's Hildie?" she cried to Ma as she burst into the kitchen.

Ma sat perfectly still in the old wooden chair, without a blanket or a shawl, her gnarled hands gripping each other. "I don't know," she said.

"You don't know?" Mim said.

"A car fetched up in the dooryard about twenty of four . . ."

John came in the back door.

"My God, my God," Mim cried. "She's gone. They took her."

"Not them folks in the car," Ma said, pulling herself up out of her chair. "Strangers, a man and two women. They never so much as opened a door. Just craned their necks and backed round and that was it."

"Where is she then?" Mim whispered.

"We was playin' cards when right in the middle she perks up her head, her eyes like saucers, and she says, "A car, Grandma." Then she picked herself right up and run out to hide just like you told her. The car went off, and I called at the door, but no Hildie. You know when you told the child to hide, you never said a word about comin' back."

"You kept a sharp eye on the car?" John said.

"It ain't the car," Ma said. "But there's no end of dangers could strike her right here."

Mim ran to the barn. In the horse stall, the hay and the old army blanket were flung about haphazardly, but Hildie's orange sweater was gone. "Hildie!" she called. Then louder and louder. Her voice hit the full hayloft overhead and fell dead. The stanchions were already looped with spider webs as if they'd been abandoned for years.

Mim ran up the stairs to the loft, but Hildie was not in her swing. "Hildie," she called. She heard the creak of steps and stumbled downstairs crooning, "Hildie, Hildie," but it was only John. "Hildie," she screamed.

"Stop," John said, catching at her shoulders as she ran for the door. "Think. Where would she think to go?"

"They took her," Mim cried, fighting his arms. "You heard him say they plan to."

John let go and Mim burst free and ran around the barn toward the sand pile.

John went into the house and called to Lassie. The old dog stood up and wagged her tail. "Go fetch Hildie," John said, motioning to the door. "Where's our Hildie, old girl?" Lassie wagged her tail sadly and flopped back down on her rug. John closed the door and leaned against it scanning the yard.

"Hildie?" he called and his voice fell flat on the encroaching night. He picked up the iron bar on its cord and struck the big rusted gong over and over again.

Mim ran up and stood breathless with him.

It was almost dark. The gong stopped sounding and there was nothing but the wind.

"You try the pond. I'll try up yonder in the pasture," John said.

Obediently Mim walked down the path toward the pond, her eyes yearning into the underbrush for the bright orange glow that would be her child. Instead, down near the gravel at the pond's edge, she found Hildie's wagon, half filled with gravel and topped by a split plastic pail and an old spoon with the silver worn off. "Hildie?" she called, but her voice wasn't loud any more. She tried to remember whether she had seen the wagon around lately. The pond was a mottled shiny gray like granite polished for a gravestone. She could not see beyond its surface. "Hildie?" she said softly. The water made quiet rhythmic rushes at the shore. And that was all. She covered her mouth with both hands and stood listening. Moment by moment, the pond before her darkened toward night.

And then she heard the quick light laughter behind her and whirled to see Hildie running down the path toward her, her orange sweater spiked with broken bits of hay.

She clasped her in her arms, her head shaking with dry sobs against the child's soft body.

Hildie pulled away confused. "I hid, Mama," she said, "the way you said. Just the way you said. I hid even better than the way you said. I heard a car and hid. I stayed hid ever and ever so long. And then I heard our truck. I heard you callin' and the gong."

"Why didn't you come?" Mim wept.

"I wanted you to see how good I was hid. You said to hide most careful of all if it was friends." The child smiled and would have laughed if it hadn't been for her sense that she had made a mistake. "I hid so good you couldn't find me."

"John?" Mim called, but her voice was small.

"I got so tired, Mama," Hildie said and clasped Mim tightly. Then, sensing that she was safe from punishment, she pulled back and said, "Want to know where I hid?"

Mim nodded. She could hardly see Hildie's face in the dark.

"Under the hay in the loft." She giggled. "In the horse stall there's hardly any hay. I'm too big for such a little hay."

But Mim was pulling her by the hand up toward the house. "Oh but you did give us a wicked turn," she said.

Mim pushed Hildie in the door of the kitchen so that Ma gasped with relief. Then she chased up the pasture running breathlessly in the near darkness, calling to John.

·10·

On Wednesday, John did not touch his breakfast, not even his cup
of chicory. He sat on the bench still wearing his pajama tops underneath his shirt and brooded into the black wall of the kitchen
range.

"When are we goin'?" Mim asked. Then louder, "When are we
goin'?"

But John said nothing, weighting the kitchen with his silence.

Finally Mim slammed her palm down on the table next to him.
"*Will* you tell me what to do?" she cried.

John lifted angry eyes to her. "Go to hell," he said.

Ma stalked out of the room and slammed the door, closing herself into the front room.

"Like it was my fault!" shouted Mim.

Then her eyes lit on Hildie who was rocking from side to side in
her corner sucking her thumb. "Hildie," she said gently. "Poor
Hildie. Come on." And she coaxed the child into her jacket.

Hand in hand she and Hildie went out to the barn and looked
around. Mim kicked at the boards under the stairs, then pulled out
a couple at random and measured them against the truck. People
turned pickup trucks into campers all the time.

She looked up and saw Ma watching her through the front
window, her lips moving as if she were reporting Mim's every

move to John. She went into the barn, still trailed by Hildie, and searched for something she could use for a saw. When she came out, Ma was still watching. Mim walked around to the far side of the truck, where Ma couldn't see her. She leaned against the door and gazed out over the still pond. Hildie jumped into her arms, and gradually she realized that the two of them could manage very well in the cab. They could share the seat. It simplified things, the realization that only she and Hildie would go. At least it simplified the building problem. She hauled the boards back to the barn and moved slowly up the path toward the kitchen door.

But, by Thursday, Mim had not brought herself to make any further move. The day was cold. Mim and John ate their oatmeal, then sat at the table drinking birch tea, almost as if the day were a normal one.

"Is it Thursday?" Hildie asked. "What will they take?"

"The tractor," Mim answered. "That's what."

Perly led the way up the path, his big body sailing in on the Moores with that silent ease that characterized all his motions. He mused without blinking on the little family clustered behind the glass in the storm door watching his approach. He stopped on the granite stoop to wipe his work boots, then opened the storm door toward himself and half bowed to the Moores.

Ma stood a little behind John and Mim, but it was to her that he held out his hands. "How are you, Mrs. Moore?" he asked.

Behind him, even more florid than usual, Gore stood on the stoop, his right hand sticking close to his gun.

Ma lifted her head so that her small features stood out sharply. She looked Perly in the eye and said, "I am bad, since you ask. And it's all your doin'. You a standin' here with your manners. And him standin' there with his gun. I was a few years younger, we'd a met you forehead to forehead from the start, 'stead of walkin' round you all the while like this." Ma had been struggling closer and closer to Perly until she stood directly in front of him.

Perly looked down on her, his face drawn together with concern.

He reached out slowly, and with his index finger, brushed Ma's hair off her forehead.

Ma caught her breath and backed off, almost tripping over John. Then she turned and moved away across the kitchen, her canes banging angrily.

"Sorry to see her slipping," Perly said to John.

John stood for a long space confronting Perly, then he turned with sudden force and threw the keys to the tractor at Gore. They hit him in the torso and he jumped back, reaching awkwardly for his gun. The keys bounced away and landed in the grass beside the stoop. Gore stood, gone pale, staring at John, his hand finally resting securely on the butt of his gun, the holster unsnapped.

"Some fall guy," John said to Gore, but Gore still stood, his knuckles white where they grasped the gun.

"Keys to the tractor?" Perly said and cocked an eyebrow. "Must be. Hope it's running good." He hadn't moved from the tight group in the doorway, not even to dodge when the keys flew by his nose. "Now don't be anxious," he said. "I just have to give my little friend here some loving." Without effort, he leaned past Gore and past John until his face was close to Hildie where she sat in Mim's arms.

Diverting her eyes, Mim tried to turn Hildie's head into her shoulder, but the child turned to the auctioneer with a dazzling smile.

"Well, Hildie," Perly asked. "How'd you like to be rich? Fancy clothes and toys. Trips downtown to see Santa at Christmas? Almost like being a princess. Bet you might even get a dog like Dixie."

Hildie beamed.

"Did you know I'm a magician?" he asked with a smile. "I'll see what I can do." He was well into the room by now, and he turned back toward the door to address John. "Such a pretty place," he said. "How many acres did you say you have? That pasture—about thirty-five right there—and what else? How much in pine?"

"You're hankerin' to know my business," John said, "go look it up in the county seat."

Perly smiled, his straight teeth bright in his dark face. "Two hundred thirty-four, more or less, if my memory serves me right."

He leaned back against the table and looked around the kitchen. "Nice range," he said. "Real antique. It sure does keep the room warm too. People are buying those nowadays to decorate their game rooms." Perly stood still for a moment, assessing the room with a half smile that was almost nostalgia.

Finally his eyes caught on Hildie's curious gaze and he reached out and ran a palm over her bright hair. "I thought I'd feel so much at home here," he said, just a touch of wistfulness softening his voice. "Here and in Harlowe." He turned a long look on Ma and one on Mim, then turned and stepped toward the door.

With the knob in his hand he whirled suddenly to John. "I never asked you for your pretty tractor," he said sharply. "Just keep that in mind. I'm not sure it's even a present I appreciate."

And then, as they watched, Perly swept out the door and down the path.

But Gore with his hand on the butt of his gun and the Moores clustered in the doorway remained where they were as motionless as animals in a spotlight.

Perly climbed into the truck and slammed the door. Still Gore stood where he was, sweat rolling in big drops down the sides of his head.

Perly tooted the horn.

"Jesus," Gore said, and stepped backward off the stoop.

John snickered. "Back off," he said. "Go ahead. Just like we was royalty."

Gore turned and trotted down the path.

"Hey," John called. "You're forgettin' what you come for."

Gore turned back to the family and side-stepped to the barn, then remembered he didn't have the keys.

"Not too put together for such a big shot," John said.

"John, for Lord sake," Mim hissed behind him.

Gore pulled the gun out of its holster and moved slowly up the path toward John, training the pistol on him. At the doorstep he stooped to pick up the keys, feeling for them blindly in the grass, his small blue eyes straining upward on Moore.

Keys in hand, he backed off toward the barn.

"What happened to all your talk, Bobby Gore?" John asked, following him slowly toward the barn at a distance of ten feet. "Gettin' tongue-tied in your old age? Lost your taste for gossip?"

"You just stay where you are," Gore said, and John stopped. He stood as if casually, his hands deep in the pockets of his overalls.

Gore stood indecisively, near the tow bar, not wanting to put his gun away to bend to his task.

Perly backed the truck around to the tractor and poked his head out the window to look back at Gore. "Put that gun away, Bob," he said. "These are law-abiding people. You're liable to shoot someone playing around with that gun."

Gingerly, Gore set his gun on the fender of the tractor and set to work. Perly rolled his window shut and leaned on the steering wheel to wait.

"Dunsmore got bullet-proof glass?" John asked. "He don't seem to put much stock by you."

Gore swept the gun off the fender. Holding it with both hands as though it were almost too heavy for him, he trained it at John. Mim screamed.

"Shut up!" Gore shouted at her, then raised his arms and pulled the trigger.

The bullet went through an upstairs window leaving a neat hole in the center of a starburst of cracks.

John stood perfectly still, his arms folded, watching as Gore leaped into the truck and the two men drove away. Perly did not drive quickly, digging out, as Gore might have wished, but deliberately, careful for the cumbersome tractor swaying precariously behind them up the dirt road away from the Moores.

"Now you fixed it so we got to go," Mim shouted at John when he came back into the house. She flew at him and stopped. "You've got no right to get yourself killed," she screamed. "No right."

"He's got no right to lay hands on you and Ma and Hildie."

"Then take us away," Mim cried.

"We won't run," John shouted.

"We will," Mim screamed. "We will. We will."

153

John looked down on her and began to laugh.

"Stop that," Mim cried. She reached for him to make him stop, but he twisted away, laughing harder than ever, doubled over with the force of it.

Mim swung her fist out on the end of her arm and landed it against his shoulder, hard.

"Ow, ow," John said, choking with laughter. "Cut it out."

Mim stepped back and her eyes filled with tears. She stood crying, not covering her face, staring at John with disbelief.

"Don't carry on now," he said, rubbing his arm. "I'm goin' out to buy us some Thanksgivin' dinner."

John threw the truck into gear and set it roaring up the road with a sense of purpose that made him slap the steering wheel in an exuberant rhythm. But instead of fading as he moved away from home, the image of the three pale faces grew more vivid, until he could almost feel the heaviness of their breath waiting on his own.

He did his errands in a hurry. At Linden's he filled the truck with gas and bought a chicken, a bunch of bananas, and a gallon of milk. Fanny handed him change and bagged his items, dispensing information all the while in her usual bored monotone.

John did not answer, but he heard, and his own breath went short at the thought of his family sitting alone so far away.

As soon as he was out of sight of the Parade, he floored the old truck so that it skidded on the gravel at every turn. He pulled up almost to the door, jumped out of the cab and burst into the room. In the doorway he stopped short. Ma was peeling potatoes at the table, and Mim was sitting on the bench by the stove rocking Hildie in her arms, singing the alphabet song with her. He could see she would say no more about going for now. The lamp cast a cheerful glow in the gray afternoon, deepening the colors of the room.

"Everything's okay!" he exclaimed, with an unfamiliar shock of pleasure.

"If you can call it that," Ma said.

154

John unloaded his purchases onto the table. "For once we'll eat decent," he said. "After all, Thanksgivin's still a holiday. You should a had a whiff of the smells from the kitchen down to Linden's."

But Mim was counting what was left in the jar when he returned the change. "A hundred and thirty-two," she said. "Fifteen dollars down in one week. A hundred and thirty-two's not much to go on."

"What the hell," John said. "It's somethin'." He was high now. Home had never seemed so precious and so comfortable. "Damn fool Jim Carroll. First he let that child go, and now he's gone and let his land go too. Him and the kids that's left, they up and went. They moved Emmie up to that nursin' home by the Circle, and took off. Even she don't know where to."

"That's what she says," Mim said. "She knows him and the kids are best off gone."

"The Carroll place must have a hundred acres clear," John said. "Dunsmore will make some hay on that."

"How can you joke?" Mim said wearily.

But John talked nonstop through dinner, and afterwards crawled around on the floor with Hildie on his back, bucking and howling to add to her hilarity. Mim frowned uneasily and Ma took her canes and left the room.

After Hildie was asleep and Ma was settled in the front room, Mim brushed her teeth, wrapped the two remaining bricks on the range in towels to warm their bed and made her rounds, making sure that all the bolts she had installed were securely fastened. At that point, John came in carrying his suit and a white shirt. "I need a bath," he said.

Mim stood before him with the bricks hugged to her.

John set the hanger with the suit on one of the hooks by the door, poured the water remaining in the pails under the sink into the big kettle on the range, took the empty pails, unlocked the back door, and headed out to the well.

When the cold gust of air from the door hit her, Mim moved. She returned the bricks to the stove, opened the damper so that the fire came up with a roar to warm the kitchen, and got the big galvanized tub down from the hook at the foot of the cellar stairs. She hung a clean towel on the line high over the range to warm.

When John came back with the water, she said, "Where you off to?"

"To blow the whistle on that Perly fellow," John said. "Past high time someone did."

John left at five in the morning, but his plans had changed somewhat. As it turned out, he was wearing the dark green work pants and red and black plaid jacket that he usually wore to town.

"Perly's got friends in Concord, sure," Mim had said. "If you happened on one, here we'd be—me and Hildie and Ma—without a way of knowin' or a truck to drive away in. You can say what you got to say just as clear on the telephone as goin' in to see him."

It was not at all obvious where he was going. Even so, as he rolled by the dark houses on Route 37, he felt that there were eyes behind each pulled shade, marking his movement. He drove warily, starting at every glimmer from the woods beyond the drainage ditches. He told himself it was silly to feel he couldn't make a trip to Concord by daylight. He generally went once a month at least to get parts for this or that. Nevertheless, his plan now was to go before light and return after dark.

He took the turnpike and changed a five-dollar bill into dimes at the toll booth. At dawn he found himself almost alone on the wide main street of Concord. He drove straight through and headed out again. On the outskirts of the city, he found a shopping center that suited his purposes. He parked his truck, noting that it was almost the only one in the fifteen-acre lot that early, and more conspicuous than it would have been in Harlowe. Nevertheless, he forced himself to eat a cold potato, and sit still on the dusty seat watching hour after hour as the storekeepers arrived, the stores opened, and cars, vans, and small trucks began to fill up the lot.

By ten-thirty, with the lot half full, the sidewalk was bustling with shoppers. John took his handful of dimes to one of the four telephone booths in front of Friendly Ice Cream. Then he stood in the booth, letting his breath steam up the glass, watching the mothers herd their pairs of well-fed children out of the ice cream shop, wiping at their chins with paper napkins and zipping up their coats.

"I can connect you with the State House, sir," said the operator and, without waiting for John to answer, she put the call through and a phone rang somewhere on the other end of the line.

"State of New Hampshire," said another woman's voice, and John again asked to speak to the governor.

"Please hold the line, sir," said the voice.

There was a long wait. Finally the operator came on and asked for another dime.

As soon as John deposited it, another woman's voice said, "Office of the governor, may I help you?"

"I want to speak to the governor," John said carefully.

"The governor is not available, sir," said the voice, which sounded as though it were coming from the other end of a rope of licorice. "If you could tell me your name and what the problem is, perhaps I could help."

John chewed on his knuckles. Women streamed by the telephone booth wheeling small children in wire baskets, their mouths stopped with lollipops.

"Are you there, sir?" said the woman.

"I am," John said. "There's this trouble I want to report."

"You want the police, sir, 225–2706."

"No," John said. "It'll take the governor for this."

"I told you, sir. The governor is unavailable at the moment. But if you contact the police, they'll take action through the appropriate channels."

John bit off a hangnail on his index finger, trying to think which detail to tell her to convince her to let him speak to the governor.

"Thank you for calling, sir," said the voice and there was a click. John's money fell into the box of the telephone and he heard the dial tone again.

He found he had forgotten the number. He dialed the operator. "I need the police," he said.

"Is this an emergency?" she asked.

"No," he said. Then, considering, he said, "I think so," but the operator was already gone.

Somewhere a phone rang and rang and rang. A family went by the telephone booth. John turned to stare after them as they passed. A man and a woman and two little boys dressed exactly alike in brand-new brown snowsuits.

Finally a weary man's voice said, "Police."

And the operator said, "Deposit ten cents please for the first three minutes."

John put his money in and the man said, this time with a touch of impatience, "Police here."

"I wanted to report some trouble," John said.

"What kind of trouble?" said the tired voice.

"Well, it's up to Harlowe."

"Harlowe? Where's that?"

"Harlowe," John said distinctly.

"If you mean the town of Harlowe, that's the state police," said the man. "Call 271–3181."

"Oh," said John.

"Anytime," said the policeman and hung up. John's money dropped and he was back to the dial tone.

John called the operator again. Each time he dialed he got a different operator.

This time the phone was answered almost before it rang. "Police, State of New Hampshire," said a woman's voice. "May I help you?"

"I want to report some trouble."

"Is it an emergency, sir?"

"Yes, sort of."

"Where are you? We'll send someone right out."

John looked around him. "I don't know exactly. It's not that kind of emergency. Not so I need someone here right now. It's up to—"

"Is it an emergency or is it not, sir?"

John hesitated. "Not an emergency this minute," he said. "You might say it's an emergency this week."

There was a pause, then, "Just what is the nature of your problem, sir?"

"Well, I see a lot of trouble goin' on," John said and paused.

"Don't we all!" said the woman. "What kind of trouble? When? Where?"

"Well this trouble's laid up seven months now under all kinds of happenings as look all right. It was April—"

"April! And you're just reporting it now?"

"Like I say, ma'am," said John. "It was overlaid with sweet talk and I didn't know as it would get so bad."

"Oh, I see. It's still going on, is it?" said the woman briskly. "What is it, extortion or something?"

"Excuse me, ma'am?"

There was a pause and a sigh, then the woman said, "Look, let's start with your district, then I can connect you with the right supervisor. Now. Where are you?"

"In Concord, ma'am."

"Concord has its own police force, sir," she said. "I suggest you call them. Then if they feel we should be called in, they'll call us."

"I called them already, ma'am, and what they say is since the trouble's up to Harlowe—"

"Harlowe?" she said. "Well, for heaven's sake, why didn't you say so? I'll connect you with—um, let's see—that's Captain Sullivan."

There was a long, long pause and again John had to deposit money.

Finally a crisp man's voice said, "Sullivan speaking. Understand you're worrying over Harlowe."

"Right," John said, relieved.

"What seems to be the problem?"

"There's this auctioneer come in, sir. A stranger. First he come round to half the town and collected up their life's belongin's to sell at his auctions. And then there was all these accidents, all to them as didn't see things his way. And now he's after land and livin' children."

"Whose land and children?" asked the man.

"Everybody's, sir. Everybody who ain't a deputy. Or the doctor or the storekeeper or some others."

"That doesn't sound like quite everybody. You personally are on hard times? That what you're trying to tell me?"

"No, sir. I mean yes, maybe . . ."

"You talked to Bob Gore about this?" he asked. "I should think he'd understand your situation better than I can. I was talking to him just last Tuesday, and he was telling me how Harlowe is just bustin' out all over. Construction, and new people, and money coming in hand over fist. If times are hard for you, maybe the town can help you out some, tide you over the winter. You able-bodied?"

"Course I'm able-bodied."

"Well then . . ."

"That ain't the point. The point bein' that this here auctioneer who's gobblin' up the townsfolk—"

"If you mean Perly Dunsmore," said the voice, laughing, "I'd best tell you he's the luckiest thing ever happened to Harlowe. Now there's a man knows which end is up. But I understand some of the old families like the old ways and don't want to move with the times. These big developers always have their enemies. You got to get with it though, mister. We're in the twentieth century. There's no stopping progress. As for that fellow Dunsmore, he's three lengths smarter than most. A real winner. You should count your blessings."

"I got no grudge with the twentieth century," John said. "What Perly's up to's got nothin' to do with any century."

"You're wrong about that, of course, but listen. What did you say your name was? Maybe you could come in here and we could talk this over."

Moore held the receiver to his ear. "Whatever you do, don't breathe the name of Moore," Mim had said. And Ma had said. "It's a sorry day when you're ashamed to say you're a Moore." John took a handkerchief out of his pocket and wiped his forehead. The telephone booth was so steamed up now that he couldn't see out at all.

"Hello?" said Captain Sullivan.

John hung up.

He opened the door and breathed the cold air. He doodled in the steam on the inside of the glass with his fingernail, thinking about Captain Sullivan knowing he meant Perly right off the bat like that.

Finally he closed the door and dialed the operator again. "Give me the State House, please," he said.

When the woman with the licorice voice answered, he said, "I talked to the police and the state police like you said and they won't help at all. You got to let me through to the governor."

"I don't 'got to' anything, sir. Didn't I speak to you before?"

"I said so, ma'am," John said, feeling the sweat start beneath the collar of his wool jacket.

"What was your problem again?"

"Where I come from, there's a man takin' people's children, their own flesh and blood. He's shootin' people and knockin' greenhouses down and jimmyin' up the steerin' so's—"

"*Who* is doing *what?*"

"The auctioneer—"

"Didn't you call me last week too?"

"No, ma'am. No. Not me."

"I think you did. This sounds familiar."

"No, no," John said, his spirits rising. "But there's plenty on the receivin' end along with me. Stands to reason. Must be others called."

"Listen. Crackpots call in here all the time. You wouldn't believe the calls we get. Obscene phone calls. People wanting him to come to their grandmother's birthday party. People will say anything on the phone. You know some guy called in here the other day, thought I was the governor's wife." The voice laughed heartily.

"Please, ma'am," John said. "In my whole life no one ever called me a crackpot. I been tendin' my business, bidin' my time, waitin' for this to blow over. I never lodged a complaint before. I let others better outfitted than me do that. But I can't wait no more. I'd be real quick. Three minutes. You got no call to stop me when I got a reason good as this."

"I'm sorry, sir," she said, resuming her licorice voice. "He's unavailable to random callers. You must understand the governor is a very busy man. There's an election campaign just over, and Christmas coming. And then there was that terrible fire over in Manchester, and he's very busy trying to organize some relief. And right at the moment all his aides are pretty well tied up too. Think of all the important things they have to look after—that broken dam up in Artemis that's left all those poor people homeless. The welfare problem in the state—you just don't know how bad it's got."

"But this here is people in trouble too," John said, but he wasn't sure, even as he stood there begging, that his problem was as important as all those other things. A broken dam was, after all, something you could stand in front of and look straight at.

"I would suggest that your problem is one for the police," said the woman.

"Gosh sakes, who?" John asked, feeling the quick heat rise to his face. "I called all them. What's a body got to do around here? Bust a dam? Burn a town?"

"That'd do it all right," said the woman, giggling. When John made no response, she said, "Look, if you're all that upset, you can come in here and make out a formal statement. The girls in the office here will tell you how to do it. If you want to bring charges, we'll help you with the forms, and get you in to see a judge. But you can't do these things on the telephone. How do I know who you are?"

"I can't do that," John moaned. "There's too many people ready to steal my child, shoot my wife—God only knows."

"If you feel the need for police protection, sir, you should discuss the matter with the police," she said, more gently now.

John held onto the phone until the woman asked if he was there still and if he didn't want to come in. Then, because he was incapable of speaking any more, he hung up.

·11·

He walked back to the truck, his body aching with fatigue. He folded his arms on the wide black steering wheel and rested his head against them. He more or less believed in the police, despite Cogswell's warning about the troopers. At least he always had. It didn't come naturally not to believe in them. In the police, and the army, and the country, and the goodness of his neighbor. He had accepted the inflation that made his milk worth less and less, and he had accepted the certification regulations which finally made it impossible for him to sell his milk at all. He accepted the fact that he was still living the way his grandfather had, while people in the towns and cities were filling their lives with expensive gadgets. He saw all the cars and the dishwashers and the cabins on the lakes and the trips hither and yon in fancy trailers and he dismissed them as a fragile tower that could be toppled in a cold wind. He let the tables and chairs go, and the tools and machinery, and even the cows, because of the land. Because the land was free and clear. Because he believed that a good piece of land was the only true security there was—the only security a family needed. Some man with a ski resort in mind had offered him forty-five thousand dollars for his land when Hildie was a baby, and he had laughed. "You could retire on that," the stranger had reminded him. "Money ain't like land," John had answered.

"Money gets stole. It loses value. Banks go bust. But my baby will always have that land."

Perhaps he should go and speak to Captain Sullivan. Perhaps Sullivan had only chanced to meet Perly hunting or visiting and didn't know him at all. After all, everybody who met Perly was impressed with him. But when he tried to picture Captain Sullivan, he saw Perly bending over Hildie, his face shining with promises of magic. Promises.

At the thought of Hildie, he lifted his head and looked around himself nervously. At this very moment, Gore and his deputies could be fanning out on all the roads from Concord, watching to see who it was that had made the phone calls—watching through rifle sights. If they had read his voice, they could be bearing down even now on Ma and Mim and Hildie as they went about their chores on the farm, alone. He had been gone almost six hours.

He headed out of Concord toward the turnpike, his stomach churning with hunger and impatience with the traffic. Once he was on the turnpike, the old truck hit sixty and the sense of rapid movement and direction and of perfect insulation from the rest of the world brought John to a sudden understanding of what he must do.

He stopped to top off the gas. Without getting out, he used the rearview mirror to watch the young boy standing jiggling to the sound of a radio as he waited for the tank to fill. He tried to decide whether it would be safe to ask him to fill the gas can. But when the moment came, he paid without a word and drove away with the gas can still empty.

Chilled at the thought of how long he'd been gone, he gave up the idea of waiting till night to return. Instead, he went past the Route 37 turnoff and circled around on back roads so that he approached Harlowe from the north instead of from the south as they would expect if they were looking. Through the last county to the north, he took fire roads all the way, rattling past old farms and a few new cottages, hoping nobody would report him. When he came to the bottom of the road past Cogswell's, it was early afternoon, gray and wintry.

As the truck labored up the road fifteen feet from Cogswell's front door, John's face and neck twitched uneasily beneath the pressure of the eyes he knew were there—Jerry's or Mickey's—following his progress through the sights of the double-barreled shotgun. But Cogswell would have recognized his truck anyway, even at night.

Halfway down his own side of the hill, the road widened out where the drive into the old Wilder place had once begun. John pulled off. He got the gas can out of the bed of the truck, and a length of plastic tubing for a siphon. He put one end into the gas tank of the truck and, sitting on the ground, sucked on the other end, slowly, so as not to get a mouthful. When it was running, he led it into the can and listened as it filled, a sound like the finger of water trickling out of the spring halfway down the cliff behind the pasture. When the gas can was full, he stood up and lifted the end of the siphon over his head so that the gasoline in it ran back into the truck.

He carried the gas can through the overgrown drive, climbed down into the cellar hole, perfectly dry now in the autumn, but overgrown with raspberry brakes. He made his way to the cold recess in the stone foundation wall where the Wilders had kept their milk and butter. He pulled out a stuffing of blown leaves, placed the gasoline can in the recess, and shoved the leaves back so that the old red can was hidden.

Probably the Wilder place had burned. That was what usually happened to farmhouses. Whatever had happened, the land had been a part of the Moore place since the Civil War. The bridal maples some ancient Wilder had planted were so overwhelming now that they would have brushed the house had it been standing. They spread their branches over a natural clearing. All the land around had been scrub when John was a boy, but now the beech and maple were eight or nine inches through and the poplar thicker still and dying out. Ma could remember when the Wilder place was mostly pasture, with views from almost everywhere.

After a house burned, the chimney stood alone awhile like a child's block tower. Then one year, the mortar completely gone, it would simply crumble in the spring thaw and the next summer there would be a heap of clean red bricks in the pit marked out by the cellar stones. He'd seen it happen. And presently the Virginia creeper and poison ivy would poke up through the bricks, and then, almost overnight, trees as thick as your wrist. Someday, someone would come and take the bricks to build a walk with, then everyone would forget—everything but the name.

"The old Moore place. Whatever happened?" they would ask.

But no, that wasn't what Perly had in mind. He had in mind to make it modern, expensive, a place for play, not work—ropes with colored floats to mark off where to swim, the barn tricked up with picture windows, hexes, and a sign for Perly Acres, ski tows running up the pasture, the dooryard paved for parking sports cars and foreign station wagons—a place no Moore could even visit.

He drove into his yard in the last light. The woods were dark already, but the pond was a pale pool of light and the pasture rose gray and wide behind the house. The soft yellow glow of the kerosene lamp shone from the kitchen windows, and from the kitchen chimney he could see a wisp of smoke, almost black against the sky. Mim was watching from the window, and came running down the path in her shirtsleeves to meet him. He caught her in his arms and held her to him in a way he seldom did. She pulled away laughing, and didn't ask him questions. She turned, almost bashful, and led the way up the path to the kitchen.

Only when he was settled at the table with his supper did she ask, "Did you tell him?"

John shook his head. "They got it fixed so you can't," he said. "And the cops want you to come in and stick your head in a noose before they'll listen. First one that let me get six words in sets right off tellin' me how Perly Dunsmore's the best thing ever happened to us."

"John!" Mim said. "You didn't let on who you were?"

John shook his head. "You got to consider, a fellow that just took a week to tie up a Harlowe boy like Gore—one that's lived down the road from us all his life—probably wouldn't find it much of a challenge at all to hogtie a bunch of strangers."

They sat at the table in silence. Ma didn't bother to eat. Hildie slipped away from the table and vanished into the front room and nobody called her back.

Finally Mim sighed. "Now you see how it is? There's nothin' to do but go."

"Maybe not," John conceded. "Maybe not."

All weekend they worked on the truck. John found a rusty saw left on a high hook in the barn, and there were pots of rusty but perfectly adequate nails. Mim worked enthusiastically, planning details, asking for shelves, thinking about how it would be, worrying about keeping warm. Hildie was as excited as a summer child preparing for a camping trip. They closed in the back of the truck with walls and a peaked roof that let Mim stand almost upright. There were no windows except the one into the cab in front. But there was a small hinged door on the back.

Ma sat on her couch by the window in the front room, straining to see through the barn doors to what they were doing. She refused to ask how they were coming, although she no longer said she wouldn't go.

On Monday morning, John said, "Tonight, late, late in the wee small hours sometime, we'll go."

They measured and found that the sofa cushions Ma was used to sleeping on would fit against the front wall of their new little house. Mim was pleased. "That'll be like a piece of home for Ma and Hildie," she said. They put the cooking utensils into the truck —the dishes, the pails, Lassie's dish. They installed the kindling box and filled it with small logs to burn in the sheet metal stove they planned to buy as soon as they were safely far away. Their bedding. All the blankets, but only their own mattress. Hildie would sleep with them. They packed all the food they had, but kept it in the kitchen yet for fear of frost. Mim made bundles of their clothing and packed a box of odds and ends for Hildie to play with.

Rather suddenly, at about two in the afternoon, they found themselves finished and simply waiting in the warm kitchen for the hour to leave. John sat in his usual place on the bench in front of the kitchen range with Hildie in his lap and Lassie at his feet, moaning in her sleep. Mim stood at the back door looking up at the pasture. The wind blew with a cold whine, laying down silver furrows in the brown pasture, then riffling them upright again.

"A good northeast gale blowin' up," John said, almost with satisfaction. "Long's it don't rain now, we'll be all set."

"That has more the sound of a wind to bring on snow," Mim said.

"Papa?" said Hildie. He rocked her. "Let's stay home."

"Yesterday you was jumpin' up and down to go," Mim said, turning to the two of them.

John could hear his mother stifling her sounds from the front room, passing the time before they could go, a stretch of time as bare and desolate as the empty house itself. Already the sounds the women made reminded him of the whimpering of the refugees hurrying across the face of the television set—mothers and grandmothers and little girls, brittle and distant as the blanched bones of birds on the forest floor.

"But why do we got to go?" Hildie asked.

John stood up abruptly, standing Hildie on her feet on the floor. "Ask Mama," he said, and went to his own mother in the other room.

She was sitting on the couch looking out the front windows, across the orchard to the pond. She did not look up when he came in. Her hair was gray and the light was gray and her very cheeks seemed gray, as uneven and fragile as ash. She had an army blanket pulled up to her chin.

"Ma," he said, and sat on her couch beside her. She dropped the blanket and pulled his head down against her shoulder. There was practically nothing left of her. There wasn't room for his head on her shoulder any more.

"You know," she said, and he felt rather than heard the catch in her breath. "When I was a youngster I had a hankerin' to see the world. But then your pa came along and he says, 'With this out your window, honey, ain't nothin' you could find wouldn't be

168

downhill.' So we set right here and never budged."

John sat up and looked at her.

"Funny, ain't it, when you think on it," she said, "how now, after all, I'm a goin' to see my blessed world."

"Ma," he said. "I'm . . ." His face was flushed as if with sunburn, and his eyes were as deep and muddy as the pond in summer. "Give me time, Ma. It may look like I'm pullin' out, but it's not in the way of quittin' quite, not like it seems."

"Never mind, son, never mind," she said. "There's some things can't be helped." And John held her in his arms as if it were she who was the child.

Outside, John and Mim and Hildie stood in the dooryard looking out over the pond. The wind roughed it up so that the light fell deep into the troughs and left the surface dark as ink. "By mornin'," John said, "I bet the pond's caught."

"It'll skim over ragged if this wind keeps up, even if the snow don't get it," Mim said.

"Crummy skating," John said.

"And how many years since you been skatin', John Moore?" Mim teased.

"Hildie's about of an age to learn," he said.

Walking three abreast, John and Hildie and Mim headed into the dim pine forest and followed the old logging road that circled around and came out at the top of the pasture. Far overhead, a restless canopy of branches broke the sunshine into tiny dancing circles. Light-starved seedlings and brush had died back and rotted, leaving an open expanse of dead pine needles which gave beneath their boots, then sprang back silently behind them. The wind rushed at the green needles overhead and they flattened against one another with a high hissing sound. Occasionally the wind reached down to sing through the dead lower branches and lift the green tassels on Hildie's stocking cap.

"He'll cut the pine," Mim said, "before he sells."

"Who, Perly?" John said. "He won't cut the pine nor sell neither."

"You figure he'll really save it for a playground?" Mim said.

"Nope," John said.

They crossed over the bridge where the brook ran in the spring and headed up a steep incline out of the pine grove. Hildie rushed ahead and clattered nearly waist deep through maple and birch and poplar leaves. Crisp oak leaves still clinging to the high branches chattered in the wind. The smaller beech saplings held their leaves too, papery thin and yellow as daffodils. The wind and sun swooped down through the branches, dappling the woods with light and hustling the leaves up into pinwheels that spun and died, then spun again. They passed through a thicket beneath a seed hemlock and came out to the Christmas grove— dozens of wild white spruce, protected far overhead by spreading maples. Underfoot, princess pine and a spiky chartreuse creeper were so thick you couldn't step without crushing them.

"Near time to cut a tree, and still no snow," Mim said.

"Dry year," John said.

"Will we come back for Christmas?" Hildie asked. She was pulling up greens by the handful. "Can I help make the wreaths this year?"

As they went on, the spruce gave way to juniper, and the creeper to the rusty orange of dried ferns. And then, quite suddenly, they stepped through the break in the stone wall and out into dazzling sunshine and the icy force of the wind. The cemetery was just as Mim had left it, except that the wind and sun had dried to gray the earth she had bared. A few curled tendrils of dead ivy still poked from the ground. "I sometimes breathe easier that nothin' grows in winter," Mim said.

Hildie stood gazing at the gravestones that she had never seen so clearly before. "My grandpa's under there?" she asked.

"Don't go no closer now," Mim said. "That stuff is wicked poison even now."

But John, whose father and grandfather and great-grandfather were there, wasn't looking at the cemetery. He stood on the crest of the hill, looking down, past the sweep of pasture and the weatherbeaten house, toward the pond. Mim went and stood next to him so that her shoulder brushed his.

He shook himself with irritation and moved away from her. "Where do you have in mind to go?" he asked her. "Just where but here can you be thinkin' there's a place for us?"

"But you said," Mim said.

"Oh we'll move into the truck and play house if you like," he said. "But nobody's goin' to cut that pine."

"Like as not, he'll keep the pine," Mim said.

"I'm sayin' *I'll* keep the pine," John said, his eyes the same color as the dead grass and the sandy soil.

Mim's eyes were the color of the sky arching over the land and away as far as they could see. "We will go?" she prompted.

John nodded. He ran a hand through Mim's short curls and picked up Hildie, who hid her face in his shoulder against the cold. Then the three of them started down the hill into the hard wind.

They ate, and Mim put the last dishes and bits of food into the cartons, even a bottle of leftover soup. Ma sat in the lawn chair with her hands clasped in her lap watching. John whittled on a stick, and Hildie and the dog watched warily, anxious at the preparations.

Mim took up the broom and started to sweep the house. The next person to see it would be Dunsmore. She prickled with red hatred, yet she wanted him, when he took what was hers by right, to see reflected in it that she was a clean and decent woman. She was swept with an awe at his power. It required a reversal of everything she wanted and believed to think that such power— whatever its devious route—could be directed at ends that were anything but right and good. It seemed that if she could only stir this man to decency, to a true vision of what it was that he was doing, he would set her world to rights. And yet she knew that if she had any way at all of touching Perly—and she burned with a guilty sense that she did—it had nothing to do with her decency or her competence as a housewife. She had no way of stirring that power in him to anything but further evil.

"I don't know why I'm doin' this," she said. And yet she finished carefully, sweeping the last dust clumps and food crumbs into a piece of newspaper and dumping them on the fire. Then she set the broom by the door to go.

One last time she put Hildie to bed on the mattress on the floor and lay down beside her to wait for her to go to sleep. The child was excited, and uneasy at the emptiness. "How could you think we'd leave you, my sweet one," Mim crooned. "It's on your account we're goin'."

But she held the child too tightly and only upset her more. "Why is it again we're goin'?" Hildie asked.

"Shhh," Mim said and lay still.

She heard the door open and shut downstairs, and thought that John had started to load the truck. But she listened on and on, and did not hear him come in again. Presently Hildie fell asleep in her arms and still Mim did not move. She lay on and on, aching at the necessity, ever, of releasing the small limp body that, given up to her like this, filled her with such peace.

·12·

THERE WAS A MOON, the shape of half an orange. The wind which seemed as solid as a living body did nothing to dim its light. Presently, stumbling up the familiar road, his flashlight in his belt, more for protection than for light, John grew accustomed to the dimness and began to detect the boulders and felled branches before the toe of his boot struck them. Carefully he climbed down into the old house foundation and plunged his arm into the leaves clogging the old dairy shelf. When his bare hand struck the unnaturally cold metal, he cringed.

He pulled the gasoline can out and put his gloves back on. The journey was four and a half miles by the road, and more by the old logging trail and the brook where the footing was so bad. He hadn't gone through the woods in decades, not since the year he had attended high school. Then the bus had let him off in the Parade, and sometimes, for variety, he had walked home through the woods. Never at night though. And never in winter either.

Now he took the heavy gas can and headed down the road. He passed his own house and gazed at the yellow light in the kitchen, wondering if they'd missed him yet and feeling shut out, the rhythmic crunch of his feet on the dirt road lost on the whine of the wind. He headed across the garden, his footsteps muffled now by the dead vines, and down the old path that passed the place where they raked away the lily pads and arrowheads to swim in summer. He paused at the edge of the pond.

There was always a lightness over the pond. Sometimes in the dark still nights of summer, way back when everything had been new to him, he had swum there with a girl—first with wild Hattie Shaw, who had had the idea, and then later, at his own insistence, with Mim when she was fourteen, then barely fifteen, shunned by his mother, and shy, but willing for him. They couldn't quite see each other, but the lightness over the pond, even on the darkest night, had been enough to assure him of the milky fact of her beside him, bending to set her clothes on the fallen pine log, then moving into the shallow water and sinking, with barely a ripple, the pale shadow of flesh. Afterwards, his own fingers puckered from the water, he touched the wet new skin, rough as his own with chill. He touched and she ran. He sat on the log and shivered until she came back. Then he took her tightly by the elbows and she let herself be forced onto the blanket he had spread.

John shifted the heavy gasoline can from one hand to the other and walked. The loss. You couldn't stop it. Not with laws or holding or thinking. They hadn't been swimming at night since long before Hildie was born. He thought about the stinging bugs now. He didn't want anything now the way he had wanted the slightest thing then. The way he needed the land was a different thing, a holding fast against more loss than he could bear. The need for the land was more like a retreat than a driving force.

The pond was frozen in ridges to about four feet out. The wind-thrashed water gurgled and sucked at the lip of ice, keeping abreast of him, a familiar presence, as he made his way along the rough path at water's edge. He stopped at the mouth of the brook. The night had unstrung him. The night and the weight of the gasoline can dragging on his shoulder. He could have clasped the pond in his arms. He put the can down and stood looking out over the pond once again, waiting for it to turn time aside for him the way it always had.

But finally, distracted, he turned and headed uncomforted into the dark woods, and followed the bed of rocks where, in spring, the brook rushed, and even now, beneath the high wind, a tongue of water rang against the scoured stones like the wooden clapper in a bell, warning that they were slippery. Twice he stepped on what looked like a windswept stretch of earth and crashed through ice up to his shin—both times with his right foot. Soon he had a cold foot and a warm foot as well as a free shoulder and a captive one, so that he felt unbalanced as he moved.

The distance was greater than he remembered, but eventually the bed of the brook grew indistinct. He worried about missing the stone wall, about turning off at the wrong wall, for walls, he knew too well, crisscrossed the woods like the paper chains on a Christmas tree. The right stone wall was the one that crested the hill and ended at the old logging road that would take him out behind the Parade. The road was bulldozed fresh the year he was in high school, but perhaps by now it would be so grown in he wouldn't be able to follow it even if he found it. The water was gone completely from the creek bed now, and the woods were growing darker. If he turned on the flashlight, it would light a narrow path for his boots but black out everything around so that he would be more than ever likely to miss the wall.

Quite suddenly, a low branch reached out and caught in the handle of the gasoline can, yanking John off his feet. He fell full length on the ground. The can struck a rock with a loud clang, and the gasoline splashed around loudly inside. He lay listening until it was still, feeling his bruised knee. He got to his knees and felt for the can. A paddy bird roared up from almost underneath him, the squeaking of wings as loud as any motor. John let out a yell that startled him still more, and settled back on his heels trembling to listen for an answer. An owl hooted not far away, and then there was nothing again but the sporadic wailing of the wind.

He no longer felt alone. But it would not be a man, not here. Only, perhaps, a deer, or even a bear, more afraid of him than he of it. Or worse, a fisher cat or a big dog gone wild. John took the kitchen knife and the flashlight from his belt. He pushed the switch on the flashlight and the woods lit up in glistening black and white. Slowly he swung the light all around him, squinting to see beyond the end of its beam. He caught the lichen on the sides of trees, the heavy ridges of fungus on a broken branch, like tumors stretching skin. And then, almost beyond its reach, the light bounced off something pale and shiny and as big as a head, and after a gasp John remembered the great chunk of quartz that marked the wall he wanted. It was behind him. He had passed it. It was the marker stone he had felt as company.

He took up the gas can and, using the light now, headed out along the wall. He moved more quickly now. He would know the old road, when he came to it, by the break in the wall. And, if he could still follow the road at all, it would take him out where he wanted to be, or close enough.

The wind still howled from the northeast. It would be at his back once he swung around onto the old road. Hour after hour it had been blowing like that, and suddenly John was struck by the thought that it could not go on like that forever. He hurried, stumbling, beginning to be afraid.

In the dark and frozen woods, it seemed clear that setting fire to a few houses served no real purpose. It was only a way of turning the rage into something he could see and touch and measure, a way of setting it apart before it burst into flame within him and burned him out.

When he thought of the three houses strung out along the Parade in front of the dry pine wood, the one he kept thinking about was Fayette's. He didn't want Fayette's to catch. He counted on the firemen to work on saving Fayette's because it was the post office. Adeline Fayette was as old as his mother, yet still she climbed onto the high stool at five-thirty every morning and sorted the mail. If you came in early you would find her blowing from the corner of her mouth at the wisps of straight white hair that fell on her face. She was almost completely deaf. She might never hear the high cracking of the pines, the fire alarm, the last commotion. The firemen might not save the post office. Perly might direct them to the deputies' houses instead. To the James

176

place, its pink paint weathered and a battered sign out front that said, "SAWS SHARPENED, APPLIANCES FIXED." He thought of James sitting on the edge of the bandstand with Cogswell, swinging his legs and sharing his coffee, waiting for Perly to come and sell the stolen children. He remembered that James had had a little girl who died of polio. That was a long time ago. Perhaps he had forgotten what it was like to lose a child. Or perhaps, like Cogswell, he was only scared.

John always came back to the auctioneer. If it weren't for Dixie straining at the gate, the window, the leash, he would have gone in and set fire to the old Fawkes place itself. But, for all the times he'd patted Dixie, he wasn't sure of her. Still, it was the auctioneer who had to be destroyed before everyone could settle back and live again. Before he himself could plant new corn, bargain somehow for a heifer and a milker, and go on living. But the fire . . . it was too much to expect the fire to understand, to shoot a long sentient tongue straight across the road at Perly Dunsmore.

Even if it did, Perly would spring up at the first whisper of smoke, cheerfully taking an interest, offering suggestions, making sure things went his way.

John came to the opening in the wall, turned off the flashlight, and let his pupils widen to the darkness. The road was filled with juniper and sticky sumac and raspberry brakes, but the thinning through the woods was still distinct enough to follow. John lifted the gasoline onto his shoulder and pushed through brush too thick to walk around. Even if the old Fawkes place should burn, Perly wouldn't be in it; he would be leading the search party, crashing through the woods behind the clever Dixie, his eyes alight in the dark, tracking down John Moore.

All Mim would know was that he had walked out on her while she was putting their daughter to bed. All Hildie would know. In a year or two, after everything was back to normal, hunters might find his bones—his bones gnawed by foxes, a rusted wrist-watch, and the can of gasoline. Such things had been happening for less. Such things had been happening and nobody was taking any notice.

John stopped. That was the worst part. Nobody was taking any notice. He felt a coldness at the base of his spine that was like an illness. It should not be left to him to make the move. It should be somebody moneyed, or educated—somebody that lived in town.

Then he remembered Sonny Pike. Somebody had shot Sonny. John started up again, the gas sloshing in the can. Somebody had gone after Sonny Pike, and Cogswell, at least, didn't seem to know who.

Perhaps he too could beat Dixie home and be gone. He and Mim and Hildie and Ma. By the time they got there, dogs barking, blue lights flashing, the Moores would all be gone. Then it would be a matter of simple hiding—from radios, television warnings, pictures in the post offices, all-points alerts, blockades on all the roads—a thousand black-and-white images of cops and detectives and star-breasted sheriffs. Yet surely, the woods, the wild stretches of woods that the trailers hadn't found yet, could hide a man live as well as dead.

Clearly though, it was much easier to hide the dead.

He thought about Mudgett and kept going. Mudgett sitting in the last row of the schoolhouse, laughing at the little kids with his twisted mouth, Mudgett crossing wits with the teachers and coming off with all the prizes, Mudgett grinning over his spotted hound as it retched blood onto the beaten ground of the schoolyard. Mudgett at the auction sitting on a beach towel with his new wife, jaws working angrily, gun bulging. Mudgett collecting up the hammer and the handsaw, the brush and dustpan, the rakes and hoes and the scythe—the simple things without which the most routine chores become almost impossible. Mudgett taking the wrenches he needed to repair the truck, the can of tar he needed for the roof over the kitchen—tossing them into the back of the truck with a clank. Mudgett knocking Ma over with her own television set.

There was no reason why any of them should ever have trusted Perly. He was an outsider with big talk and they should have been more wary. But Mudgett was one of them. Mudgett should have been one of them. And Mudgett's was the closest house of all to the pines he had in mind.

And John began moving more forcefully through the brush on the old road, his right foot warming up and the sweat starting beneath his shirt and woolen hunting jacket. Even with the brush and the weight of the gas can and his plan, he felt freer than he had in months. The point was not so much to accomplish anything as that it had become necessary to do something. That he must not be pushed to abandon everything without leaving some mark.

John knew that he had entered the stand of pines from the sound of the wind combing the needles, the silence of his footsteps, and, even in the cold, the fragrance of the pitch. Under the pines, the wind at his back was so strong that he never heard the traffic on Route 37, so the lights from Mudgett's house caught him before he was quite ready. He stopped.

He was there, standing thirty yards back into the woods, staring out past the pines and the abandoned apple orchard at Mudgett's house. Though it must have been nearly eleven, every light was blazing and the spotlight under the eaves threw long ropes of light into the woods.

To the left was the James place, too big for Ian James and his wife and their one grown son. There was a light on in the ell, probably in the kitchen. The son would be watching television. The house loomed through the dark the color of driftwood, dry as driftwood.

And to the right, Fayette's, all dark. Adeline must be in bed already. Over the chimney he could see the pale outline of the tower on the old Fawkes barn. Standing still and listening, he could hear, when the wind hushed, the sounds of the town—a distant motor, a door slamming, a cat crying.

John put the gas can down. He would have to build a fire about a hundred feet long; he hadn't much reckoned on the actual work of it. He began to act, moving stiffly, unconvinced, now that he was about it, that he could do what he had planned. He picked up dead branches from the ground and tossed them into an elongated heap. When the pile was five feet high and six or seven feet long, he stopped, restored by the rhythm of work to a sense of normalcy. He broke two green branches off one of the smaller pines, and using them as a rake, gathered in layers of nearby pine needles and sprinkled them over the top of the dead branches. Then, putting his makeshift rake down where he would recognize it again, he moved back into the woods and began collecting more dead branches to continue his pile. Bending and straightening, bending and straightening, it was like pitching hay or drawing water or splitting firewood. He worked now without weariness, strong in the faith that the long funeral pyre he planned would be complete in time, just as the raked piles of hay ended up in the loft of the barn each year before the weather cooled.

The gusts of wind piled upon each other furiously, then scattered down the hill into the Parade, occasionally leaving John in a hole of silence. In such moments the branches crashed into the pile like thunder and John straightened up and held his breath, waiting for the wind again. Far away, he had been hearing a dog bark. When the wind died, the sound leaped closer. He stopped to listen. Then he whirled to face Mudgett's house. The back door was pulled ajar and a white husky came bounding toward him, outlined in silver by the spotlight. Then the spotlight and the light in Mudgett's kitchen went dark, the door clicked, and John felt rather than saw Mudgett standing in the doorway with a rifle. The big dog barked frantically, dashing halfway across the clearing toward him, ghostlike in the dark, then back up again toward the house.

"Hey, King, hey, boy," he heard Mudgett call. "What's up, dog?" Then, "Go get him, boy!" The dog went on barking. The wind was blowing John's scent straight toward the dog.

John took out the knife and the flashlight. If he ran now, Mudgett would hear him. The gasoline can was sitting out in the open, its red clearly visible in the light from the half moon. The dog was getting bolder now, dashing right up to the edge of the woods, so close that John could see the dark shading on the sides of his muzzle.

Mudgett was moving into the yard, his dark shape clear against the yellow house. John crouched, watching Mudgett through the branches he had piled. He should have spent the last money and bought a gun. Mudgett was a perfect target as he peered down the barrel of his rifle into the woods, moving gingerly but steadily toward John.

Suddenly Mudgett dropped the barrel of the gun and grabbed the dog by its collar. "Damn you, King," he said. "Damn fool dog. Don't know the difference between trouble and a coon." He turned and moved rapidly into the house, and the kitchen light went on again.

The dog stopped bounding at the woods, but went on barking. Gradually it dawned on John that the other noise, the new noise underneath the barking and the thud of the jumping dog, was the sound of a chain pulled and loosened, pulled and loosened, as the dog strained toward him.

John rose stiffly and went to work again as quietly as he could. He swept the pine needles away from the base of a tree and buried the gas can under them. Then he stood still until the dog got tired of barking. When he grew bold enough to take up the rake again, the dog started again. He stopped and the dog stopped. He started and the dog started. This time he kept working. Suddenly the woods were lit up and John jumped. They had turned the spotlight on again. Mudgett's wife came out in a red robe, screaming, "Shut up. Shut up. You son of a bitch. You're drivin' me crazy. You're worse'n him." The dog yelped. She hit him across the nose with the flat of her hand. The dog rolled over on his back whining.

Then Mudgett was standing in the doorway, careless of his outline in the light from the kitchen. "God damn you!" he shouted. "I'll lock the both of you in the cellar. Get him in here."

And, in the brightness from the spotlight, Mudgett's wife dragged the cringing dog into the kitchen after her.

John laughed. The work did not seem so hard now he was used to it. And eventually he found that he was working in back of James's house. The light was out in the ell now. And all of Mudgett's lights except the spotlight in the back yard were out as well.

It was about four o'clock in the morning and still pitch dark when John finished his work—a seventy-foot-long arc of piled branches stretching around the backs of Mudgett's and James's houses. In an admission that Perly was beyond his reach, John did not continue the pile, as he had planned, behind Fayette's, which was the house directly opposite Perly's. The firemen would never let the fire jump the road. He would have to settle for Mudgett and James.

John walked back the length of his pile, giving it a kick here and there, shaky at the thought of setting it on fire. He poured a trickle from the can of gasoline along the back edge of his heap, careful not to leave any gaps. Then he walked back the length of the pile again, dribbling out the gasoline until it was gone.

He carried the can a good way back up the road, screwed on the cap, and left it there. He dropped his gasoline-soaked gloves beside it, and fished the big box of wooden kitchen matches out of his jacket pocket as he walked back. He listened. All he could hear was the wind. The town at that hour was as silent as the woods. The line of gasoline smelled so strongly that he wondered if the town weren't rousing itself for the chase already, alarmed by the fumes.

He backed up six paces. Then he struck the match on the box and threw it as it flared, starting to run with the same motion. He was almost to the gasoline can before he paused to look over his shoulder. Darkness and silence. He stopped. The match must have fizzled.

He returned, moving cautiously, to within eight feet of the gasoline. If he stood too close there wouldn't even be any bones to tell the tale. He struck and threw.

This time, before he had run four steps, the earth shuddered and he was knocked forward by the whoop of the explosion. The woods before him lit up with a flash of yellow light. John could feel the flickering light of the gasoline-fed flames burning into his back, framing him with brightness. He caught up the can as he went and kept on running.

The pine crackled and split loudly as it burned. Mudgett's dog was howling frantically. John crashed through an almost solid wall of juniper. Now Mudgett was hollering. He must be at the door already. John kept running. It was harder and harder to find his footing as the layers of brush accumulating between him and the fire began to obliterate the light. Finally, John risked one quick look over his shoulder as he ran.

He stopped short. Through the brush he could see the ragged wall of flame rising higher and higher. He stood a moment, mesmerized, held by the beauty of the fire he had made. High above the soaring needletips of flame, the green branch of a pine caught fire and a shower of sparks ran off before the wind in the direction of Mudgett's.

John ran then. He ran wildly, leaping through raspberry brakes as if they weren't there, barely feeling the thorns as they raked his face. He ran until his chest was burning and he had left behind the last trace of light from the fire. Then he stopped, confused, and found he was already at the wall. He went on, pushing hard but too spent to run, stumbling against stones, bumping into trees. He turned on the flashlight and raced along the wall within its jerky light a hundred yards, then fell full length and smashed the face of the flashlight on a boulder.

The moon was down and it was darker than when he had come. He used his hands, feeling as much as seeing his way along the wall, watching intently for the landmark quartz, stopping now and then to stroke a pale granite boulder that looked, in the dark, as if it might be quartz. The way was endless. He kept listening behind him for the dogs he expected, for the alarm, for the sound of people leaping and shouting. All he could hear was the racket of his own body, panting and crashing through the dense undergrowth. Then, finally, his groping hands were caressing the quartz, its crystal faces slippery as ice.

He started running down the creek bed, slipping and floundering in the confusion of rocks. Before he had traveled twenty yards, his feet flew up before him and he fell backward on his spine and the base of his skull. He lay on his back across the rocky bed of the brook, looking into the wavering dark gray of the sky beyond the darker lace of branches.

At first the noise seemed a new dimension to the pounding in his ears, or the water running underneath the rocks. But stock still and listening as he came to, he recognized the sound fighting its way upwind from the far edge of the world. It was the alarm in the Parade, clanging from the top of the firehouse to rouse the firemen.

As he lay, almost peacefully now, he knew that in town people were throwing off covers, setting bare feet on cold floors. The volunteer firemen, many of them deputies as well, were pulling boots and rubber raincoats over their pajamas. Their wives were covering their curlers with kerchiefs and following more slowly, pouring out into the Parade to see the fire, his fire. Calmly he hoped, the way he hoped a cow would calve without trouble, that someone would think to wake up Adeline Fayette. But the image he fastened on was that of the auctioneer, gliding fully dressed into the road, Dixie waving her tail at his left heel as he indicated with a raised eyebrow just what he had in mind for the firemen to do. He would wait only until his eye, like a fisheye lens, had gathered in the whole scene.

And then he would start. It would be foolhardy to expect flames or underbrush to slow down Perly. He would simply slither through, silently following the dog along John's trail. It was a matter of minutes now.

John struggled to his feet and floundered on. As he got closer to the pond, dark patches of ice kept giving way beneath him, trapping a boot and yanking him to a stop. When he reached the path around the pond, he started to run again. If they were there already, he would see the commotion in the dooryard: the state police with radios blaring, perhaps Captain Sullivan himself questioning Mim. Perhaps taking her from Ma and Hildie. Perhaps taking them all as hostages to coax him out of the woods. He paused to listen. He could no longer hear the noise from the Parade, but he realized that the sky had brightened from navy to royal blue. He went on, clinging to the edge of the pond, his left foot skidding on the embankment from time to time. Finally, he rounded the twin oaks by the swimming place and came out in view of his own house and yard.

Dark. Peaceful and dark. No light, even in the kitchen. He slowed to a walk and let the empty gas can swing at his side.

But when he got to the road, he started to think about the dark. Mim asleep, or gone without him, or running in the dark somewhere searching for Hildie. He ran up the path to the door and leaned against it. Locked. The sounds of his body beat against the familiar wood. He had no key and was afraid, even in his own yard, to call out. Then, in a burst, the door gave beneath his weight and Mim caught him as he fell in.

They stood a moment in each other's arms. Ma moved laboriously across the front room in the dark.

"Are you all right?" asked Mim, supporting him.

"Don't know," he said, his voice foreign to him.

As a child, he had come running up the path from school, burst in at the door, and let the dammed-up stream of failure overflow. "Be a man. Be a man," Ma had crooned in the way of comfort. And now he longed to be a small boy, to overflow, to refuse the command to be a man.

"You been runnin'," Mim said.

John straightened himself up away from her and leaned panting in the doorway.

She struck a match. Her jeans and sweater showed she had been waiting up for him after all. She lifted the chimney from the kerosene lamp on the table and put the match to the wick so it flared. John watched the small yellow flame, caught up in the comfort of fire.

"Dear God. You been fightin'," Ma said, moving toward John for a closer look.

John shook his head, then he thought to set the gasoline can down. By the door were the piles of cartons just the way he'd left them. "Not packed!" he cried, panic pounding up in him again. He lifted a carton of dishes and turned to go out.

"John," Mim said, clutching his arm. "Where you been?"

"Let go!" he screamed at her.

Mim let go and John opened the door and faced the cold again.

"Set that thing down," Ma said, her voice clear and muscular in the dim room.

"Ma," John said. "We got to get out of here. Quick."

"Not all that quick," Ma said, and John hesitated.

"How'd you . . . I never seen such a . . ." Mim said. John leaned his face against the cool door as he closed it. "John, that's gasoline. It's that you reek of."

"We can't stop for talk," he said. "They'll be a good way after me by now." His throat was dry now and his body throbbed so he could hardly stand. He looked down at the box of dishes coming in and out of focus through layers of red.

He let Mim pull him to Ma's lawn chair and push him into it. She handed him a glass of water from the pail. "Who?" she asked.

"Him and the dog," he said. "Dunsmore and that dog."

"John, what've you been up to?"

"Best you not know," John said.

"Me and her got to know," Ma said. "We're in on it sure as you." As she stood over him leaning on her canes, her face, lit from below by the lamp, was drawn in strong lines he had almost forgotten.

Mim knelt in front of him with a wet rag. "Here," she said. She touched his face with the warm water and the scratches started to sting.

Unstrung not by the pain but by the care, John said, "I set them pines back of the Parade on fire. And the wind by now must a blowed it clear through Mudgett's and James's and maybe the post office too."

Mim dabbed at his face. "You got caught?"

He shook his head.

"Chased?"

Again he shook his head.

"You know that stretch of road where the fields run level on both sides?" Mim asked. "Gores could've seen you there, walkin' along with the can."

"He was never near the road," Ma said. "He cut through the woods like he done as a boy. Runnin' scared through the woods in the pitch black. It's the woods beat him up like that—no man."

"Woods never stopped a dog a minute," John said.

"You heard them after you?" Mim asked.

He shook his head. The blue on the windowpanes was giving way to gray. When they went, they'd have to go out past Cogswell's to avoid the Parade.

"We might as well put our name to paper as go tonight," Ma said.

John sat in the chair, letting Mim take off his frozen boots. "We're so helpless here," he groaned. His body went limp as the truth of Ma's comment exploded in his head. They would have to stay at least another day or two. Again they would have to sit home and wait. Now he could see the colors of the trees through the windows, and knew that the first day of waiting had begun.

"You was ever a scared of dogs," Ma said gently.

Lassie banged her tail on the floor at the soothing words.

Mim shook his arms. She began to unbutton his jacket. "Undress," she said. "They mustn't catch you like this." She poured a pailful of water into the big kettle, and shoved a new log through the top of the big range.

John stood up and looked around wildly. The great belching explosion of gasoline and his helter-skelter retreat were written all over the room. "Hurry!" he said. "Unload the truck." He started to pull his boots on again. "Oh my God. Am I foul with the smell of it? If they find us awake and all the signs . . ." He got up and blew out the lamp.

"Sit still," Mim said. "Don't be spreadin' the smell all over. And you're like to catch fire yourself, you take yourself too near the stove."

John pulled off his jacket, then his sweater. "My gloves!" he cried. He picked up the jacket and jammed an arm into the sleeve again.

Mim clapped a hand over her mouth. "Your pockets," she said. But they weren't there.

"Too late now," Ma said. "The woods are half growed in the dust of lost gloves. And what good's a glove if they find it? Ain't like you had your name on it."

"Dogs, Ma," John said, pulling his sweater back on and still searching his jacket for his gloves. "Now we've got to go. Now I fixed it so we've got to go. The gloves is just settin' out there in plain sight like a red flag."

"John," Mim said. "Undress. It's me as wants to go the worst. But now it's clear enough we can't. Not now. Now we got to just set and listen for the truck again." She took up the pails. "Not that I'm sayin' I like what you did." Without a coat, she headed out the back door toward the well.

Ma stood over John, barely leaning on her canes, and to John, looking up in the early light, it seemed that the terrible transformations of age dropped away for a moment. "Move, son, move," she urged. "Get yourself cleaned up. I'm sayin' I do like what you done. If they catch us out now, at least they'll know that Moores don't knuckle under like a pack of fools." She banged her cane with pleasure. "Nope. That's a fact. I always did know it too, from the time I met your pa. Moores don't knuckle under."

·13·

THEY PUT HIM to bed in his clothes, so that if they heard a car, they could wake him and no one would know he had been sleeping into the bright hours of morning. Mim had hauled the mattress from the truck back up to the bedroom and now he lay under Ma's old quilts watching the first fuzzy stripes of sunshine spread like gauze across the floor toward Hildie. She lay curled in a ball with her head thrown back, her cheeks chapped to a bright pink, breathing noisily through her mouth. He lay awake and tense, tuned for trucks, sirens, state cars—the final visitation that would break up everything. But all he heard beneath the great lid of winter silence was the breathing of his daughter and Mim's quick orderly steps below. Out the side door for more wood, out the front kitchen door to the barn. In again. Out again. The bars of sunshine grew shorter and more definite, tinted with blue as if filtered through ice. Wide-eyed he listened. The wind, he realized, had stopped. The wind was gone.

Presently Hildie sneezed, and sneezed again. Then suddenly she erupted from her bed and rolled into his. "Where's Mama?" she asked.

"Downstairs," he said.

"Sure?" the child asked, sitting up in her faded blue pajamas. "She said we was goin' away before I woke up."

"No, no," he said. "Listen. That's her downstairs."

Hildie listened until she heard the footsteps and the women's

189

voices, then she cuddled down close to John, her teeth chattering. "We didn't go," she said.

"Nope," he said.

"I knew it," she said happily. She put her arms around his neck and breathed into his stubby face. She was barely settled in before she said, "Time to get up."

"I know," he said, and as he said it, the drowsiness came on him so strong he could scarcely respond to the child. By the time she crawled out of his bed and scampered down the stairs to the kitchen, he was nearly asleep.

At first, as she worked, Mim trembled. She set the clothes to soak in a tubful of water, then went to the well for more water. She stoked the fire, then set the front kitchen door ajar to the icy weather so that she would be sure to hear them coming before they were upon her. Hopefully, too, the air would thin the gasoline smell in the kitchen. Ma was too excited to be shut up in the front room where it was warm. Mim wrapped her in a blanket in her chair and, glad for the company, moved her in close to the stove.

Mim washed the clothes in three different tubs, waiting impatiently each time for the water in the kettle to heat. Then she wrung them out hard and hung them from the line over the roaring stove. She and Ma rehearsed as she worked what to do when they came. Hide the clothes. The quickest way would be to stuff them into the oven. Shut the outside door. Damp the stove. Run upstairs to warn John.

Mim scrubbed the boots with a brush and yellow soap. And scrubbed them again, but couldn't get rid of the smell of gasoline. Finally she ran out to the barn and rolled the wet boots in the dust of dried cow dung and hay that still covered the floor. Then she brushed them off and took them in and hid them in a closet.

But still, with all the air and the washing, the kitchen smelled of gasoline. "The gas can, Mim," said Ma and laughed. "What a pair of dolts we be."

Mim's heart beat. She caught up the can and ran to the barn.

She rubbed the bits of dried leaves and the sticky gas stains off with her hands and thrust it into the back of the truck where it belonged. Then, rubbing her hands clean on the frozen grass, she started and straightened, as she had six times that morning, thinking she heard a car. But the wind had died and the dawn was so still she could almost hear the faint crackle as the pond skimmed over with ice. A mallard cried and she first heard the beating of its wings on water, then saw it, dark and graceful against the gray sky of the new day.

When she went inside, she stood at the door looking out over the pond as she had several times a day for twenty years. "Black ice comin', after all," she said to Ma. "And we'll be gone."

"Never mind. She'll make a pretty skater anywhere. Just like him."

Mim pictured her child grown tall, green stocking cap flying as she spun dizzily across the pond on a cloudless winter day. Was Ma remembering such an image of her own child? John a pretty skater? Those were the things you gave a child—the spirit and the pond and the memory.

Mim put her hands to her face, stunned with happiness at the fullness of her world there on the edge of the pond.

"Hey, Miriam," Ma said softly, and reached out a hand to her. "You always was such a feelin' girl."

Mim touched Ma's hand, then roused herself and set to work again. Soon she was unloading the truck, unpacking each carton entirely and throwing it into the cellar before she went to the barn for the next. She had just come out of the barn carrying the fourth carton when she heard the car coming. She ran back into the barn with the carton still in her arms and found herself standing in the horse stall wondering what to do. The truck was only half unpacked and John was sound asleep and vulnerable upstairs. Mim held her breath and listened. She could hear the low hum of the car motor, but there was no sound of car doors opening or of footsteps in the gravel. She placed the carton noiselessly beneath the window and stepped up onto it to look out.

An orange Datsun station wagon sat in the middle of their yard. Inside a bearded man, a youngish woman, and two small boys sat looking peacefully around at the barn, the pasture, the pond. They moved their lips and talked. Finally the man nodded and got out, and, with an easy smile of curiosity, strolled leisurely around the barn. Almost directly below Mim's window, he stopped to kick at a sill. Then he went back to the car and revolved slowly, examining everything he could see. His eyes stopped at the kitchen window. He grinned and waved. Hildie, Mim thought. She must be right out in plain sight. Finally, the man climbed back into the car and said something. His wife and children started laughing and waving toward the house. Finally they went away, the two children staring from the back window until the car disappeared over the hill.

Mim waited until the sound of the motor was altogether gone, then ran for the house. She dropped the carton just inside the door and stood over Ma. "How could you let Hildie stand up there in plain sight?" she demanded. "How *could* you?"

"Just tourists," Ma said. "Got to be. I never seen a bunch more like."

"In December?" Mim asked. "On a Tuesday? The next time that happens, you see she's hid and hid good, you hear?"

Ma held Hildie tight and didn't answer.

Mim went back to work, more frantically now. Before the sun was quite high, she took a breath and realized that, except for the wood superstructure on the truck—which indicated only that they were thinking of leaving sometime soon—things were back to normal. It no longer looked as if the Moores were poised to run. Clothes and food and cooking implements were all in place. Hildie sat with Ma under the blanket in the chair drawing pictures. Dirty cereal bowls and cups created a comforting litter on the table. Even John's clothes were nearly dry enough to hang on the hooks in the bedroom where they belonged.

Almost without transition, Mim found herself settled into the familiarity of everyday chores. She filled the woodbox, got in two pails of fresh water, swept the floor, and tidied up the breakfast dishes. She made herself a cup of chicory and heated up what was left of the oatmeal. Finally she closed the door so that the room began to warm up. Now there was nothing to do but wait.

Mim sniffed. "I wonder, would a fresh nose still catch the gasoline?"

"We got any onions left?" Ma asked.

Mim stooped to the onion bin beneath the sink and came up with six small onions. "Enough for one more soup," she said. Then she sighed. "I hope we get to eat it."

John woke up hungry. The bedroom looked dingy in the bleak last light that he momentarily mistook for dawn. Then he remembered and took up listening where he'd left off. Perhaps it was the sound of the auctioneer's truck that had awakened him. He stumbled to the window dragging the quilts and looked down on the empty dooryard. There was no sound, even from the kitchen, and, like Hildie, he wondered if he'd been left behind. He dropped the blankets and ran downstairs.

Mim was sweeping the kitchen for the third time. Ma and Hildie were playing cards. Hildie spilled her cards and ran to him. "You slept *all* day," she said.

"Shh," Ma said. "That's a secret. Now don't forget."

John sat down at the table, unable to speak. For a moment he couldn't remember why or how he could have risked it all.

"We had some company," Mim said, "though they seemed . . ."

John clutched the edge of the table, quizzing Mim about the visitors. Finally he got up and went out into the dooryard in his stocking feet. He shivered with the cold and looked at the sky toward the town. It was cloudy and silent, and the air in his nostrils was as fresh as wet snow. He came back in. "Nothin'," he said.

"Who knows?" Mim said. "Harlowe's a long way off."

She gave John a bowl of soup, Hildie climbed into his lap and he ate, swallowing too quickly as if he might be interrupted at any moment.

It grew dark, suppertime passed, Hildie was put to bed, and the heavy part of the night settled in for its long stay. The wind came up again. The branches on the trees in front of the house snapped free and thumped against the ground and the wind blew across the long vibrating reed of the pond, singing up and up to the pitch of sirens and screams. They listened, trying to block out the racket around them in order to detect sounds from town, or the whine of a car approaching, or the subtle rustle of footsteps in the yard.

John worked at a piece of kindling, whittling it away to nothing with his knife. Lassie snoozed on her blanket behind the stove. Ma sat wide awake in her chair. And Mim, at the table, gnawed on her fingers and did nothing.

"I keep wonderin'," John said, "how far it spread. If they found the gloves."

"Lassie'd bark if there was anyone about," Mim said.

"You remember somethin' about Gore?" John said. "True of all of them Gores. Dogs never bark at them. Never did."

Ma picked at the fringe of her blanket.

At ten they let Lassie out, then in again, and, after some discussion, decided that the least suspicious thing they could do was go to bed. Hour after hour, John, so recently awakened, lay listening. All the tumult of the night outside the windows came to him as an echo of the smashing of dry woods around him in his long flight.

Suddenly, not knowing whether he'd been full awake, he sat up and shook Mim awake. "You hear sirens?"

She listened. He could feel her shivering, as much at being shaken out of her heavy nervous sleep as at anything. "I do," she said.

But as they listened the sirens stopped and they were listening to the wind again in the tops of the bare maples.

"Sounded so close," Mim said.

"Could it still be goin'?" John asked.

"Wrong direction for the Parade," Mim said.

"The night twists things," John said. "And the wind. Could of been Powlton fire engines on the way to the Parade—"

"Or Harlowe fire engines on the way to Powlton," Mim said. "Just as like. Who knows what's burnin' where or why."

The night passed and morning came again, with sunshine and Hildie. Curiosity grew as heavy on their shoulders as fear. At twelve o'clock, taking Hildie in case they came while she was gone, Mim went to Linden's.

They rattled over the last familiar potholes in the dirt road and rolled onto the hardtop, sudden and smooth, starting abruptly in the middle of a stretch of unbroken woods like the hostile finger of the town probing the wilderness. In the blackness of the tar, she anticipated the charred ruins of the Parade. But the sunshine stretched in peaceful bands across the road, darkening the cracks and lighting up the bits of mica imbedded in it. Nothing could seem quite sinister in sunshine.

As she rounded the last clump of pines and found herself at the far corner of the Parade, she saw at once that there had been no fire. It was like waking up from a dream and finding everything the dream had upended settled back into place—restored. She tried to remember just how the dream had gone and found she couldn't.

James's house looked as empty as ever, the front blinds drawn as always and the dormers lopsided—one weathered to gray and one pink with new paint that was already peeling. Mudgett's house sat unchanged in its clutter—the six-month-old pile of lath and plaster outside the parlor window, the same stock car in the front yard, missing fenders and wheels, the big 14 dripping white paint down the door. As she drove by, craning her neck, Mudgett's wife paused with her mouth full of clothespins to peer back from her station behind the half-filled clothesline. Adeline Fayette herself stood under the American flag in front of the post office, chattering at some stranger. He was listening. He couldn't have done much besides listen, since Adeline couldn't hear.

Mim drove around the corner toward Linden's. Her back set on the three solid houses, she glanced at the still green grass on her right, at the locked town hall, Stinson's repair shop, the doctor's house with its tidy sign, and the pair of greenhouses on her left, still caved in at the peaks like broken legs. The precise normality of the Parade fell over her like a dark blanket, and she tried to remember the story her husband had told her, the drama, the far-fetched sequence. Then she thought of Agnes Cogswell, of John pitching the money into the stove, of Ma banging her cane at the tale of her family name revenged.

At the far side of the Parade she backed into Linden's parking lot and leaned on the steering wheel, gazing out across the green at the three untouched houses. No monsters, no armored tanks, no cross voices—only Harlowe Parade as she had known it ever since she could remember, glistening with sunshine at the time of year when autumn falls to winter. Hildie stood on the seat beside her, leaning on her shoulder, dreaming too, it seemed.

It was the Thursdays that were hard to come to grips with. People came to visit—familiar people, people whose mothers and children she remembered—and they smiled, and they never did so very much. The auctioneer came and looked at her and filled her with guilt.

Mim shook herself, and suddenly, like the hidden picture in a puzzle, what she should have seen immediately jumped out at her. In the space between Mudgett's place and James's, the line between orchard and sky was drawn in angry charcoal. Where the pines had been were brittle black stalks, some broken over and some pointing to the sky, like the rubble in a cornfield stripped and darkened by frost. The black extended out across the cut hay in the orchard to include half a dozen apple trees. In several places the dark river lapped at the edges of Mudgett's yard then ran away again into the woods.

Hildie pushed the door open and danced to the case which held the candy and plastic toys. She pressed her nose against it until her breath frosted up the glass and she couldn't see. Then she pulled back and started to draw a face with her finger in the mist.

"Get away from that case, Hildie," Fanny said, sitting on her high stool behind the counter, so still she seemed only a voice in the dark store.

Mim pulled the child away from the case. She had a comment planned, like the first line of a play. "Some weather for December," she managed. "Can't complain about this." She moved shakily to the milk cabinet and took out a gallon in a glass bottle. *Pulver's Dairy.* Maybe milk from her own cows. She put the bottle on the worn pine counter.

"That be all?" Fanny asked.

"No. I'll be needin' some flour," Mim said.

"Takin' a trip?" Fanny asked, nodding at the roof over the truck.

"Just considerin'," Mim said.

"Hard to say about the weather," Fanny said, writing down $1.41 for the milk on the back of a paper bag. "A good snow'd put an end to them fires."

Mim picked up a bag and found it was sugar instead of flour. She stooped to put it back.

"*If* you want to put an end to them," Fanny said.

Mim turned, frowning. "Fires?" she repeated, feeling the heaviness of her motions, sensing she had answered too slowly, wondering if she had already given John away.

"Ayyup," Fanny said. "Some year for accidents, this one. Most beyond belief."

"You say you had a fire?" Mim asked, standing at the counter holding out three crumpled dollar bills. Hildie was whining and pulling on her hand, trying to drag her toward the candy case.

"You mean you ain't heard?" Fanny said.

Mim shook her head.

"Well, don't know how you would, all alone up there. Guess you ain't got no phone these days?"

Mim shook her head again.

"You stop that now, Hildie," Fanny said, handing the child a Mars bar with a greasy wrapper. "These here are gettin' kinda old. Now no more fussin', hear?" She turned to Mim and took the money. "Comes of bein' the only child. You always spare the rod when you got only the one. You put too high a value on them."

"What about the fire?" Mim asked softly.

"Up to Gore's."

"Gore's!"

"Yep. Funny thing. House burned to the ground. But that old barn ain't touched. Got a charmed life, that barn of Toby's."

"Anyone hurt?"

"Hard to say at first."

Mim took the change without counting it to see whether Fanny had charged her for the candy bar. She stared at Fanny.

Fanny chuckled. "They thought Bob was cooked, 'cause he weren't nowhere to be found. Then they took note that that spiffy new truck with the sirene was gone too. And they found the old man in the barn. He just took a blanket and moved right in. His everlastin' cows. All he ever cared about, his cows. That barn's goin' to collapse on him, first big snow. You wait."

Mim tried to think of something to say. "He's gettin' on the old side to be livin' all alone," she said.

Fanny shrugged. "You don't figure Bobby'll be that eager to come back? Guess the old man's goin' to fall on the town after all. Nineteen kids and not a one worth a plugged nickel."

Mim smiled uneasily.

"Or maybe that auctioneer there'll do for him. Ought to, you ask me."

Trying to sort out the pieces, to think how John's fire could have burned down Gore's place, Mim stood at the counter holding her bag of flour, and let the silence stretch too far. "I guess so," she murmured. "Tough luck."

Fanny shoved the brown paper bag with the milk and flour across the counter toward Mim with a sharp look. "Breaks your heart, don't it, dearie," she said.

Mim's heart somersaulted. She took the bag in one arm and crowded Hildie toward the door with the other.

"There's a firebug loose, all right," Fanny added. "Tried to set the whole Parade alight the night before."

Mim looked back. "What?" she said.

"You heard me. Take a look up yonder past Mudgett's. You mean that's not what you was lookin' at, sittin' in the truck afore you come in?"

Mim threw another look over her shoulder at Fanny, unable to answer. Outside, she stood by the gas pump openly squinting once again at the charred spikes of trees clinging to the hill beyond Mudgett's.

That night after Hildie was in bed, Mim sat at the table turning and turning a mug of birch tea. "We've got to go now," she said. "Tomorrow's Thursday."

"All my life, livin' near forests, I never saw a forest fire," John said. "Remember the fires in Bar Harbor? The 4H was ever after us about fire, like they figured we'd be trippin' over fires every load of wood we cut." He had his knife out and the bark peeled off a new maple stick, but he was stabbing at the table, leaving a circle of small raw marks. "A forest fire. I figured a forest fire ate up houses like kindlin' sticks. I figured a forest fire went—"

"John!" Mim cried. "Tomorrow's Thursday. At the very least, they'll be comin' after the truck. Will you set your mind to that?"

John looked at her absently and went on talking. "They got no dogs at Gore's these days. No dogs to warn them . . ."

Lassie, thinking she was summoned, struggled to her feet and waddled to the table wagging her tail. John ignored her.

"John," Mim asked suddenly, lowering her voice and leaning closer to him. "Was it you set that one too?"

"What a question, Miriam," Ma snapped. "Wasn't you up there sleepin' with him the whole night through?"

"But, John," Mim cried, "if they figure out you set the one, they'll lay the blame on you for Gore's as well. They're like to come for *you* tomorrow, let alone the truck."

John got up, paced to the door and looked out into the darkness. "I didn't set but one fire, and that one fizzled," he said. "But, could be I set a good idea goin'. There's plenty have the same reason's us to want trouble for Gore."

"Sit down, for the love of God," Mim cried, springing up herself, then sitting down again. "You make a perfect target there." She pressed her palms to her eyes. "I wish we had some shades."

"Well, for myself, I'd rather burn up in my bed than be turned out like a tramp," Ma said.

"We plan to *take* your bed, Ma," Mim said, "or at least the cushions. John, why can't we go? Now. Tonight."

But John wasn't listening. His eyes were bright. He was carving away at the kindling now.

"John!" Mim cried. "Lord sake. You're actin' both of you like you lost your wits. Tomorrow they'll take the truck for sure. And then we *will* be stuck. Stuck! And you keep settin' like we had a world of time to kill."

John threw his knife on the table and stood up again. "We go and he'll say, 'Look, the Moores are runnin'. Must be them.' Perly don't give a damn who done it really. All he needs is a body to crucify."

"But if we go . . ." Mim started.

"How far do you reckon we'd get with the truck lookin' the way it looks? Lucky to make it to Powlton."

"If he's goin' to crucify a Moore," Ma said, "I'd sooner he found us at home than runnin' like so many hippies."

Mim slammed down her cup so that the tea leaped out and spattered on the table. "What about Hildie?" she cried. "You just sit here and wait when you know sooner or later . . . It's her they'll come for." She dropped her forehead on the table. "At least in the truck, we'd stand a chance."

The wind blew hard all night, and John, listening as the hours passed, kept thinking he heard sirens and alarm bells, even the crackling of fire. Hildie, Mim, and Ma. He kept counting them over. He listened to Hildie's labored mouth breathing and felt Mim's warm foot resting against his knee as she slept. Ma, sleeping alone downstairs, made him uneasy. He wanted to bring her up into the little room with the rest of them so that he could count her life over too in the sound of her breath. He kept hearing cars in the dooryard, footsteps in the gravel, the sound of rifles being cocked. He remembered stories of people held prisoner in farm-houses—torture, rape, children tossed on bayonets. In the cities they shot people walking down the streets. In Vietnam they had shot whole villages.

At some point, lying in his own sweat, he pulled Mim to him and said, "We'll go, Mim. We'll go. You're right. We'll go first thing tomorrow before they come."

But in the brave light of morning, he stood at the door watching the wind feathering the needles across the tops of the enormous white pines lining the pond. They were twisted and scarred and halfway ruined, yet Ma always called them the "virgin pines." A bunch of them had gone over like dominoes in the 1938 hurricane. He had climbed on a chair when he was smaller than Hildie and

watched through the window. And even after that, the ones that
still stood they called "virgin pines." Maybe the point was that if
you stood through enough you would come back to something like
what you started from. If you lost everything but the main trunk
itself, there was some mysterious return to sweetness. Hildie was
telling Ma a story about tree frogs. That was sweetness—Hildie
and the spring erupting every year the same, fed by the earth that
had always kept them. He had always planned to die on his land,
sooner or later.

"We'll just sit tight and see if what you think's goin' to happen
really happens," he said, and turned to stand fast against Mim's
flaring temper.

But Mim wasn't listening to him. She had stopped midway in
one of her journeys across the kitchen and was standing, her eyes
glazed, listening to something outside.

John and Ma caught their breath and listened too.

"Tractor comin'," Ma said.

"No," Mim said. "Somethin' bigger."

The high hard groan grew suddenly louder as the invisible
machine crested the hill and began to move steadily down the road
toward them.

The sound dulled momentarily, then burst forth anew in a
harsher gear. There was a high whine, a lull, then a shuddering
crash giving way again to the grumble of the motor.

"Jesus," John said. He grabbed his jacket from the hook and set
off down the lawn at a run.

"That's our woods," Mim gasped. She fixed Hildie with her eyes
and said, "You stay here. I'm goin' too."

Mim caught up with John as he crossed the bridge over the
stream. They ran together around the bend and started up the
hill.

The bulldozer was smashing out the beginning of a new road
where an old logging trail had been. It had knocked over a dozen
spindly birches and was running a sizable pine off to one side.

"They can't do that," John cried, but his voice was sucked away
by the commotion of the bulldozer. "They can't *do* that!"

He started to run again. "John!" Mim called, and then ran after him. At the edge of the raw space, John stopped, insignificant as one more tree beside the huge yellow machine. The driver wasn't anyone they knew. A sign stenciled on the door said, "Lynch, Inc., Concord."

John signaled to the high cab, but the machine just backed up and made another rush.

John loosened Mim's hold on his arm. When the buldozer moved again, he ran into the clearing in front of it and stood windmilling his arms at the driver.

"Johnny," Mim screamed. She started after him, but stopped when she saw the ram of the machine bearing down on her. The bulldozer came to within eight feet of John, then stopped.

The driver rolled down his window. "Out of the way," he shouted over the roar of the machine.

"It's my land," John shouted back. "You can't do this."

The man was big and overweight and ordinary. He could have been from Harlowe, though he wasn't. "Look," he hollered. "You them characters squattin' in that house down by the pond? I been warned about you. This is what they told me you'd do. Well give up, will you? You can't argue with a bulldozer."

"It's my land," John insisted. "I'll get the law on you."

"Look," said the man, cutting the motor and leaning out further. "I got my orders from the president of the corporation. He wants a road in here and four house lots. And the guy he sent up here with me last week to mark it off's a cop in Harlowe. If he don't know who the land belongs to—"

"What corporation?" John said. "President of what corporation?"

"Perly Acres?" said the man sarcastically.

"Perly Dunsmore's a crook and so is every cop in town."

"Oh yeah?" said the man. "Funny, they told me you'd say that too. You must a pulled this before, huh? The big cheese showed me his deed, Mac. The cop showed me his badge. Now who'm I supposed to believe?"

John stood silent.

When it looked as though the man was about to start up again, Mim cried, "But it *is* our land."

The man looked at her and at John. "Sorry you feel that way," he said. He began to roll up his window.

Suddenly John came alive. He leaped onto the step leading to the cab. "You son of a bitch," he screamed. "I'll kill you!"

"You will, will you?" said the man, looking down at John from his high perch. "Guess I'll worry about that when I see a gun. The cop claims you're one of them peace types that don't keep guns."

The engine raced and the man eased it forward again, aiming at a large beech only a few feet from where Mim was standing. John jumped free of the machine, and he and Mim backed into the road.

The bulldozer made such a racket that they didn't hear the car until it was practically upon them. It swept past without hesitating —a blue Dodge with two people in it.

"Hildie!" Mim cried. "She's just settin' there with Ma." She started off down the hill toward the house at a hard run. At the bridge she had to stop, a pain knotting in her side with every breath. John pounded past her and she ran again, stumbling.

The Dodge had stopped in the dooryard, but the two people were still sitting in it. John stopped in back of the car and Mim joined him without speaking. Looking down into the low car, they watched a white-haired couple pass a thermos cup of something steamy back and forth, gazing around them as though they were parked to look at a Scenic Vista.

When the woman caught sight of John and Mim, she started slightly, then laughed and spoke to her husband. She opened the car door and stepped out a bit stiffly. "How do you do?" she said. "We're the Larsons—Jim and Martha. We're thinking of buying into Perly Acres, and we're interested in the site of the recreation center. Is that the barn they plan to make over? Does that bulldozer up there mean they're really on schedule? You know," she said with a short laugh, "when you're as old as we are, you can't afford to . . ."

Mim's face had gone taut with astonishment. She felt John stiffen beneath her hand, then expand gradually as he took a deep breath.

"Get off my land!" he roared, taking a step toward the woman. "I'll wring his goddamn neck for sendin' you up here."

"Heavenly days," murmured the woman, backing hastily into the car and pulling the door to after her. Her husband fumbled

hurriedly with the car and managed to get it going with a jolt. He
made a hazardous U-turn and rumbled off up the road.

John paced the kitchen as if it were a cage. Hildie retreated to a
corner with a blanket and sucked her thumb. Ma sat in the chair,
shivering and ignored. And Mim, determined that they must go—
that nothing mattered now but that they go—silently arranged and
rearranged the things they had to take, trying to make it possible
for them to sweep everything into the truck and go in two
minutes flat as soon as John said the word.

The caterwauling of the bulldozer filled the room. When they
spoke, their voices were dimmed as if with distance and, although
they could see the trees by the edge of the pond bending and
straightening, they could hear the wind only in the pauses between
the bulldozer's assaults.

At about ten, a truck glided into the yard, materializing on the
waves of sound as if it were perfectly silent. Mim swept Hildie
into her arms, then paused. It was Mickey Cogswell, alone. "He
wouldn't be the one to . . ." she said.

John put his knife on the table and went out. Mim stuffed
Hildie into the chair beside Ma. "Now don't say a word, hear? Not
one word."

Hildie hid her face in her grandmother's lap. "Stop tellin' me. I
know," she cried, her shout muffled by the folds of Ma's dressing
gown.

Cogswell didn't get out of the truck, just opened the door and
waited. His flesh and clothes were stained dark gray. The lines on
his face were traced in black and his eyes were rimmed with red.

"What on earth . . . ?" Mim asked as she approached. Then she
smelled the smoke on him.

He shook his head. "God knows," he said. "The whole town's
goin' up in smoke. We been fightin' a fire at Sonny Pike's. Not
enough he gets shot, but now forty acres of his pine are gone and
his barn's started. Seems like the house is a goner too. Then there
was fire bustin' through the roof of Pulver's barn when I went by.
They was wettin' down the house, but it's attached and the wind's

all wrong." Cogswell stopped and rubbed his face, pushing the soot into dark streaks.

The wail of the bulldozer rose and fell around them. Cogswell shook his head. "Perly sic that on you?"

John stood with his arms folded. He nodded.

"Couldn't even wait . . ."

"We ain't goin'," John said. "Thought I told you that."

Cogswell looked at John, his blue eyes more focused than they had been in months.

"What I want to know is what you're doin' here," John said, "with your deputy buddies in all that trouble?"

"Well, you know, they got the Powlton fire department now, and Babylon and Walker comin'. Trouble is, we just heard that the Ward place they cut up and sold—that's on fire too, in a couple of different places, and it's way to the other side of town. That was about the last straw. Me and James and Stone and a bunch of other deputies with houses of their own to worry about took off. Poor Sonny was jumpin' around screamin' at us to help. But I got visions of my own dry fields. Half of them ain't even cut this year. And some of them from Powlton quit workin' too and got to arguin' about whose town is it anyway, and why should they risk their necks with us takin' off. Meantime, the fire's runnin' up the hill curlin' up trees like leaves, workin' its way up to the Geness place."

John stood listening, his face grim.

Cogswell ran his hands through his hair. "If I shoot off the shotgun three times, will you come give me a hand?" He glanced at Mim, then at John. "Look," he said, swallowing, "I know it's your side settin' them fires. And I don't say my side ain't got it comin', but does that mean you and me got to be at war?" He reached for John and touched his sleeve. "What can I do, Johnny? There's no fire department left to come."

John looked up the road toward the sound of the bulldozer, considering. "So, half the town's on fire," he said slowly.

Cogswell pulled himself wearily around behind the wheel. "Maybe you're right, Johnny," he said, slamming the door. "We don't any of us deserve to live till mornin'."

205

As he headed up the road, Mim ran past John to the truck and pulled the door open, running to keep up with it. "Why don't you all leave, Mickey?" she cried.

"I can't, Mim," he said, braking to a stop. "Agnes keeps askin' till I can't hardly stand it. But I can't. How can I? It's just another way of dyin'."

John came up behind Mim and leaned past her to grasp Cogswell's arm. "You hear that fellow up there knockin' over my woods?" he asked. "You think you can do somethin' about that?"

Cogswell looked startled. Then he fingered the gun in his holster and took a deep breath. "Yeah," he said. "Guess maybe I can. I can try anyhow." And, instead of going home, Cogswell turned around and went back up the hill toward the bulldozer.

John and Mim stood together in the yard, listening. The bulldozer stopped work almost immediately. There were no shots and they were too far away to hear voices. Presently, the big motor roared again, then gradually began to recede.

Mim looked at John. "He was only up there an hour," she said.

"This time," John said.

Mickey drove past them with a grin. John returned his salute with a shout of reassurance.

The wind curled around the chimney and slid off the steep roof with a whine. It rattled the doors and worried the plastic over the windows. In the room that had been Hildie's, splinters of glass continued to pull away from around the bullet hole and sift to the floor. The rest of the day passed somehow and no one else came.

"Thursday gone," Mim said in their bedroom that night, "and no one from Perly except that bulldozer."

"Fires are keepin' them busy," John said. "But you can bet Perly's already switchin' and schemin' how to have us dead and buried one way or the other, all of us, deputies included. And him left to sell off the whole empty town."

It was so cold they took Hildie into their bed and piled her quilts over their own for warmth. Impatiently, they waited for the long night to pass. Finally, the dawn appeared over the frost line on the windows and they could see gray clouds blowing like dust balls over a dead-white morning sky.

"Snow up there," Mim said. "We ought to go this mornin' quick, before we get snowed in."

"Back of that truck'd be cold as the bottom of a well," John said.

"We'll get a stove in Concord. You said yourself he's goin' to bury us all, and we're the first ones in his path." She was pleading now. "Johnny, please."

John got up without answering, pulled on his overalls and jacket and went down to see to the stoves. After breakfast, he took up a stick and his knife. Hildie climbed up next to him and watched, wide-eyed and still, as one by one the chips fell away and the stick disappeared.

Mim pulled on her jacket and went out to the well for water. "That snow won't wait," she insisted when she came back. "It's comin' any minute and here we'll be." She was fretful and peevish. She kept making work for herself in the kitchen, then abandoning it halfway through. "We're gettin' this one last chance," she kept saying. "And you two won't budge."

"Go then," said Ma. "You and the child."

"How can I, Ma?" moaned Mim. "And leave you and Johnny here?"

The clouds piled up overhead thick as pudding. They waited all morning for the next move. But nothing happened. Even the snow held off.

Four o'clock was already darkening into another night. They heard the motor and said nothing. Mim swept up Hildie, lifted their coats off their hooks, and moved to the door.

It was the yellow truck. She stared, half believing that what she saw was only one more repetition of the vision she had suffered so often during the long days of waiting. It was not until the truck was so close that she could pick out the features of Dunsmore and Mudgett that she took Hildie's arm and rushed her out the back door.

207

Ma made her way into the kitchen and stood by the sink, upright between her canes. John stood behind the closed door waiting.

Perly led the way up the walk, unarmed as always, moving with big-boned ease. He was a perfect target for a sniper hiding, say, behind the unmended upstairs window. As if he read John's thought, Mudgett, following warily behind the auctioneer, his hand near his gun, glanced upward at the second-story windows, then with a quick darting motion, turned to his left to check the dark opening to the barn.

John opened the door himself and the two men stepped inside and stopped with their backs to the door, the cold spreading from them.

"Where are Mim and Hildie?" Perly asked.

"Gone," John said.

Perly raised an eyebrow and considered. "Harlowe's filled with trouble lately," he said.

"Guess you heard about the fires all right, seven of them in a week and a couple more that never got goin' good," Mudgett said in his quick high voice. "And that bloody fool of a Gore took off."

John said nothing. He stood perfectly still with his hands in his pockets.

"That makes Red here, as first deputy, the acting police chief," Perly said, looking Mudgett over as if for the first time.

Mudgett stood rocking nervously on his toes as if to the rhythms of a transistor radio in his head. "Relax, Johnny," he said. "We ain't collectin'." He gave a short laugh. "Unless collectin' people counts."

Both John and Ma listened impassively.

"People are getting panicky," Perly said. "With good reason. We have to do something to keep the town safe. Somebody clearly has to take some initiative to straighten things out. And I've grown so attached to this town . . ."

"We want to know who's settin' them fires," Mudgett said. "I hear tell you been lettin' your temper hang out lately, Johnny. You got any idea who it could be?"

"Who, me?" John said.

"It's the lightning strikin', Red Mudgett," Ma said, turning on

Mudgett almost with relief, her voice confident against the man she had known as a child. "It's the lightning strikin', and it's a goin' to come after you too. Just you wait."

"Mrs. Moore," Perly said reproachfully. "Red lost the ell on his house last night."

"And it ain't lightning neither, Mrs. Moore. It's some two-legged skunk. One that ain't long for this world, I promise you."

"We haven't decided yet what to do," Perly said. "We've called a meeting for tonight in the town hall to talk things over. We really need you as one of the old families. All of you," he added, looking around, "if Mim and Hildie come back."

Ma took a step toward Red Mudgett. "Goin' to set fire to the whole lot of us at once, that's what," she said. "I wouldn't put it past you."

Mudgett snapped his fingers. "Maybe we oughta take the truck after all, Perly," he said, watching Ma.

Perly turned half-hooded eyes on Mudgett. "We can't do a thing for the town till we get it back to normal," he said. "Just keep that in mind." He kept looking around the kitchen as if he half expected to find Mim and Hildie hidden in some corner—at Ma in her flannel robe leaning on her nicked canes, at the mutilated kindling stick on the table, at Hildie's hair ribbon and rag doll in Ma's lawn chair. "You will come?" he asked John. "We need all the input we can get. And what we don't need is more trouble."

John took his knife from his pocket and began absently stabbing at the table with it.

Mudgett gathered himself together and stood still, but Perly, his eyes on John's face, continued to wait for an answer.

"I'll think about it," John said without looking up.

"Good enough," Perly said, showing his teeth in a smile. He turned back toward the door. "See you there."

"If not . . ." Mudgett said, and flicked the gun in its holster with his trigger finger so that John reflexively stepped back. Mudgett grinned.

Perly moved quickly down the path without a backward glance. Mudgett danced behind him, side-stepping and wheeling to keep a constant eye on John.

·14·

THE PARADE was so crowded they had to park the truck half a block away. Hildie danced on ahead, but not too far, excited and a little awed by the experience of being out after dark. Mim and John, one on each side, helped Ma as she limped down the road and up the long sidewalk toward the door of the town hall.

"I got a feelin' there'll be nothin' but cinders left to go home to," Mim said.

John said nothing.

"That there's a man thinks he's God. Thinks he can move the mountains and dry up the seas," Ma said. "And there's them as believes him too."

"Not me, Ma," John said. "But you might's well sign a confession as stay home."

Ma snorted. "He thinks we're nought but a passel of witless ninnies, and we ain't done nothin' to show him otherwise."

They moved slowly. People piled up behind them and stepped around them. A number stopped to say, "Why, Mrs. Moore, how you doin'?" as if they were half surprised to find her still alive. The men she had taught as boys in Sunday School, and the women she had made bridal bouquets for—some were deputies and some were not, but they all greeted Ma as if she were part of some prior life, before the town had been drawn off into parties.

The town hall served also as the theater and the movie house and the gymnasium and the selectmen's office. It was heated by a crackling wood stove with a bright stainless steel exhaust pipe that ran glittering half the length of the room before it turned into the cinderblock chimney. The folding wooden chairs, the same ones they used for auctions, were set up in rows facing the stage.

They settled Ma in the middle of the hall. She took off her kerchief, unbuttoned her coat, and settled her canes between her knees. Then she peered nearsightedly around her, looking for Hildie.

Hildie had found the French children and tagged after them as they clambered up the stairs of the stage and jumped off of it. The Frenches looked unkempt. The smallest boy had a large rip in the knee of his overalls and his black boots were mended with adhesive tape. The doctor's daughter, a tall shy child about ten, walked slowly toward the other children, sucking the end of her pigtail. Finally, with a grand burst, Cogswell's three youngest joined the fray.

Mim fretted. "Fetch her back," she said to John.

"Let her be," Ma said. "What harm can come to her here?" Ma hadn't been to town since the day they'd gone to church. She kept recognizing people and asking about others. And now and then someone would lean over her to ask in a whisper about her health. It seemed to comfort them to find her there. She sat up stiffly in her chair. "Everyone's here," she said, "just like always."

Mim nodded. "Whatever they have in mind, we won't be alone."

The adults were subdued, and the shouts of the children stood out in sharp relief. Presently, Walter French approached his children and herded them to their seats on the side, watching the back door from the corner of his eye.

Mim turned her head to see what he was looking at. What she saw was a proper city policeman in a navy blue uniform with a light blue shirt, a peaked cap, and a badge.

John snickered beside her. "Red Mudgett playin' dressups," he said. "Bobby had more sense."

Mim looked again. The policeman was rocking just slightly on his feet and chewing gum. She stumbled into the aisle and ran to the front to catch up Hildie.

With Hildie safely in her lap, Mim felt the strength in her own body. She still had that. She could still run. She felt she had the energy to run for miles—away from everything. As a girl, when she had first known John, she used to run across the fields, through the woods, around the pond. She remembered the way the long muscles had obeyed her. She had known that in some way it would come to this—to the old woman and the child, John and his land, nailing her in place like a deerskin stretched on a wall. And yet she had always come back.

Mudgett stepped quickly up the stairs and onto the stage. His glance flickered from side to side. He moved precisely to the center of the stage and stood on the line where the maroon curtain closed when it was pulled, under the big painted plaster town shield that Linden's grandfather had designed and donated in the days when the store did a good business and he was one of the richest men in town. To his left was the American flag, to his right the flag of New Hampshire.

His blank-eyed contemplation of the townspeople snuffed out the last noise in the hall so that even the chairs barely creaked. Mim noticed suddenly that Perly Dunsmore was sitting three rows in front of them, way over to the right. He sat as still as the others, his eyes resting easily on Mudgett as though he were watching images on a screen.

When Mudgett spoke, the people of Harlowe found that the man before them was no longer an old schoolmate or neighbor, but a tough vice-squad cop—anonymous, steely, professionally mean—a figure familiar to everyone from the late movie reruns.

"The Harlowe Police Department has called this special town meeting because there's an arsonist loose in this town," he began in correct, snarling, radio-announcer English, his usual quick tenor speech lost entirely. "Well, we're planning to catch him, but we need your help."

John crossed and uncrossed his legs uncomfortably, and Mim

glanced sideways at him in a warning to be still.

"For a start," Mudgett said, "you've got to stop wandering around at night. That way everyone can sleep safe—at least everyone who doesn't happen to be on the police force. If we find anybody more than fifty yards from home after dark, we're going to assume he's up to no good. Until we stop these fires, you're not going to be in any mood for partying anyhow. So just stay home after sunset. We'll send someone round every night to make sure you all got home all right."

Mudgett chewed on his gum for a moment and glanced around the room, touching only on the familiar faces of his fellow deputies. "The other thing we're going to do is keep track of the people coming in and out of Harlowe. We're going to put roadblocks on the seven roads out of Harlowe. So try to stay in Harlowe. If you really have to go somewhere, give us a call and we'll be expecting you." He paused. "Can't think why you need to go anywhere though. Linden's got most everything a body needs." Mudgett waited as if he expected some response.

There was none. The people in the hall barely stirred.

"So that's the deal," he said, almost lapsing into his normal voice. "And just to show we mean business, Perly's got a gift for the town. So, uh . . ." Mudgett scowled at Perly.

Perly stood and side-stepped out along the row, excusing himself to the people he moved past. Wearing his everyday green work clothes, he climbed the stairs up to the stage, with Dixie trotting prettily at his heel. He took over Mudgett's place in the center of the stage, and Dixie traced out a circle beside him and lay down with a sigh. Mudgett moved over and stood in the lee of the American flag. Perly frowned as he squinted out over the people.

"Some of you have sunk so low, you've been setting fire to your own town," Perly announced sternly, his voice cutting through the stillness in the hall and making everyone sit up a little straighter. Perly looked out into the watching faces, absorbing their expressions as if the proper degree of guilt would register by setting off an alarm in his head.

"Isn't that right, Paul?" he said.

Paul Geness let the child in his lap slide to the floor. He squinted up at Perly with his close-set brown eyes. Geness had eleven children. He managed by looking after the town dump and salvaging what other people threw away.

"I said, 'Isn't that right, Paul?'"

Geness opened his mouth but didn't answer.

"I know it hasn't been easy," Perly cried. "But we're undergoing the fastest change in the history of civilization. All I want to do is harness that change. Make it work for all of us. And I pride myself I've made a beginning. A fine beginning." Perly raised his fist and slammed it down into his other hand. "But since when have the people of Harlowe been so fond of their creature comforts? Since when have the people of Harlowe been afraid of a little hard work? Since when?"

Perly's voice grew louder and deeper. "A few have even run away. Well, damn it, if they're that low-minded, we don't want them. Do we, Frank?" he asked, pointing a strong brown finger at Frank Lovelace, a stocky man who had been a fairly efficient truck farmer before the auctions.

Lovelace was not a talkative man, and now he shifted in his chair, tightened his lips, and swallowed.

"And now this madness," the auctioneer cried, his voice seeming to come from everywhere at once. "This insanity. This lunacy." He shook his head as if to rid himself of his vision, then looked out over the people with an intensity that made them turn away from him.

He pulled a sheaf of bills from his shirt pocket. "Well, here's three thousand dollars," he said. He held the bills high so that everyone could see that they were hundred-dollar bills. "Three thousand dollars," he repeated, playing his eyes over the crowd. "Anyone gone by your place at an odd hour? Anyone smelling of gasoline lately? Anyone in your house acting peculiar this last week?"

Perly focused on a heavily made-up woman sitting next to her husband, who had recently had a leg amputated after falling under his tractor. "What do you say, Jane Collins? Do you know anyone sleeping all day?" he asked. "Do you?"

She dropped her eyes and shook her head. Her husband gripped his crutches and looked at the chair in front of him.

"Let us know," Perly said, his voice low and smooth. "We'll pay cash and we'll pay in secret. Trust us." He snapped the elastic band back around the bills and returned them to his pocket so that the figure "100" poked out with its elegant elongated zeros.

"Does anyone have any questions?" Perly asked.

No one made any noticeable move, but no one was quite still either, and the stiff folding chairs gave off a sound like radio static.

"Well, then, we ask you for your own protection to get right on home. The deputies will be making rounds in about half an hour to make sure you all arrive safely."

The people of Harlowe sat in their chairs as though they had not heard their dismissal.

"Good night," Perly said more gently. "We're all in this together. Let's try to remember Harlowe's heritage of strength and courage. We'll make a new beginning yet."

Perly started off the stage, and very slowly the people in the hall began to pull their coats around their shoulders and stand up.

"Hey there, young fellow," said a voice from behind the Moores. "Them proposals you're makin'. They supposed to be laws or what?" It was Sam Parry. His sky-blue eyes were as piercing as ever, but he was less ruddy than usual after taking a bullet in the shoulder during hunting season. "We goin' to get a chance to vote on them new rules?"

Perly paused and smiled a moment at Sam before he returned to the center of the stage. "Vote, Sam?" he said. "Who could possibly object? Simple temporary regulations for the protection of all of us. But, of course, if you think we should take a vote, let's take a vote." Perly looked out at the townspeople as though they were co-conspirators. "Why not?" he said. "All in favor, say 'Aye.'"

There was a pause, then Ian James shouted a throaty aye and there were scattered echoes around the room.

"All opposed, say 'Nay.'"

There was silence in the room.

215

"Sam?" Perly said at last, raising an eyebrow in challenge to the old man.

"Well, I'm opposed," Sam said abruptly and sat down.

After a pause, Ma lifted her cane high and pointed it unsteadily at Perly. "I'd just like to know why it's you, Mr. Perly Dunsmore, that wants so bad to catch that firebug," she cried, her voice harsh with effort. "Ain't nobody set fire to your house."

Fanny Linden, sitting in front of the Moores, ducked to avoid the cane, and Mim grabbed at it and lowered it to the floor against Ma's struggles.

"Mrs. Moore," Perly cried, his hard face twisted, "how can you ask? Harlowe is my town. You were here and never had a choice, but I *chose* Harlowe. After twenty years in forty different countries, I chose Harlowe to be my home. And to a bachelor like me, a community is mother, father, son, and daughter. It's my family."

Dixie turned nervously at Perly's side, but Perly stood easily. "Now I know what's going on in the world. And if you turn on your television set at night, almost any night, you can see too. You see a picture of young America—usually violence, rebellion, shouting obscenities. This is the new wave. These things are happening everywhere. But Harlowe—Harlowe is hanging on to the old ways. And now this quality of life—this treasuring of human values—is in danger. Nothing can be the same with everyone living in terror of his neighbors. And, if a place isn't good for my neighbors, it's not going to be good for me either. That's why I care, Mrs. Moore. I can't think of a better use for my money than to save our community."

"He gave the town the ambulance, didn't he?" called Tom Pulver, a short barrel-chested man who had lost his barn and part of his house in the fires.

"And glad enough I was too, when my father took pneumonia," said Vera Janus.

Perly watched, his eyes unblinking as onyx.

Sam Parry was standing again. "Course, if you ain't got a phone, you can't phone up for the ambulance. Not that I'm complainin'. My old jeep was plenty good enough to get me to the hospital. And, of course, ain't nobody offered a reward yet for the damn fool as shot me. And it ain't strictly necessary neither to be wanderin' about in the dark to get shot at these days. I managed it just by goin' out to my own pump house in broad daylight, now, didn't I?" Sam put his good hand to his forehead and shook his white mane vigorously. "But I'm gettin' off the track. Just like me to be gettin' off the track."

Sam paused and the crowd murmured.

"Anyhow," he went on, "what it was I wanted to say is how come it's Perly up there? He ain't town moderator, as I recall. He ain't a selectman. Why he ain't even a cop, though we got so many nowadays. What the dickens is he doin' runnin' this here town meetin'?" Sam finished and scowled around at his neighbors.

The answer came, finally, from Ian James, a burly deputy who had been elected to serve as selectman for eight terms running. "Jimmy Carroll's supposed to be moderator," he said, standing in his place behind the Moores. "And he's moved away. As for selectmen, Ward's out of town, and old Ike Linden's been sick. So looks like that leaves me. And I hereby appoint Perly moderator. And anyway, it's only regular town meetin's got to be run that way. And it's Red, not Perly, who's runnin' the meetin'."

Perly smiled gently at Sam. "Who'd you have in mind, Sam?" he asked. "Yourself, perhaps?"

Slowly, the old man sat down. There was no laughter. The rows of faces tilting toward the auctioneer were stolid and noncommittal.

Mudgett stepped up to Perly and darted a sideways glance at him. "I guess we all ought to give Perly a hand," he announced.

Again, nobody moved.

Perly pulled himself up and his black eyes seemed to penetrate and tally the refusal of every person there to start the applause. "Of course you feel angry," he acknowledged. "Some of you even suspect that I'm personally to blame. You need to blame someone for the evils of the twentieth century—and you include these fires among them.

"But, believe me, someday you'll understand what I've been doing. Movers and shakers have always had their enemies at first.

217

Five years from now, in the new Harlowe, every person in town will leap at the chance to give me a standing ovation."

Dixie got to her feet and shook herself, and Perly moved smoothly toward the New Hampshire flag and the steps down into the audience.

"Wait just a minute," said someone near the back and everyone turned, recognizing the voice instantly—the flat matter-of-fact voice of one complacent in his power. It was Dr. Hastings. "Harlowe's got more cops per capita these days than New York City," he said. "It's got three sophisticated patrol cars, a radio-alert system, and a network of what we used to call 'informers,' which seems to include about half of Harlowe. I'd like to know why, with a force like that, the cops are having so much trouble catching one lousy firebug."

"Give us a chance," said Ezra Stone. The big deputy sat on a high stool near the wood stove with his arms folded. "Don't worry. We'll catch him."

"And," said the doctor, without even turning to nod to Stone, "as the doctor around here, I'd like to know how come the more cops we get, the more accident prone we seem to become."

Perly had returned to the center of the stage and stood there, his eyes glistening on the doctor.

Dr. Hastings peered back unflinching behind his glasses. "And incidentally," he added, "I'd also like to know why so many of my longest-standing patients are moving out of town."

"If you want to make comparisons," Perly said in his cool luminous voice, "have you looked at the per capita statistics for New York City on arson—let alone mugging, rape, murder, armed robbery? Why a New Yorker can hardly expect to get through a month in peace. Harlowe may be facing the first serious problem in its history, but most places are exploding with crime. And the reason, Doctor, that we're better off than most, is that in a country town like this people act promptly before things get out of hand."

Perly held out his arms to include all the people in the hall. "People in the country know what brotherhood means," he said.

"Everyone takes an interest in his neighbors. It's the good will in a town like this that's going to help us put an end to these fires. And, as for moving around, people still don't move around half as—"

"There he goes again," shouted Ma. "Standin' words on their head. Down comes out up. Wrong comes out right. Shoot you in the back comes out the Sermon on the Mount."

Perly shook his head at Ma. "Slipping," he commented to the doctor.

John sprang from his seat and stood facing the auctioneer.

"Ask him about the auctions," Sam Parry growled before John could think what to say.

"The auctions?" asked Perly, breaking into a jaunty smile and ignoring John. "Now you're on my favorite subject. What about them? Never a town loved an auction like Harlowe. When I came here, I had in mind three—maybe four—auctions. But you folks just wouldn't let me quit. Oh, I paid for everything. Maybe that's why you kept showering stuff on me. All I did was float along on the crest of the wave. And a wonderful ride it was—the most American experience anyone can have. It's like the very eye of a hurricane—where the sellers and buyers come to terms."

"Ask him how bloody much he paid," Sam Parry shouted.

Perly turned on him with his quick black look, then gestured to the people in the hall with quiet control. "Nobody has ever complained," he said slowly. "Of course, I am a newcomer. My knowledge of prices around here is limited. But just let me ask. Is there anyone here who ever complained?"

In the silence, a log settled in the wood stove with a crash. Perly, standing light on the toes of his boots, leaned down over the people spread out below him. "Did anyone ever complain?" he repeated.

Finally, he put his hand on Dixie's head and turned to Mudgett with a smile.

Ma had been shaking her head. Now she started to bang her cane on the floor, her gray head bobbing angrily over it. Every-

219

one turned again to look at the Moores. Mim sat perfectly still. She felt she'd been caught in this moment a dozen times before, with the jacklight and the gunsights trained full on her. "Ma, please," she murmured.

"I complained," Ma cried, her voice hoarse. "I complained loud and clear. Just like I'm a complainin' right this minute."

Mim put a restraining hand on her knee, but she brushed it off.

"Mrs. Moore . . ." said Perly, raising his brows and lowering his voice. "You didn't complain when I made you a gift of a more comfortable couch." He raised his head to the hall and said, "Mrs. Moore's losing her grip. . . ."

"The hell she is," John cried, still on his feet.

Nearby, Cogswell lifted his flask to his mouth in a sudden sweeping motion, tipped it back, and drank. Then he put the cover on, wiped his face on his sleeve, and pulled himself to his feet. "She complained all right," he said. "And if there ain't too many did, it's because the pickup men had their orders. We had to make sure every soul knew about them accidents. Every time people got in a mood to complain, they heard about another accident."

Perly straightened up in horror. "Good God, Mickey," he cried. "You *are* muddled. We had to demote Mickey," he announced to the townspeople. "I offered to send him on a cure, but he insisted he didn't have a problem. In fact, he's been nursing a grudge against me for even suggesting it."

Cogswell swayed slightly as he faced the auctioneer.

"You see . . ." Perly said, gesturing sadly.

But the people kept their eyes on Perly.

"He turned us into a pack of thieves," Mickey muttered.

"Well, why'd you let him?" shouted Arthur Stinson, clapping a hand over his mouth before he was quite finished. Stinson had married four years ago at sixteen, and, despite a reputation as a hothead, he had settled down and managed to support his young wife and then his child as a general repairman.

"I didn't see you sayin' no either," cried Sonny Pike, standing in his place and leaning toward Stinson over the sling that still held his wounded arm. "You think we liked it? We thought we

was doin' the town a favor. By the time we found out different
. . . Well, look what happened to the Carrolls when Jimmy
quit."

Perly watched the exchange, his chiseled features composed.
"Sonny's lost his nerve," he said in an even voice. "Nothing's quite
so shattering as a secret ambush."

Sonny dropped his eyes and shook his head, but remained on
his feet, his free hand resting heavily on the chair in front of him.

"It's hard . . ." soothed Perly.

"And what about them children, Perly Dunsmore?" Ma cried,
her question rasping through the hall. "What about them children?"

Dixie began to whine, but Perly almost visibly relaxed. Without taking his eyes off Ma, he motioned to Dixie to lie down. He
spread his feet wide and put his hands in his pockets so that he
was planted firmly in the center of the stage. He waited. In the
shadow of the American flag, Mudgett began to jiggle his foot
impatiently.

When Perly spoke, his voice was low and easy. "Naturally, it's
hard for someone nearly eighty to keep up with the new ways,"
he said. "Still, it makes me sad. Mrs. Moore is a symbol to me of
everything I'm trying to save in this town."

John was still standing in his place, hugging himself with both
arms. But Perly looked at Ma, and a pale pink flush spread across
her face. Mim, sitting near her, could feel her tremble.

"She asked about the children," Perly said. "I'm glad she asked
about the children. I'm proud of my—"

"We seen him Tuesday," John interrupted. "Sellin' children at
auction just like slaves. One of them Jimmy Carroll's—"

"Like slaves!" Perly cried. He took his hands out of his pockets
and leaned toward the townspeople. "What was I to do with
those children?" he asked, indignant. "Me. A bachelor. Me, who
never had wife nor child. Me, who'd love so much to have some
children of my own. You all know I love children. Hildie Moore
can tell you I love children. Mickey Cogswell's poor neglected
little ones can tell you I love children. But what kind of a life can
I offer a child? Two young mothers came to me with their chil-

221

dren. What should they do, they asked me. They couldn't look after their children. Just couldn't manage. What was I supposed to say? All I could think of to suggest was that people sometimes adopt children."

Perly paused. "And those mothers begged me to find good people to adopt their children. Now I'm no social agency. I know that. But Harlowe doesn't have a social agency. Maybe someday, if my changes go through, we will. But those parents couldn't wait. I've been around. I have some money. So they came to me. And, by golly, I found those children homes. Good homes, with parents who were eager to love them, and able to support them in style. What more could I do? What does this town want of me?" Perly stopped. He was breathing hard, his face dark.

People shifted before him like reprimanded children. John and Mickey and Sonny Pike were still standing, high and conspicuous among the seated townspeople.

"Ask him," Mickey said, his voice fuzzy, but his head erect with the easy confidence of a man who has always been a favorite, "ask him how he got people to part with their own flesh and blood. That took more than talk."

"Ah, Mickey," Perly said, his anger apparently lapsing. "You mean well by your children, for all your problems. If only everyone were as loving a parent as you." And Perly looked over the townspeople almost wearily, as if he were looking in vain for loving parents.

"Look at Sally Rouse, a settin' there as slim as ever," said Fanny Linden. Fanny didn't stand. She sat perfectly still and subjected Perly to the flat uncompromising stare familiar to everyone who had ever tried to bargain with her as she sat on her high stool behind the counter in the store. "Ask Sally how he done it and what he paid with. She must think I ain't got a woman's eyes in my head. Ain't more than a month ago, she was prancing around the store, far gone. But I don't see as she's got no baby with her now. So I ask you where that baby went to."

Sally Rouse sat with her parents in the back part of the hall. People craned to see her. She was a tall clear-featured girl with a long blond braid down her back and a grace that stood out in the plain crowd. She raised a strong chin and let her blue eyes rove slowly around the room, meeting the stares of the people, then coming to rest on Perly.

Dunsmore met her gaze for a long moment before he spoke. "I don't think this is quite kind," he said gently. "Is it such a terrible sin? Would you have her wear a scarlet letter just because she wants a better—"

"Oh, Sally, Sally," cried Agnes Cogswell and rose out of her seat, her hair and eyes wild. She would have stumbled over to Sally to comfort her, but Jerry pulled her back. "What did he do to you, Sally?" she sobbed.

"Out of the goodness of my heart," Perly said, standing straight now and lifting his shoulders in the beginning of a shrug, "I took responsibility for some other man's child." He leaned toward the people, his voice gaining momentum. "I said I'd find a home for it. And now you're—"

"He never said he was a goin' to *sell* her," wailed Sally's mother, a broad pale woman, flushed now with anger. "Poor babe. Poor tiny girl." She fell sobbing against her husband's shoulder. He didn't move. Sally sat erect, her dry eyes firmly fastened on Perly.

"And was it *you* got the money, child?" asked Ma.

Sally turned to Ma. "Me?" she said. She looked back at Perly and gave a short laugh.

"Not a cent," said Dan Rouse, standing slowly in his place. He was a tall man with a heavy stoop as though he had spent his life with his head bowed to keep the sun out of his eyes. "Not a cent," he repeated. "And he used his power over the child to make us keep contributin'." He spoke slowly. "I'm a fool. I should have let him shoot me. I thought I could save Sally, somehow. But now that's gone, I say it out. The man's a devil. Sally ain't the only one as did his bidding. Scarce a soul left in Harlowe can call hisself a man." And Dan Rouse stood in his place, looking at Perly from under his brows.

Perly cocked his head to one side and said casually, "Sit down, Dan. You're making a fool of yourself."

But Rouse remained standing.

This time Perly fixed his eyes on him and commanded him. "Sit down."

Rouse didn't move. Slowly, Sally rose to stand beside her father, her head thrown back as if to avoid the curiosity of the townspeople. She was almost as tall as her father, and her figure, under blue jeans and a loose shirt, was still full from childbirth. Her mother tugged at her shirt but she didn't move.

Then Sam Parry rose, his figure straight even at his age. "They half got me once," he said. "Let them finish me now."

Mudgett had his hand on his gun.

"How would you have had me dispose of the child?" Perly asked, almost in annoyance, his eyes darting over the crowd.

"Oh Emmie. Poor Emmie," moaned Agnes Cogswell.

Without a word, Frank Lovelace pulled himself to his feet. And John tugged at Mim's elbow to make her stand too, with Hildie in her arms.

And people noticed that the doctor was still standing in the back where he had been all along, standing casually with his arms folded, watching the proceedings.

Sam Parry began, slowly, to smile.

The silence stretched. Dan Rouse stood bolt upright, his brown eyes on Perly. His wife switched from side to side in her chair. Finally she stood up and cried, "He never gave her nothin' for all her pain—nothin' but that child itself, and used that agin us too. And soon's she was born, he took her too."

The crowd began to whisper.

"He come in here," the mother went on, "with that animal way of his. And he fastened his eye on Sally, her only just fourteen and headstrong. Nothin' ever to suit that child. And he come in here with all that power and money and a knowin' full well what he wanted. Well, our Sally, she went a dancin' off after him like he was the Pied Piper. Ain't like we didn't try to teach her right . . ."

Perly stood on his toes, his chest thrust out and his head back, his mouth open with his answer before the mother finished. "Wait a minute. Wait a minute. Let's get one thing clear. That's not *my* child," he said. "I came to this town exactly two hundred and

224

eighty days before that baby was born. Count for yourself. The doctor here can tell you the human gestation period is two hundred and eighty days. You give me too much credit. No man on earth could arrive in town, search out Sally Rouse, seduce her, and conceive a child at the first shot—all between sunup and sundown. I'm flattered you think I could, but it's not humanly possible. And that child was eight and a half pounds—full term or over. This is one accusation that just isn't feasible. You'll have to dream up something better than that."

Perly shrugged, mischief spreading across his face. "Not that I deny that I've had my times with Sally Rouse. A tough little number she was too, whatever her age. Not much I could teach her. Look at her."

Some of the townspeople turned and looked. Sally forced her head back further still and held her blue eyes hard on Perly, though now the color was rising through her fair skin.

"Look at her," Perly repeated. "What red-blooded man could possibly refuse?"

Mrs. Rouse stood in her place. "And then . . . And then . . ." she screamed, unable to finish.

Perly shook his head and frowned. "Still, my fault or not, I offered to do the honorable thing—"

"To kill the helpless babe, not marry her," shouted the mother. "Evil upon evil."

"No girl ought to marry a man nearly thirty years her senior," Perly said softly.

There was a muffled undercurrent of talk and motion in the hall.

Perly stood perfectly still beneath the town shield, watching.

With the help of her canes, Ma got shakily to her feet and leaned against the chairs in front of her.

Perly's face flushed darker and darker.

John reached to support his mother and cried, "And what about that four-year-old blond beauty you promised for next week? What about the barn and the steep pasture?"

"What, just what, did you think you was a goin' to do?" Ma demanded.

"Silence!" shouted Perly. "You're wrong. You're all wrong! You misunderstand everything. I'm only one man . . . only—"

"I say we understood too damn much for too damn long and kept too damn quiet," cried Mickey, his words slurred. He pulled Agnes up to stand beside him.

"There's no law," cried Perly. "Nothing I've done is against the law. You have no authority to put me on trial like this. What are you charging me with? With having ideals? With teaching Sunday School? With falling in love with . . ."

Silently Walter French stood up, then Arthur Stinson, and Ezra Stone.

Now the color began to drain from Perly's face. "Ezra . . ." he said.

And one by one the men and women in the room stood up. The rustling in the hall grew to a babble.

Perly stood as if frozen in place, watching the turmoil beneath him spread. "Just remember this," he said in a deep voice that cut neatly through the confusion. "Whatever I've done, you've let me do."

Then, after one last survey of the people of Harlowe, he turned adroitly on his heel and headed swiftly toward the wings on the side of the New Hampshire flag, with Dixie trotting at his heel.

Perly took six steps before the crowd began to push at one another to get into the aisles, shouting at him to stop.

Then he drew himself up short.

In the shadow of the flag, Bob Gore, in his usual sagging denim shirt and Levi's, blocked his way. He held the gun awkwardly in both hands, pointing it at Perly, just as he had pointed it at Hildie's bedroom window.

Across the stage, Mudgett leaped nimbly out from behind the American flag, and everyone saw that his gun was also drawn.

Gore swung his gun away from Perly and onto Mudgett.

The noise in the room vanished, sucked in on the breath of the crowd, and for long seconds nobody moved at all. Perly stood facing Gore. Gore and Mudgett stared into the muzzles of each other's guns.

Then Dixie sprang through the air, a tan streak, and landed on Gore's shoulder. His gun arm flew into the air and the gun went off. The town shield over the center of the stage shattered and crashed to the stage in a cloud of plaster dust. Gore roared and rolled over and over, embracing the snarling dog. Mudgett stepped forward and danced after them, keeping his gun on Gore.

There was another shot, and the children cried out. Mudgett shrieked and dropped his gun to the stage with a thud.

"Red!" shouted Perly and rushed forward, his arms stretched toward Mudgett. But instead of stopping to tend him, he ran past him without a pause, off the stage and out through the wing by the American flag. Dixie, who had turned at the shot, abandoned Gore and galloped after Perly.

A shout went up in the hall. Mudgett stood white-faced, grasping his right arm. Blood soaked through his sleeve and dripped to the floor. And Gore got shakily to his feet to search for his gun in the swirls of plaster dust.

It was Ezra Stone who raced up the stairs to the stage two at a time, his gun drawn, and headed toward the wing where Perly had disappeared.

Gore picked up his gun and followed him. Then a number of other men detached themselves from the crowd and rushed for the exits.

Mudgett clutched at his bloodied arm, his eyes glazed with fear. His wife, bulky with his child, stumbled up to him, then stopped, wide-eyed, afraid to touch him.

·15·

MANY OF THE townspeople had fallen to the floor at the first shot. Now they stood up and reached out to touch the other members of their families. Everyone talked. Agnes wept loudly. Mim cuddled Hildie who had awakened crying at the shots, and John put his arm around Ma.

The double doors in the back of the hall were thrown open and cold air swept over the close hall. Ma untangled her coat and her canes from the jumble of wooden chairs, and the Moores moved slowly down the main aisle. When they reached the doors, they paused. Instead of going home, the townspeople were crossing the green in clusters, drawn as if mesmerized toward the auctioneer's house.

Lit up brilliantly enough for a wedding or a ball, it cast a glow across most of the green. Every window shone, even in the auction barn. Six spotlights on the front lawn gave a sheen to the new white paint and an icy sparkle to the fretwork under the eaves. The glistening façade was broken only by the unsteady black shadows cast by the bare maples. And overhead, the lynx hunched, as always, restless and shifting on its weathervane.

The Moores followed the others across the Parade toward the house. Bob Gore was shouting at the people, "Stand back. Stand back."

The Moores stopped at the outskirts of the crowd. Bob Gore, Ezra Stone, and Tom Pulver were moving in on the house with their pistols drawn. They crouched like cats, sheltering behind yew bushes and honeysuckle, and seeking out the denser darkness behind the trees.

"Stand back," Gore shouted over his shoulder. "He may be armed."

The people in front fell back a step or two.

"Who, Perly?" John asked.

"Ezra claims he's in there," said Sam Parry, turning to scowl at John.

Ian James came running across the green from the firehouse with a bullhorn on the end of a long cord. He looked up at the dazzling house for a moment, glanced back at the people, then lifted the bullhorn to his mouth. His amplified words seemed to be coming from all corners of the green at once. "All right, Dunsmore. Come on out with your hands on your head."

The house with its lights seemed to twinkle in the stillness. The lynx on the weathervane turned from side to side, and a few last leaves fluttered down from the tops of the maples.

People waited, scanning the transparent windows.

"Let's go get him," yelled a stinging tenor voice from the edge of the crowd.

Turning, the people saw Jimmy Carroll, looking thin and hard in his old denim jacket. No one had seen him since he left Emmie in the nursing home and vanished with their remaining children.

"Jimmy!" cried Agnes.

He began to run. As he approached the front door of the house, he wheeled around and faced the people. "I'm goin' to kill him," he warned. "For Emmie."

"Don't!" shouted Bob Gore. "Hey!" He ran to the bottom steps of the porch and waved his arms to intercept Carroll. But Carroll leaped into the air with a grating yell and shouldered him out of the way.

Gore staggered and paused.

Carroll hit the latch, and the heavy front door fell open before him. He vanished inside, and moments later the hushed crowd heard the jangle of shattering glass.

"Let's go!" cried Cogswell, shaking loose from Agnes, but hesitating, waiting for others.

The people began to jostle one another fitfully, but they held back.

Suddenly, they were stilled by a cry like the yelp of a wounded fox. Molly Tucker ran up onto the porch and turned to bang her hand on the railing. She was a small brown woman whose thin wrists and ankles protruded sticklike from a frayed blue coat. Her family had not let her come to town since her youngest son was drowned in a well. Now her whistling syllables shrilled out over the heads of the people, garbled by the commotion and her frenzy.

Mickey broke out of the crowd and galloped up the stairs, past Molly and into the house. Arthur Stinson and Frank Lovelace followed him, running. Ian James and Ezra Stone exchanged a look and moved deliberately up the porch steps together.

John pushed Ma's hand away from his arm and headed for the house. By the time he reached the porch steps, he was in a crush of bodies trying to get inside. A few people at the edges broke away to try the other doors.

Bob Gore was shouting objections and shaking his gun at the people, his face contorted with frustration. But the noise on the green had risen to such a pitch that his effort to protect the house had no more effect than a dumb show.

Pushed from behind, John could do nothing as he moved past Gore's gun except eye it warily. Finally, Gore turned away, shaking his head. Already, dozens of dark figures flowed back and forth across the lighted windows.

Once he was inside, the press of people dissolved, and John was free. He paused. Everything gleamed. The deep color of oriental rugs over polished oak floors had replaced Amelia's linoleum, and a delicate crystal chandelier hung where her pink glass fixture had been. Everywhere there was light and the glow of well-oiled wood.

John started up the broad staircase three stairs at a time, his feet silenced by the deep blue carpet, his fingers touching the dark banister at the curves.

Upstairs, he ran until he was stopped by a door at the end of the hall. He pulled it open and found himself in a bedroom. A row of lights near the floor made the white walls glow. John turned slowly, examining the bed with its green velvet spread, the oak chiffonier, the small painted table and chair. Quietly, he moved to the closet door and jerked it open. Inside, a row of dark suits hung on hangers. John jabbed at them with a stiff arm, and they began to swing back and forth without a sound. Despite the fact that the three pairs of shoes on the floor were clearly empty, John kept staring, expecting Perly to materialize before him.

From the corner of his eye he caught a glimpse of something that made him whirl around—a dark green figure gliding smoothly by the door. He ran for the hall and shouted. But the man who turned, his face white with alarm, was Walter French.

John moved to the next door down the hall and yanked. Behind it was a bathroom, everything blinding white—the tub on claw feet, the flat walls, the four fluorescent lights. John turned to leave and bumped into a running figure. It was Tom Pulver. The two drew away and looked at each other, almost without recognition, then backed off and, carefully skirting one another, continued in opposite directions.

John started running again, gathering momentum, rushing from door to door down the hallway. Finally, in a bedroom, he paused. His eyes were stinging and he was gulping for air.

Dan Rouse was tearing the curtains off the windows, grunting with satisfaction as the silky stuff ripped. A traverse rod fell with a clatter.

John kicked at the fallen curtains and watched. It was only after Rouse had moved to the next room that he saw the dressing table—its walnut polished to a dark richness, its elegance more in keeping here than in the plain bedroom at home. John turned away and leaned in the doorway, pressing his hands against the doorposts in an effort to hang on to his anger.

Cogswell lurched out of the bedroom opposite. "He's gone!" John cried. "Mickey, is he gone?"

Mickey's face was red with temper. "I'll find him," he promised.

"God damn . . ." He stopped, and he and John found themselves looking at one another, their faces gone slack with bewilderment.

Without sound or warning, all the lights went out. A stunned stillness fell over the house, as if life had been snuffed out with the light.

A woman's voice rang out, "He's here!"

There was a soft impact near John and a man shouted in surprise.

Slowly, John backed away from the darkness, returning to the bedroom he had just left, where the pale oblongs of two windows revealed at least the contours of the room. He backed up against one of the windows and waited.

As his eyes adjusted to the dimness, he thought he detected a dark figure standing perfectly still against the wall opposite him. He opened his mouth to make some casual remark, and remembered that he had just been through that room and left it empty. His mouth went dry.

When the figure didn't move, John began to slide slowly along the wall toward the door. Almost imperceptibly, the figure also inched closer to the door. John stopped. The figure stopped. John started again. And again the figure moved.

John made a furious dive for the figure. He was caught in a muscular embrace, and fell to the floor with his face pressed to the other man's neck. The two rolled over, kicking and grunting. Then the other man took John firmly by the shoulders. "Let go of me," he commanded in a detached and unfamiliar voice. "What on earth are you thinking of?"

Reflexively, John loosened his grip.

Then, without knowing how he got there, he found himself lying on his back making his way through layers of sleep, trying to reach and stop the hard pain at the back of his neck. Somehow, he got his feet beneath him and stumbled toward the black shape of the door to the hall. But the man was lost. John tripped over the threshold and fell against the banister. "I had him. I had him," he moaned.

"You had him!" repeated a man. "You mean he's here?"

John grasped the banister for support and, in an effort to collect himself, peered down over it into the murky pit of the downstairs front hall. "I don't know," he said. "How the hell should I know?"

The other man moved off, his footsteps sounding on the uncarpeted stairs to the third floor.

In the hall below, the glimmer of pocket flashlights began to move cautiously back and forth. Someone cried, "Candles!" and soon people were moving up the stairs, each one cupping a fragile flame.

John started slowly down the stairs. At the bottom, he found himself looking into the living room. In the shimmering orange light from newspapers burning in the fireplace, Frank Lovelace was stamping methodically on a spindly pine rocker and feeding the broken pieces to the fire. "There's a hundred people in this house," he said in his slow heavy voice.

"Perly's too sly to hide in his own hole," said Dan Rouse.

"Then what are we doin' here?" cried Arthur Stinson. "Damn!" He swept an arm across the mantel, sending a clutter of candlesticks and knickknacks crashing to the tile hearth.

Lovelace threw the solid seat of the rocker on top of the fire, damping it momentarily. "Good question," he said soberly.

John turned away. Seven candles lit the dining room on the other side of the hall. Fanny Linden and Janice Pulver were fishing in the drawers of the buffet. John moved toward them and saw that they were filling a shopping bag with silverware.

"Fanny . . ." he said.

She turned her moon face to him. "It's stolen goods, ain't it?" she said flatly.

Janice Pulver examined a fork in her hand and did not look at him. "He left the lights on and the door open, didn't he? You go right ahead and hunt for his big self, if you think he's that much of a fool." She threw the fork into the bag. "Myself, I'll settle."

"Them too," said Fanny, jerking her head in the direction of the front hall.

Walter French had an easy chair jammed in the front door, and people were piling up in the hall behind him, complaining. Jane Collins was at the top of the staircase, feeling gingerly for the steps with her feet, unable to see over her armload of ornate mirrors and paintings. Agnes Cogswell and Jerry were carrying a harvest table, and old Adeline Fayette was waiting by the door with her usual frail dignity, weighed down by a pair of silver candelabra.

Suddenly Jimmy Carroll shoved his way down the stairs. "What are you doin'?" he shouted. He grabbed Jerry by the collar. "Where's Perly?" he asked the boy. "Don't you care?"

The people paused and looked up at him in the uncertain light. Sam Parry was leaning on the wall at the foot of the staircase.

"He's here," insisted Carroll.

"Says who?" said Parry.

"He's got to be," Carroll said, but he let go of Jerry. He looked around at the dubious faces and shook his head. Near the hall fireplace he spotted a metal wastebasket filled with mail and old magazines. He took a lighted candle from the mantelpiece, and dropped it in. With a sound like a gust of wind, the trash flared up. Hovering behind it, his features insubstantial and mobile in the dancing flames, Carroll gave the wastebasket a kick that sent it skidding across the polished floor into the center of the crowd. "Smoke him out!" he shouted as people backed away. "We'll smoke him out!"

John stood watching the flaming wastebasket. In minutes the hall was filled with smoke. There were cries of "Fire!" and people began running for the door, hollering at the people ahead of them to move. They coughed and jockeyed for position, but they did not abandon the chairs and tables or the armloads of appliances, china, linen, and clothes that were making the exodus so slow.

John looked up at the crystal lobes of the chandelier, their bright faces twinkling with gold light caught from the flaming wastebasket. Every night the auctioneer had walked under its great luminous symmetry into this house. John swung up his arm, grabbed a handful of crystal pieces and yanked them free. As he pushed into the crowd waiting to get out the door, the chandelier jittered and rang out in sour dissonance.

In the living room, Arthur Stinson was pouring from a five-gallon can of kerosene, wetting down the sofa and cushions. Rouse and Lovelace were looking on, frowning, their arms hanging loosely at their sides.

"Smoke him out!" shouted a voice and someone elbowed John aside and burst into the living room. Stinson straightened up with his can of kerosene. "See how you like it, Perly!" shouted the newcomer, and John recognized Sonny Pike by his sling.

Outside, the townspeople who had not gone into the house—mostly mothers and their children—were strung out in a long thin line across the road from the house. Near one end, Mim knelt on the ground with Hildie asleep in her arms. Ma leaned on her canes nearby.

"Johnny," Mim called in relief as he approached. Then, as he came close, she shifted Hildie and asked, "John, what on earth . . .?"

John turned and faced the house. He dug his hands into his pockets to keep himself from shivering, and his right fist closed over the icy crystal teardrops. "He ain't in there," he said. "There's just a lot of junk."

"You don't think so?" Mim said. She watched the people pour from the house with their booty and move across the road to join the gathering crowd.

Tom Pulver and Arthur Stinson ran out the back door, each carrying a red can of gasoline.

In the dining-room windows, there was a faint flutter of light. It died and then sprang up again, this time with the orange taint of fire. Then a flash of flame lit up one of the living-room windows and moved in spurts around the room as the draperies caught fire.

Bob Gore ran across the green toward the firehouse. It was lit up and wide open to the night. Inside, sitting idle, were Perly's ambulance and the two big firetrucks bought with the proceeds of a dozen annual auctions. "Come on!" shouted Gore.

No one followed him.

He stopped and looked back at the line of familiar people. There was only the wavering firelight from inside the house to

235

mark their features, but their bunched forms were clear and utterly still. Gore stared at them for a few minutes. Then he folded his arms and moved slowly back toward them.

The living room was filled now with yellow flames, and suddenly the glass curtains in the dining room burst in a shower of sparks. In two of the upstairs windows, a tremulous gold light became visible through the dark panes.

"What if he *is* still there?" Mim whispered. She turned Hildie's sleeping head to her shoulder and bit hard on her knuckle.

"He ain't," John said, choking with anger. "It's all a waste."

"But if he is?" insisted Mim.

The barn was on fire now, too, but people were still running in to carry out water pumps and separators and power mowers. As flames became visible in more and more windows, the stillness was broken only by the footsteps of the people and the muted panting of the fire itself. The townspeople gathered closer and closer together, leaning into each other to stare in trancelike silence as the fire rolled through the house.

"There he is!" shouted Sally Rouse. And then, her full voice rising, "He's in there!"

But still, during a long silence, the glimmer of the fire within seemed the only life behind the sooty windows.

Then, one by one, the people saw it. In the central attic dormer, still unlit by fire, a ghostlike whiteness floated in and out of focus. And beneath it, the shadow of torso and arms moved against the black glass of the window. Pale fingers began to move against the mullions, touching the panes, trying, with ritual slowness, to open the window. It would not give. The hands struggled—distant, ineffectual, and dreamlike.

Then, with a jolt of convincing energy, the figure straightened up and smashed a foot through the bottom of the window. Glass sprayed down on the roof of the porch below and everyone had a clear vision of the scarred yellow sole of a work boot.

Smoke billowed from the break and in moments the golden glint of fire appeared in the attic room. The dark shadow sagged against the top of the window. Behind him, something caught fire. In the brief blaze, the townspeople recognized the green work

clothes and the length and strength of the man they were looking for. The whiteness was a towel wrapped around his head.

"Get a ladder," yelled Sam Parry. "Somebody get a ladder."
He himself ran a few steps toward the firehouse, then stopped and
looked around for help. Bob Gore ran past him and veered around
the house toward the barn. None of the other townspeople
moved.

A surf of smoke washed up and down over the roof around the
dormer. Here and there, a ball of flame slipped down the steep
pitch and disappeared. Then, with a shudder, a pillar of fire burst
free and leaped against the sky.

Now steady flames inside lit the blank white towel and en-
larged and blackened the silhouette in the window. Slowly, both
arms moved up, palms outward. The hands began to beat against
the upper sash, shaking the panes and finally breaking one. The
swaddled head leaned into the hole for air, but the smoke
gathered to it also, and spun in gagging gray spirals around the
head.

Only then did anybody notice Bob Gore climbing a ladder to
the flat porch roof directly beneath the window. Ian James followed him up and the two pulled the wooden ladder up onto
the roof and set it against the sill of the high dormer window.

Molly Tucker cried out, clearly now, "Let him burn!"

The figure groped at the window. Bob Gore started up the
ladder, a hatchet in his belt. As he climbed, the townspeople dis-
integrated into commotion.

"Stop!" cried Jimmy Carroll. "Let him burn!"

Gore paused and turned to look down at the crowd.

"Go get him," Ma urged. She looked ancient and tired in the
quivering light.

A gunshot punctured the hubbub and reduced the Parade to
stillness except for the sound of the fire, roaring now through the
roof.

Gore looked behind him and began to scuttle down the ladder.

In the window, the figure did not move. He stood erect, his
arms still raised against the wooden framework that held him.

"Get up there!" hollered Sam Parry.

237

Gore hung on the bottom rung. This time, Ian James headed up the ladder, pushing Gore ahead of him.

But before they were halfway up, four or five shots rang out. They came from all directions and they came at almost the same moment. The unbroken panes in the high dormer window shattered. The figure slowly crumpled, clawing at the jagged edges of broken glass as he collapsed, gradually disappearing inside the house.

Bob Gore stepped to the edge of the roof and faced the crowd. The people confronted him without expression and without motion. No guns were visible in the black shadows, and every eye was fixed on the burning house with its empty window.

Gore turned and headed up the ladder. He hit the window frame with his hatchet, splintering the old wood and releasing a wall of smoke. He coughed and ducked. Then he took a deep breath, threw one leg over the sill, and leaned into the room.

The once-graceful limbs in the fresh green work clothes flopped about awkwardly and resisted his efforts to get a grip on them. Finally, he got the arms across one of his shoulders and the legs across the other. James steadied the ladder, and Gore backed down with his burden.

The body jerked from side to side as Gore moved, and the towel around the head, soaked and brilliant now with blood, gradually unwound. When Gore turned at the bottom of the ladder to lower the heavy body onto the porch roof, the towel loosened and fell away.

The hair was not black and curly. It was straight and silky and brown. The eyes, staring now without sight, were not black, but grayish blue. And the face was that of Mickey Cogswell.

With a sigh, the fire broke through the roof of the barn. It rose higher and higher, converging with the fire from the house and ending in a dainty pointed tip a hundred feet overhead. In time, the walls of the house and the barn were transformed into a ragged blanket of orange flame, broken by the outline of the main timbers.

The people of Harlowe didn't stay to watch as the timbers broke and fell, forming black diagonals and reducing Perly Dunsmore's mansion to rubble. Each family huddled together and drew away.

John took Ma by the elbow and guided her toward the truck. Mim followed, carrying Hildie.

Ma pulled free of John and limped heavily between her canes. "You just stood there," she said. "Mickey Cogswell . . . and you just stood there."

Mim pressed Hildie to her. "We loved Mickey," she said. "We didn't know."

Ma turned abruptly, forcing them to stop. "Are you God Almighty to stand there and let a fellow human burn?" she cried.

John stopped. "Wasn't me shot him, Ma," he said between his teeth.

Ma raised her cane. "I didn't see you scurryin' up there to get him down."

"John was busy lookin' out for us, Ma," Mim said, reaching to touch Ma's hand.

"No," John said sharply. "I wanted Perly dead."

Ma looked at the ground and leaned hard on her canes. "Johnny," she said, her voice shaking, "I gloried too."

Presently Ma lifted her face and began to move forward, tears finding the deep creases in her skin. "The only thing we had to stop him with was right," she said. "Now we gave that too."

John helped Ma into the cold truck and Mim climbed in after her with Hildie. John started the motor and the family sat in silence as it warmed.

The snow that had been holding up for days was beginning to fall. The big heavy flakes fell into the fire and melted with a tiny hiss. They fell on the tarpaulin pulled up over Mickey's face, and on the townspeople as they moved away from the Parade. On Constance Hill, they piled up quickly, sticking to trees and roofs, catching on the new skim of ice over the pond, and blanketing the frozen earth. Somewhere, perhaps, they fell on the auctioneer.